Praise for *Class Dismissed*

"*Class Dismissed* is pitch-perfect and elegantly plotted. That would be enough happiness for a reader—but it's also very funny. Not to mention harrowing. And, of this moment. Patrick Lynch practicing the art of teaching is heroic in a way that illuminates why teaching is a calling and indeed an art. This book is a joy."

—Jane Hamilton, author of *The Book of Ruth* and *A Map of the World*

"*Class Dismissed* explores the triumphs and tragedies of teaching—and the Kafkaesque bureaucracy that one gifted New York City public school teacher finds himself in after an accident involving his most difficult student. Simultaneously as cynical as the city he now calls home and as sincere as his midwestern roots, Patrick Lynch is an unforgettable narrator, one you'll root for as he buckles under the weight of his own mistakes. This novel is both laugh-out-loud funny and deeply moving, and marks an impressive debut."

—Lisa Borders, author of *The Fifty-First State* and *Cloud Cuckoo Land*

"Kevin M. McIntosh's *Class Dismissed* is competing for The Great School Novel title, alongside classics such as Kingsley Amis's *Lucky Jim* and Bel Kaufman's *Up the Down Staircase*. McIntosh writes with humor and a sardonic appreciation of life's all-too-expected travails. In *Class Dismissed*, the world tries to teach Patrick Lynch a lesson. He proves to be as apt a pupil as he is a successful teacher."

—Alex Beam, *Boston Globe* columnist

CLASS DISMISSED

Kevin McIntosh

Regal House Publishing

Published by
Regal House Publishing, LLC
Raleigh, NC 27612
All rights reserved

ISBN -13 (paperback): 9781646030675
ISBN -13 (epub): 9781646030927
Library of Congress Control Number: 2020941113

Interior and cover design by Lafayette & Greene
lafayetteandgreene.com
Cover images © Kris Schmidt/Shutterstock

Regal House Publishing, LLC
https://regalhousepublishing.com

The following is a work of fiction created by the author. All names, individuals, characters, places, items, brands, events, etc. were either the product of the author or were used fictitiously. Any name, place, event, person, brand, or item, current or past, is entirely coincidental.

Author photo credit: © Small Circle Studio, Inc.

"It Had to Be You" copyright 1924, Jerome H. Remick & Co., WB Music Corp. (renewed), music by Isham Jones, lyrics by Gus Kahn

"Oh, Lady Be Good!" copyright 1924, Harms, Inc., WB Music Corp. (renewed), music by George Gershwin, lyrics by Ira Gershwin

Parts of this novel were originally published in different form in the following: Beloit Fiction Journal: "Special Needs"; Bryant Literary Review: "Who Is We?"; Chicago Tribune Printers Row Journal: "The Scheme"

For Karin

1

WRITE WHAT YOU KNOW

It begins with Patrick Lynch's swollen, aching eyes. Then funnels out past the bank of gleaming white computers, past the gleaming white boards, over the heads of his gleaming white students. Above them all, tacked to either side of Old Glory, Steinbeck and Harper Lee gaze down on Tiffany Strohmeyer as she shares page two of her critical essay.

"The pâté in the Princess Cruise buffet wasn't heavy or greasy, as foie gras can so often be, and was superior in every way to that in the smorgasbord of the Royal Caribbean ship," Tiffany asserts, swiping that renegade blonde lock out of her face, securing it behind her right ear. The floor fan in the back is cranked to high and it flutters Tiffany's honeyed tresses like they're shooting a shampoo commercial. A long pink nail flicks forward to page three.

After an entire year, Patrick still can't believe he gets to teach in this classroom—his classroom—for one more day. And so familiar now were the three Tiffanies, two Maxes, two Jasons, and twelve others in second period, though strangely indistinguishable when they met last fall. Minnesotans through and through, these kids, his tribe. More or less. He'd have had no problem sorting them by degrees of freckled dirty-blondness back when he was an eighth grader in Peterson's Prairie. But they were so different from the kids he taught in Manhattan and so similar to one another that he took to calling them Ms. Thorsten, Mr. Swenson, just to keep them straight. Another Mr. Lynch quirk they added to their list of his New Yorkisms.

He shakes his head. The Guy from the Midwest. Now the

New York Guy. Perhaps he is both, neither. A man without a country, a teacher without a classroom.

Brilliant June sunlight streams in the window, filtered through the horse chestnut blossoming in the courtyard. Without question the tree is the loveliest classroom view he's ever had but also the source of his bloodshot eyes. The chubby gray squirrel that lives in the courtyard is leaping at the bird feeder, a covered disk that hangs from a pole near the chestnut, trying once again to knock some birdseed to the ground. As he descends on the feeder, he manages to smack it with one paw, sending the feeder swinging, seed intact, and falls on his side. The squirrel shakes himself and scrambles up the tree. Has he finally exhausted the supply of chestnuts he gathered in October? And didn't squirrels always land on their feet?

A soprano throat-clearing brings Patrick back to center stage. Tiffany Strohmeyer—Tiffany Number One—hand on one hip, critical essay in the other, is uninterested in her teacher's nature musings. She merely wants feedback on her review of the cruise her family took last Christmas. Tiffany may be the sweetest, prettiest girl in the class, but she has trained her considerable intelligence on a withering dissection of the calorie-laden food, antiquated gym facilities, and corny entertainment to be found aboard the Scandinavian vessel. She smiles demurely, as if she hadn't just left the Norwegian national honor in tatters.

"Thank you, Ms. Strohmeyer," says Mr. Lynch. "Very specific and relevant details. Well done."

And though their forebears, like those of many in the class, hailed from Greater Oslo, Tiffanies Two and Three nod their lovely heads in agreement, having endured the same cruise on winter breaks past.

Ms. Strohmeyer smooths her short pleated skirt, returns to her seat and sits, snapping open her binder, slipping her essay in, snapping it shut. She folds her hands on her desk and looks up alertly, and it isn't hard for Patrick to imagine her leading board meetings, as does her mother and, indeed, her father.

Write what you know, he tells them, and they do, they do.

Patrick leans back in a student desk in the last row, his shirt slick against the plastic. He tucks a bit of shirttail in and the sweat that has pooled above his belt trickles below. Twenty more minutes of reviews of horror movies, boy bands, skateboard brands, teen clothing lines, and he can plop himself onto the lime green sofa beneath the air conditioner in the teachers' lounge.

Erik Lindstrom is next. He shifts from foot to foot, swaying rhythmically, pulling at his dress-length Timberwolves jersey, plucking at his spiky red hair. Boys sway more than girls, and Patrick tries to alternate genders at these year-end readings, lest he get queasy. Erik's review of *Death Match 3*, the computer game he got for his fourteenth birthday, is also full of specific, relevant details. Erik is tiny, half the size of the largest eighth-grade boys, but Zoltar, hero of *Death Match 3*, is massive, his biceps "awesome," and when he swings his two-headed axe, enemy heads "spin through the air like so many basketballs," the blood spurting vividly, aided by "twice as many pixels as they used in *Death Match 2*."

The boys are captivated by Erik's account; the girls shoot glances at Tiffany Number One, covetous of her long shiny legs and the tight pink top that so cunningly matches her nails.

Patrick stares at Erik, spouting gore in his half-changed contralto, and is amazed, still, at how well-behaved the students are at Lake Minnehaha Junior High. June nineteenth, the penultimate day of the school year, a day for battening down hatches, a humid ninety-two degrees, and yet they sit, if not attentive, respectful as only upper-middle class Midwestern teenagers, weaned on politeness, could be.

It's impossible not to like these kids, so hard-working, so well-trained. Not always kind, perhaps, but generally nice at an age notoriously cruel. A small wave of guilt bathes him, remembering the resentment he'd felt in September. Susan's voice was keen—keening—in his head then. "Look at this place!" he could hear her wail, hands planted on those slender hips. If she were here, she'd survey his nineteen students, his sparkling classroom with its just-out-of-the-box Apple computers, its crackling new textbooks; she'd follow him into the high-buffed hallways, past the display cases filled with trophies and student art. And the supply room!—pencil and pen boxes, staplers, markers, transparencies, rulers, folders of every size and color. And paper—lined, graphed, copier—reams of it, pallets of it, stacked from floor to ceiling. "What do they spend—ten grand a kid?" Susan would huff. "These aren't the kids who need it!" She'd fling that long dark hair over a pale shoulder, daring him to debate the point, though, of course, she knew he agreed. Then the eyes would narrow and out would come data on the socioeconomics of this community, the evils of funding schools through local property taxes.

True enough, Susan, he'd answer her, answering himself. But you couldn't hold all that against these kids. Not their fault, being oblivious of their privilege, he thinks, watching Erik Lindstrom sway in his Air Jordans. No fault of theirs, being raised at the Mall of America.

Ted Sturdevant sticks his handsome head in the doorway, same time as every second period this year. Patrick nods at him. Ted nods back and disappears down the hall, but his forced smile tells Patrick just how unfocused he must look.

Patrick never blames him, checking in like he does. Focus has been a struggle each of the previous 891 class periods this year, and today the heat and antihistamines aren't helping. But he's fought the good fight every class, given the Lake Minneha-ha school board its money's worth. And it's the least he can do for Ted after he used his juice as the department chair to bring him here, taken that risk. Ted still insists Patrick did him a favor filling Cindy Sperling's maternity leave. *Buddy*, Patrick thinks, *you don't have to teach an English teacher about suspension of disbelief.*

But they were never buddies, growing up. Which makes his hiring even more a mystery. Of course, Patrick's mother called Ted, put that bug in his ear. Which explained why Ted didn't ask too many questions about why he'd left New York so suddenly, why he was "coming home." Good thing, too; Ted was not a man to understand free fall. An optimist, a can-do guy, same now as in high school: square-built, square-jawed, firm handshake. He strides the halls of LMJHS like he's still president of the senior class at Willard County High, still blocking back on the football team. Having spent his whole career at Lake Minnehaha, Ted would not appreciate Patrick's ambivalence about teaching this population. Ted is compassionate—even Susan wouldn't argue otherwise—but he is not from the school of Life is Unfair.

And as the squirrel scrambles back up the chestnut tree, Patrick envisions Ted and Susan in a lively dustup: state spending versus federal; racially biased testing; whether the mighty economic stream gushing from Lake Minnehaha trickles down its tributaries to the less fortunate neighborhoods of Minneapolis. Oh, the battle royal if Susan were here!

If Susan were here. Patrick taps a pen on his forehead. Ridiculous. Here could never be "there," with Susan, and with those other kids, the ones who need him. Patrick stops tapping. His head hurts.

Prolonged silence is seldom a good thing in an eighth-grade classroom, Patrick is reminded as he looks away from the courtyard window to where Erik stands, twitching, expectant, the text of *Death Match 3: The Final Episode?* dangling at his side. The entire class stares at Mr. Lynch, making Patrick wonder just how long they have been watching him watch the squirrel.

He clears his throat. "Good job, Mr. Lindstrom."

Erik doesn't move. Something more precise is required to salvage this moment. "Your description of the sound effects, particularly the exploding...Kray-gon *debillitators*—was very sharp. Nicely done." Erik, convinced, relieved, exhales loudly and sways back to his desk.

Focus, Patrick tells himself as Tiffany Number Two launches into her review of *SassyGrrrl* magazine. You've made it this far, *focus*. And he does manage to watch, listen, respond through Tiffany's, the Maxes', the Jasons' presentations. Then the bell rings, as it must, ending Mr. Lynch's 892nd class of the year.

"Thanks, everyone. We'll wrap it all up tomorrow," Mr. Lynch says to the backs of his students. They flee his classroom with their usual astounding speed, despite the heat. Patrick leans back in the desk, extracts a balled-up tissue from his khakis and blows his nose.

"Have a good day, Mr. Lynch," chirps Tiffany Number One, the last to leave.

"You, too, Tiffany." Patrick looks up to catch her farewell smile, but her symmetrical features are bemused, like Ted's some minutes earlier. He offers something like a smile and she vanishes into the hallway. He rubs his eyes, stares out the courtyard window. The squirrel hangs from the feeder, swinging, a furry little man on a disk-shaped trapeze, unable to scramble on top or let go.

2

WHO IS WE?

New York City, One Year Earlier

Patrick was handing back personal narratives to his second period. He used to call them *memoirs*, but his students always laughed. He checked the clock on the back wall: 9:23 it read, as it had for the past seven years. The clock, end point of an exclamation begun by the fissure that ran down the back wall, reassured Patrick. The one constant in his classroom. Beneath it, Emily Dickinson, poor defaced Emily Dickinson, looked over the proceedings with equanimity, alarmed neither by her disfigurement nor by her function as cover for the section of fissure beneath the clock. Mr. Lynch handed his narrative back to Jamar, a pudgy, bright-eyed boy in the front row.

"Are they pretty, Mr. L?" Jamar smirked at his favorite Lynchism.

"Some are pretty, Jamar," Patrick said, "some less so."

Jamar frowned at his A-, which was pretty, but he wanted to be beautiful.

Abdul said, "You always give me Cs 'cause I'm Black."

"'Cause you Black and don't study," said Jamar, who was blacker still, and studied, and was hell-bent on pushing his A-average to an A. Everyone laughed, even Abdul.

"Don't play yourself, Abdul," Patrick said, an expression he liked. Still, you had to be judicious with street lingo. It could only be used as self-parody: Look at the feeble white man, reaching out. You couldn't let them think you were trying to be hip or, worse, making fun of their culture. Patrick remembered Mr. Graves, sophomore English back in Peterson's Prairie, Willard County High. Mr. Graves caught the '80s wave just as it crashed on the '70s beach. "Let's forget old Will

Shakespeare," he'd say, plopping *The Tempest* on his desk. "Let's just rap. What's goin' on? What's happenin'?" Then he'd pull at his bushy Elvis-length sideburns. Mr. Grooves, his students called him, in the hallways. Fifteen years later, at the Science & Tech Academy in Marcus Garvey High School, the same rules applied. "Snoopy Dog, I'm down with him," sleepy Phil Sitkowitz declared last semester, without irony, a desperate grab for street cred that was met with howls, then barks for weeks afterward.

That week's narrative, "My Role in the American Dream," one of Patrick's lesser inspirations, had yielded predictable results. But they couldn't expect a home run from him every day, could they? Not after Gladys Hellmann decided late last June that her tetchy hip would not, after all, allow her a thirty-fifth year of ninth grade American History. Principal Silverstein had left a terse, enigmatic message on Patrick's answering machine that day: "Mr. Lynch, how would you feel about teaching American Humanities?"

Silverstein later explained that American Humanities, a new course, would give Patrick the chance to broaden his teaching repertoire, synthesizing English and history. And, yes, it would save the principal the task of scrambling to find a replacement for Mrs. Hellmann. And save the district money. And, since Patrick was certified to teach both subjects, students would get credit for both. Unquestionably, he was the man for the job.

"But Mr. Silverstein—Steve—I'm licensed in secondary English. I'm not licensed in history," Patrick stammered.

"Oh, really? Wally said you were." Walter Kupzcek, vice principal, not a man to let facts stand in the way of expediency. Patrick listened to the static on the line, to Silverstein's raspy breathing. "Hmmm. Well, Patrrrick," the principal pulled on his name, "they'll never check." Silverstein hung up before Patrick could ask what would happen to him if "they" ever did.

And so American Humanities was born, bastard child of AmLit10 and AmHist12, reconceived every night at Patrick's desk, and sometimes in the morning as the No. 1 local screeched into the 103rd Street station, Patrick's lesson plan book in one sweaty hand, sesame bagel with a schmear in the other.

It was late February, the meat of the school year; now the heavy lifting began. The first two quarters were always given over to taming and training. He and Abdul had gone toe-to-toe every day into mid-December, until one morning when Abdul decided Mr. L was for real.

"Where is your essay, Abdul?"

"I don' got it. Didn' do it."

"Why not?"

It was such a stupid question, repeated so often, Abdul finally laughed and slicked down what he liked to think of as his mustache. "You not gonna stop askin', are you, Lynch?" (Sounded like lunch. He knew they called him that. Are you ready for Lunch? they asked each other before a quiz.)

Patrick shook his head.

"Well, a'ight then," said Abdul.

The next day Patrick found Abdul's essay on his desk. It wasn't pretty. Abdul was chairman of the too-cool-for-school crew. But, as chairman, he was able to do occasional work without damaging his rep, for the act of handing in an assignment was understood by his cronies as the highest form of satire. Let him think you care. Much wittier, in the end, than being empty-handed; anyone could do that.

Yes, February was good. If you were going to make serious headway with a class, it was between now and spring break. Manhattan was slushy, the new TV shows had lost their novelty; it was still too cold to hang out in the park drinking 40s or smoking blunts with your buddies. Mid-April the big black puffy coats came off and you were competing with some buxom girl's cleavage, an alpha male's biceps, a contest that was no contest. But February was fun, February was productive—a veteran teacher could finally smile and not be thought weak; you could get in the face of an unprepared student without provoking all-out war. Usually.

Patrick made his way back to Amina, Fadwa, Muna, and

Hegira, the Afghan girls perched on the ledge at the rear of the classroom, beneath Emily Dickinson, above the splintered boards that once were bookshelves. He still felt that twinge of guilt when they nodded in thanks as he handed them their narratives, their eyes cast down, faces obscured by their head coverings. Thirty-six students, thirty-two desks. Who else would sit back there, shoulder to shoulder, silent, listening, taking notes? Hegira, spokeswoman for their group, still paused every day after the bell rang, waited at the door, focused her large brown eyes on Patrick's chin and said, "Thank you, teacher, for teaching us today." The way she said *teacher* humbled him. The other three nodded and filed out behind her. Hegira's father, who made it out of Kabul just ahead of the Russian tanks, had a little smoke shop in Crown Heights. She spoke not a word of English three years ago but got an 87 percent on the citywide writing test last spring. Abdul could learn a thing or two from Hegira, were he the kind of boy to pay attention to a girl who covered every square inch of her body.

There were thirty-six students in period two, but, as with every class, the flavor of the group was established by a handful. In this class, Jamar, Hegira and, of course, Abdul. Also Angela Wong and Maria Lopez. Angela worked nights in her family's restaurant, waiting tables, folding won tons, and broke boards in karate class after school. Maria was an angel-faced femme fatale. Wicked smart, Maria, but, as they said, at-risk. Patrick couldn't look into her first-Communion eyes without remembering the note he'd found on his floor a few weeks ago. *Did you like what I did in lab?* it said in her loopy, girly script. *You want some more of that after school?* Sitkowitz's chem lab. Procreation—nuclear fission—could be going on in the back row without his knowledge.

Then there was Josh Mishkin.

He was quiet today, slumbering at the little round "editing table" to the right of Hegira's girls. *Joshua requires preferential seating* said his Individualized Education Plan—by which they meant front row, center—but back row, right corner was what

Josh preferred and was the only spot where he, and the class, could function.

Mr. Lynch tapped a finger on the table, next to Josh's head. He learned early this fall not to rouse Josh with a tap on the shoulder. *While shouting and upsetting furniture is clearly unacceptable behavior in a classroom setting,* Dr. Mishkin, Josh's mother, wrote in her November 7th missive to Principal Silverstein, *it is behavior consistent with the psycho-pharmacological and socio-cultural issues detailed in Joshua's IEP.* She concluded with a snappy, *I urge Mr. Lynch to familiarize himself with this document*—and a final shot across his bow—*as federal law mandates.*

Josh opened one blue eye, then tilted his head up toward his teacher, short pale dreadlocks bobbing over his freckled forehead. How could one sleepy eye convey so much disdain? Then Patrick had to say it: "Josh, where's your personal narrative?"

Josh waited until Abdul and Jamar had swiveled to take in the show, then hoisted his lanky torso up. He smoothed down his Bob Marley Lives! T-shirt so the cannabis leaf that outlined Bob's head like a halo was clearer. "Hey, yo, I forgot it at home again." He puckered his lips, making visible the surrounding reddish wisps of facial hair. "Sorry."

Jamar shook his head; Abdul and his minions chuckled.

"Bring it in tomorrow if you want credit," Patrick said, and moved on.

He felt his throat tighten, his stomach swirl. He had always made it his mission to find something to like in the unlikable student—good penmanship, nice hands. Sometimes you really had to dig.

His father's dictums, however corny, were still his guiding lights. "Education is a relationship," Superintendent Lynch would pronounce, carving the turkey in smooth, even strokes, "an unspoken contract between the teacher and the taught, based on trust." It was tempting to dismiss these archaic notions—the Upper Midwest wasn't the Upper West Side, after all—but his father had had plenty to deal with back in Peterson's Prairie: pregnancies, pot, rural poverty. His son. But

Patrick couldn't recall anyone like Josh or his mother back in Minnesota, nor had he encountered their like in his seven years at Marcus Garvey.

Patrick had never come this close to hating a student before, and it was that, more than any of Josh's antics, that ate at him.

Patrick came back to center stage. "Okay," he clapped his hands, rubbed them together, "who read the Declaration last night? Who looked up the vocabulary?" The usual hands popped up: Hegira and her girls, Jamar, Angela; Maria raised her hand shoulder height (she looked up half the words, before the lucky recipient of the chem class hand job telephoned), and a few others from the front two rows waved uncertainly. An inauspicious response to Patrick's latest brainstorm, introducing Jeffersonian democracy by weaving it into their previous unit on *The Autobiography of Malcolm X*. The Malcolm X part of the American Dream unit had gone well—Spike's film version was out in video, X-caps and T-shirts were still everywhere—so most of them had read most of the book. He'd put up a poster of Malcolm as an experiment, to see if he'd wind up with the same Frankenstein scars and bandito mustache as Emily Dickinson. Patrick was out in the hall one morning when he saw Abdul, fine-point in hand, prepare to perform cosmetic surgery on Mr. X. Before he could say a word, Patrick heard Jamar scold softly, "Hey, man. That's Malcolm." Patrick watched from behind the door as Abdul paused and capped the pen.

"Jefferson states that some truths are 'self-evident.' What's he mean? Angela?"

Angela consulted her notes. "Obvious."

"Obviously," said Abdul, to titters from his people.

"If it's so obvious, why the long letter to King George?" Patrick asked.

"Not obvious to the *British*," declaimed Jamar, adjusting the silver-and-black frames that appeared midway through chapter nine of Malcolm's autobiography.

Jamar's pride in appreciating the distinction was justified; it had been a long hard slog through the national, regional, and religious issues of the rebellion. None of it seemed to stick. For most of them, the only meaningful signifier was race. And Mr. Lynch had done himself no favors by drawing comparisons with the Bolshevik revolution and using the term "White Russian." (Abdul: "How many Russians is Black, Lynch?" Patrick: "None that I can think of, Abdul. It's a political term." Jamar, nudging the glasses up his nose: "Pushkin was Black, Mr. L. Don't forget Pushkin.")

Attempting a brief summary of the American military campaign, Patrick had explained: "We were a disaster here in New York City—worse than the Knicks. We were a frozen mess at Valley Forge…but we triumphed sneakily at the Delaware River." He was halted in his march toward Yorktown by Maria's fluttering hand, perhaps raising a question, perhaps perfecting the arc of shiny black hair that shaded her almond eyes.

"Yes, Maria?"

"Excuse me, Mr. L." She'd patted a few strands back into the arc. "I don't mean to be rude or nothin'," she wrinkled her petite, caramel-colored nose, "but *who* is *we?*"

Being New Yorkers, they got *pluribus*; the *unum*, Patrick finally realized, would take time.

"'Unalienable,'" Patrick said, "that's a weird word. Who has that one?" He waited. Seeing no takers, he called on his go-to girl. "Hegira?"

She looked down at her notes, her face shrouded. She shook her head. "It's in the wrong form, Mr. Lynch, I think."

"Go for it."

"My dictionary is no good." She looked to her fellow ledge girls for support. They stared back solemnly. "Foreign, it says. Strange."

Mr. Lynch nodded. "Yes, 'alien.' That's on the right track."

"Strangers from another planet," said Abdul, followed by his famous intergalactic noise, half-hum, half-whistle.

"Oh snap, d'joo see *The X-Files* last night?" squealed Julio, Abdul's right-hand man. He waved his long, praying mantis arms. Julio's father was Dominican, his mother Haitian. This parentage, coupled with his extravagant gestures and slender prettiness, led to the stairwell graffiti claiming that Julio slept on "both sides of the island." Being Abdul's boyhood chum and court jester spared him additional physical abuse.

"Illegal aliens, next on Fox," intoned Abdul.

"My uncle Ramon's illegal," said Julio.

"Yo' whole family's illegal," said Abdul.

"Yo' mama's illegal…"

"Oooooo…" said Patrick's American Humanities class, in sudden hope that something more exciting than an explication of Lockean philosophy might develop second period.

"Enough," said Mr. Lynch, knowing that Abdul and Julio could easily burn forty minutes with this routine and, according to accounts of Sitkowitz's class, frequently had.

Strolling the aisles, a quick survey confirmed that homework completion lacked critical mass. Jefferson was dying. Plan B had been to introduce *The Adventures of Huckleberry Finn*, but he'd miscounted in the book room and was six copies short. Plan C—this being a new course, he had no Plan C.

The jackhammers on Columbus Avenue started up. The ancient radiator, which produced much noise but little heat, began its *ping-ping-ping*. Maria was evaluating her crimson nails. Abdul was about to punch Julio's shoulder. Josh was sleeping. Angela—Angela!—was sketching on her desk. She was his canary in the coal mine; if he lost her, it was really over. Patrick looked through the metal meshwork that covered his windows. A red Corvette was gunning up the ramp of the Park 'n' Pay across 103rd. A damp, early spring breeze leaked through the baseball-sized hole in the front windowpane. His first year at Science & Tech, Patrick put in a work order to have it fixed. A braver man would've sent in another work order, but Bernie, the hollow-eyed, brandy-breathed head custodian, was the only person in the building who scared him.

Patrick faced his students. He looked over their heads at the clock. Nine twenty-three. It would always be second period.

Help me, Emily. Her gaze was unyielding: *You let them do this to me. You never said a word.* The teacher's eyes came down on Julio, who, forgetting which class he was in, was slipping his Mets cap on, tilting it backward. Mr. Lynch strode to Julio's desk, snatched the cap off his head.

"What the—"

"No hats in class, Mr. Aguilar."

"Yo, Lynch—"

"But..." Patrick knew without looking that all eyes, save Josh's, were now on him, "you can have it back—you can wear it in class the rest of the *year*, Mr. Aguilar—if you can tell me what Thomas Jefferson and this man," he did a little hop, skip, and jump to the poster of Malcolm, rapped it with his knuckles, "have in common."

Julio's narrow face crumpled in despair. Who knew this would be the day doing homework actually mattered?

"They're both men," offered Abdul. "Can I have Julio's hat?" Julio glared at him.

"*When in the course of human events it becomes necessary to dissolve the bands...*" Patrick quoted, waving the cap in front of them as if it were his quill pen.

"They're both rebels," said Angela, her jaw set at the angle he'd seen after school in the gym, when her fist went through a board.

"A rebel? Jefferson? On his hilltop plantation?" Patrick flipped the cap, caught it by the brim. Jamar raised one hand and thumbed his text with the other. "Jamar?"

"*And for this we pledge our lives, our land, and our sacred honor.* Yeah, he owned a plantation and slaves, but if the British found him, he was gone."

"And he got all his rich friends to agree," said Maria, who had forgotten her nails. "Their names are on it same as his."

"Hmmm. I don't see the connection yet." Patrick tried the cap on for size. Julio squirmed.

"Malcolm used to work those crowds on 125th, up by the Apollo," offered Jamar.

"My dad heard him. He say everybody be screaming. Say brother could really talk some sh—stuff." This from Abdul, who'd said little during their discussions of the autobiography. A first for him, invoking his father, who, apparently, was moved enough by Malcolm to leave his son with the Nation of Islam name before he left for good.

"They were both persuasive, okay." Patrick stalked the room, taking off the cap, running a hand through his retreating hairline. "But to what end? Their philosophies?"

"The white man's the devil."

"The British are the devil."

Mr. Lynch threw his head back. "That's lame." He scowled. "That's weak."

"Tyrants," said Jamar. "The British were tyrants."

"Better," said Patrick. "What to do about it?"

"Fight back."

"How?"

"Protest."

"Arm yourself."

"*When in the course of human events it becomes necessary…*"

Julio sprang to his feet, pointing a long finger at the teacher. His eyes were wide. He thrust his shoulders back. "By any means necessary!" he shouted.

"Bravo, Mr. Aguilar, well done. A+." Mr. Lynch frisbeed the cap back to Julio, who snatched it out of the air and yanked it on his head to the class's applause. He gave a deep bow and sat with theatrical flourish.

Patrick let Julio and the class savor their collective brilliance for a moment. He glanced at his watch: twenty-five minutes left in the period. This could really go places. Patrick hugged his sides, which were a little damp. He put a fist on each hip. "So—Tom and Malcolm, a couple of homeboys, lookin' to stir somethin' up. Let's take it further. Who were their audiences? To whom were they appealing?" Half a dozen hands went up, several for the first time this year. That vein in Patrick's jaw pulsed.

A rat poked his nose and bristled his whiskers through the broken boards beneath the dangling feet of Hegira's girls. "Mickey!" screamed a familiar voice from the editing table in the back-right corner. Sleepy Josh had been driven off by his evil twin, Manic Josh. He stood with his arms outstretched, ready to embrace their visitor. Since construction commenced on Columbus Avenue, the sewer vermin had sought higher ground. It was Patrick who named the first one Mickey, in hopes of defusing the situation, of evoking a kinder, gentler rodent. Until now, the rats had always stayed back by the wall, amidst the boards, often noticed only by the teacher, but Josh had succeeded in spooking this one and he hopped out, sniffing the air, thrashing his hairless tail. The ledge girls, unruffled, peered down through their feet at Mickey, pulling at their skirts slightly, flashing a rare glimpse of ankle. Such creatures, perhaps, had been pets in Kabul, or dinner.

The rest of Mr. Lynch's second period American Humanities class was less composed. A number of the girls and more than a few boys scrambled atop their desks, hugging their knees in fear and delight as the rat darted from row to row. Abdul and his crew did the same, in parody, bleating falsetto cries, Julio leading the way, his mouth opened wide, his reedy fingers framing his face in a silent Munch-like scream. Jamar and Angela took in the proceedings with disgust, but their classmates, in the main, were enjoying themselves immensely. Any distraction—fistfight, fire drill—was a welcome change, but this was really good, surefire Topic A in the hallway.

Josh was gleeful. He leaned against the editing table, shaking his shoulder-length dreadlocks, Bob Marley's beatific stoned face looking on from his chest. "Mickey," he clapped his hands, "come to Papa."

"All right, everybody," Mr. Lynch said, finally, in a voice that sounded weary even to himself, giving last rites to their class discussion with that universal admission that things were irretrievably out of control. "Remain calm."

Mickey finished his circuit of the room and disappeared

into the broken boards. Patrick scanned his options, knowing he had only one, the one he'd hoped to save for May, Plan D: "Please open your texts to chapter six." Second period moaned but submitted. As his students hauled out their texts, a text their teacher loathed more than they, a text that portrayed the moon landing as a recent event, Patrick noted that Sleepy Josh was back, slumped on the editing table, his Medusa head nestled in the pillow of his arms.

That hard place returned to Patrick's throat. He cleared it with a cough. "Page 127," he announced. "A nation is born."

"A nation is bored," muttered Abdul. Julio giggled.

Sleepy Josh—who'd lost his third American history textbook two weeks before—sighed deeply, as if already dreaming. But as Patrick read the first sentence aloud, "Nations, like people, are often born in turmoil," he lifted one eyelid, dropped it, and puckered those fuzzy lips.

3

SUSAN

I don't know what it is with this kid, Susan. By this point I've usually got them in hand. He's running my class. It's humiliating."

"You've been complaining about Josh all year, Pat. Have the mother in for a chat. You can bring her around. You always do." Susan tugged the blue comforter over her lap and slapped the three pillows behind her into a more comfortable shape.

"But she's not like the other mothers. The other mothers don't have PhDs. The other mothers don't use Latin in their 'please excuse my son' notes."

"She doesn't."

"When I left a message that Josh hadn't finished his Malcolm X reflection, she wrote back 'Nolo contendere.'"

"Didn't happen."

"Did."

Susan looked doubtfully over her glasses. Chauncey, Susan's cat, followed the conversation from his perch on her dresser, blinking his clouded ancient eyes, shifting his puffy head back and forth like an overfed Wimbledon umpire. The judgmental edge, thought Patrick, when did that sneak in? She looked so uncompromising in those glasses, her dark hair pulled back, a style he used to enjoy thinking of as naughty librarian.

Patrick didn't like the turn this was taking, that too many nights were taking. But he had to defend himself. He set the stack of papers on his lap and turned to her. "Josh can't fully express his disdain for his mother as an Upper West Side, middle-class white boy; it's easier to do in blackface. And Dr. Mishkin likes telling her pals at NYU how much her son loves his public school—their kids, of course, are at Collegiate and

Spence. No armchair Marxist, she. Her son has friends in the 'hood. Which was all good, until he decided to *be* Black. And she didn't count on him getting the same attention as the other thirty-five kids in my second period. She wants public school props and private school perks."

Susan, ignoring his bon mot, let her book rest against her chest. "I think Dr. Mishkin is a bright, hard-working woman who wants her privileged but learning-disabled son to grow up in a racially and economically diverse environment. And she's trying to make that work while he goes through a particularly difficult developmental phase." Susan hunkered down into her pillows and hoisted her tome, *Aspects of Modern Social Work,* concealing, he knew, that expression of disapproval that had become her face when they were together. "God, Patrick, when did you get so cynical?"

He sucked in a breath, ready to respond, but it was a question that couldn't be answered without self-indictment. And clearly she had meant it as the end of their discussion, as her face remained covered by her book. He picked up his stack of papers and continued his grading.

This had once been a cherished ritual, she reading a novel or something from her social work program, he editing papers from his creative writing classes. They'd interrupt one another when they came across something significant. Susan especially loved the raps. *I'm the greatest mack in this whole world/ now don't you front, jus be my girl.* The boys' raps moved her. They always said the same thing—I'm the baddest, my dick's the biggest—but to her they always meant respect me, love me, don't hurt me.

Providing entree into inner-city life was, amazingly, how he'd won her. No other woman in New York City had been so moved by his choice of careers.

He'd followed a college girlfriend to New York. Helene. Raised in an old-world Armenian neighborhood outside Boston. In her family, teaching was viewed as a woman's task. Not a profession, really, teaching children. A professor, yes. Helene had slept with her classics professor. He was refined and worldly. Business, law, medicine—these were acceptable pursuits for a man. Soon after Patrick settled in New York and it became clear that this urban teaching gig was more than a short-term, domestic Peace Corps affair, she dumped him. The rest of Patrick's twenties were years in the romantic wilderness. There was the occasional interlude with females equally at loose ends: undiscovered actresses/barmaids, office temps, publishing house gofers. No real connections, just things that went bump in the night. But there was always teaching to consume his days and working on his master's degree to absorb his nights.

It was Oscar, Patrick's college chum and sometime roommate, who pulled him into the swim. Oscar was short, dark, proudly half-Puerto Rican. Hunting women struck him as a noble venture; he claimed it was his "Latin blood."

"I know just the place," Oscar said as they stalked Columbus Avenue. The saloons they passed seemed interchangeable to Patrick and some held unfortunate memories. They were always crammed with brokers, lawyers, bankers and, although he was tall, reasonably attractive, and appropriately groomed, the body language always constricted at the words *public school teacher*; the hair-flicking and arm-touching stopped and the pretty associate from Smith, Fletcher & Boyd would cross her arms in front of her little black dress and begin looking over his shoulder. *This man will never summer in the Hamptons* said the suddenly hunched shoulders; *his children will never attend Dalton* said the elbows that now hid the breasts.

Oscar tugged Patrick into Jake's Last Chance and ordered a couple of upmarket beers. He pointed his chin at a group of young women, maybe five or six, in after-work dresses.

Oscar ambled toward the pack. He glanced at the TV behind the bar and shook his head. "Can you believe how lame that show is?" He smiled at a petite blonde. She smiled back. That's all it took. The circle opened; they were in. So obvious, Patrick thought, so manipulative. Then again, all his Midwestern ingenuousness had gotten him nowhere.

The place got louder. The girls got looser, flirtier. The little blonde, assistant to an assistant on Wall Street, offered that the men in her office were all jerks.

"What kind of men do you like?" asked Oscar.

"I like my men the way I like my coffee," she smirked.

"Café con leche?" asked Oscar, playing the Latin lover card. She asked him how he liked his women. He showed off his white teeth. "Like my beer." Dirty laughs from the group.

Thus began a can-you-top-this of sexual preference similes:

"Like my universities, well-endowed."

"Like my paintings, well-hung."

The quips circled round and Patrick no longer heard them above the ambient hum of chatter, TV, and ice-on-glass, so focused was he on his turn. He'd not made a dent yet; the wingman had barely kept up with the leader. It was like the fifth-grade spelling bee: they were all standing, and he was waiting, waiting for his turn. He'd get one shot and spell it right and remain standing or miss it and sit down in humiliation. His turn was coming. His mind was empty.

"I like my men like my cheese: hard, French, smelly." This from a slender, pale, dark-haired woman with tortoise-shell glasses, her head canted at a saucy angle. How had he not noticed her? Everyone laughed, but she just looked up at him, expressionless.

"I like my women…" he began, and seconds passed as they do on stage when an actor forgets his line, "…like my oil: light, sweet, crude."

She smiled at this. He had, improbably, named her.

Ultimately, Susan pried *him* away from the herd. And though she looked, in outline, like the rest—young and lovely and rather corporate—her response to him was the reverse of all he'd experienced in Manhattan watering holes. She'd come to Jake's straight from her job at her father's insurance company, but she'd recently decided that her parents' suburban dream wasn't for her, that she wanted to do something *valuable* with her life. Her background may have been East Coast cliché, prep-schooled and Darien-bred, but to Patrick's Midwestern eyes she was exotic: that rare pretty girl—unknown in Peterson's Prairie—with the crush not on the quarterback but on her English teacher.

And so, to his surprise and delight, the very thing he was loath to reveal was the thing that captivated her. She nodded earnestly at the mention of his occupation and listened, rapt, to his teacher war stories. Her pupils dilated at the knife fights he'd preempted; she laughed and tossed her head at the stairwell couplings he'd forestalled; her hand went to his knee as he described the scrawny Haitian boy who'd slashed himself with his own box cutter, how he'd helped him wash off the blood in the custodian's sink and wrapped his hand with a T-shirt from Lost and Found, only contemplating exposure to HIV later, after an oblique inquiry by Kupczek. And your doctor? Susan said, raising an eyebrow. He gave you the all clear? Patrick laughed a little too loud and smiled. She took his hand and took him home.

Soon Oscar was looking for a new wingman and roommate. Patrick gathered his few effects and moved into the little condo near Columbia, where Susan was getting her MSW, which Susan's parents had purchased as an "investment."

Susan's parents, Bryce and Pepper (parents in Darien had names that retrievers had in Minnesota), were impressed by Patrick's manners, and that his father had been a school superintendent. But Patrick detected a bemusement, bordering on concern, over his prospects. There was cachet, a reverse-snob appeal, in having one's daughter choose social work over running the family business, but Patrick couldn't help noticing that those of Susan's girlfriends who had also chosen morally elevated careers had, in addition, the good sense to mate with investment bankers and litigators.

Though Susan referred to herself as a "refugee from Darien," she carried on a love-hate affair with her class. She was embarrassed by her privilege, fought it in ways large and small: never taking a taxi when she could hop a bus; ordering chicken instead of the shrimp; refusing to let Patrick pick up a check, a custom both "sexist" and "bourgeois." But vacations at her family's place in the Adirondacks were a cherished tradition. Patrick kept finding tiny jars of Corsican anchovy remoulade from Zabar's on their shelves.

The differences in class and region were both their core and fault line, and the first fissures spread in an argument over money. Susan paid a token, below-market "rent" to her parents every month and only expected Patrick to pay half of that. When Patrick insisted that he pay what he'd been paying for his previous apartment, that he didn't expect her parents to subsidize him, she called him stubborn. What did it matter who paid what, as long as it was fair? She was going to be a social worker; he taught poor kids. If her parents underwrote those projects, where was the harm? From each according to his ability, she argued. Susan gave in, though, publicly miffed but secretly pleased at his self-reliance. He overheard her discussing this with her mother on the phone. Her words revealed little, but her tone said See? I found a *man*. Not one of those trust fund babies my girlfriends married.

And that was the newest and widest crack in their relationship: marriage. She broached it first, in the abstract. I'd want to get married outdoors, she'd sigh as they strolled the rose garden in Central Park; Venice would be a fun place to honeymoon, she'd say, thumbing the *Times* travel section. He would nod, agreeing in the abstract, not tipping his hand. Susan was annoyed, though, then hurt. And who could blame her? He was thirty-one; she was twenty-seven. It wasn't an unfair expectation, Patrick could see that. Even Oscar, ever the hound dog, said "*Cabrón*, she's hot, she's smart, she's rich. Don't know what she sees in your sad schoolteacher ass but jump that train before it leaves the station."

Eventually, there were fights. Yes, he loved her. No, no, he wasn't carrying a torch for Helene. Or anyone. He wanted to get his master's degree first, make a little more money. Why is it always about money? she said. Only someone from your background would say that, he thought but never said.

Something essential changed, though, some emotional jujit-su took place, with her internship at the women's shelter. Later and later she came home at night, exhausted but exhilarated, her dark eyes shiny, those pale cheeks flushed.

"She is the sweetest woman, Pat," Susan would say be-tween bites of the now overcooked stroganoff or stir-fry or enchiladas he'd made. "She's had the hardest life, but she's still really hopeful," she'd continue, listing the abusive step-fathers, baby-daddies, and society that had led this client to this place. Then Susan's eyes would widen as she detailed the job counseling she'd scheduled, the gynecological exams, the day care arrangements for the woman's children. She'd tilt her head in that adorable way, her favorite shiraz from that little wine shop on 106th staining her lips, adjusting those funky glasses, geeky-beautiful. Then she'd look at him, dreamy, the way she used to after he'd told one of his long teacher war stories, or after they'd had sex—back when they had regular sex—and say, "You can't imagine, Pat, what it's like to help someone who has never been helped before. Who has no idea why some white lady cares one way or the other about her life." She sipped her wine. "It's the greatest feeling."

He could imagine, actually. But, clearly, he was no longer the source of her greatest feelings. Now every teaching move he shared with Susan was deconstructed according to the latest lefty theory they'd fed her at Columbia, and found wanting. Where once he'd been her Sidney Poitier in *To Sir, with Love*, now he was a functionary, a drone in the public school hive. Later and later she came home from the shelter, aglow, afire. Fleetingly, he wondered if it was another man who was keeping her out, some hyper-feminized, goateed, over-educated Mar-cusian, and not the addicted, abused, hyper-fertile women she described with such fervor.

Finally, desperate, he'd even dipped a toe in that marital pond.

"Venice," he said, perusing the Sunday *Times*, "that *would* be a great honeymoon."

"Hmmm," Susan said, erasing an answer from the cross-word, dismissing more than that faded, sinking city.

She was withdrawing, Susan was, pulling in on herself, just as the blue comforter always ended up wound around her, girding her loins, that social work tome her breastplate.

Chauncey leaped down from Susan's dresser and up on the bed, circled a spot at the foot two times, and plumped his fat body down. (Why always two times? Patrick asked when he first moved in. I don't know, she'd replied. It's what cats do; it's how they find their place.) This *was* his place, Susan made clear. He had slept there since she was in junior high; she wasn't sure she could sleep without him. And so, though Patrick was mildly allergic to him, there he stayed. No amount of sleepless thrashing could unseat him. Patrick, awakened by his own sneezing, would find himself bolt upright, glaring at Chauncey; the cat would be sitting up, staring back, blinking occasionally. Back in the early, steamy days of their relationship, Chauncey liked to sit there and watch. It alarmed Patrick at first, looking up after a frantic bout of lovemaking, sheets, pillows, underclothes all about the room, to see Chauncey in his place, placid as the Sphinx.

The cat opened wide his jaws in a slow yawn, thrusting out his tongue at Patrick. Patrick sneezed.

Susan looked over her book. "Did you get the cat food?"

"We still have some Purina."

"The vet said Chauncey needs the special food for senior cats. The Purina's bad for his kidneys." Susan swept her long black hair from the pillow and smoothed it with one hand, draping it over her freckled left shoulder. This had always gotten to him, and still did. Even now.

"I'll get some on the way home from school. I promise." Susan lifted her book, nodding her head behind it a little too vigorously in that way that said, *I know you won't.*

Patrick could feel *he's your fucking cat* worming its way up his esophagus, but he swallowed as it reached his soft palate, remembering the new regime, how Chauncey was *their* cat now.

Having taken marriage off the table, Susan had renegotiated their contract: Patrick was now the *primary caregiver*, removing Chauncey's litter-leavings and swabbing his nocturnal regurgitations, giving Patrick the chance to prove his worthiness as a mate. Somehow that obese, blind, fur-vomiting creature had become the measure of the husband, the father, he was likely to be.

Susan closed her book and stretched to stroke Chauncey, who was sprawled at her feet, lapping the thick fur on his belly, gathering material for his next eruption. She clicked off the light on her nightstand, the understood signal for Patrick to turn off his light and go to sleep, or, in better times, make his move. He turned to put the stack of papers on his nightstand, paused to consider its heft and that most of the papers had to be returned first period, and leaned back. Normally he would have gotten up early and dealt with them, but he wasn't feeling generous.

Susan turned to him. "You weren't that different, you know," she said, gently.

He ignored the shift in tone. "Different from what?"

"Josh. When you were a kid."

"Says who?"

"You." She smiled. "Drove your parents crazy, didn't you?" She nudged him with that freckled shoulder. It was a delicate subject.

He'd told her bits from his Midwestern youth, highly selective bits, the parts that conformed to her romantic ideal. She liked to think he'd been a bit of a scamp, a bucolic bad boy. Take me to Minnesota, she'd pleaded. He'd put her off: There's nothing there to see. His mother had been out to visit briefly, a year ago. She'd said Susan was "lovely," which meant a little intimidating.

"Drove them crazy?" Patrick considered, softening. "I believe I did." She didn't know the half of it.

4

PETERSON'S PRAIRIE, 1978

Preachers' 'n teachers' kids," said Gunther, "you've got two choices." He tugged his black watch cap down on his forehead and stretched against the red pleather of the banquette, surveying the Full Moon Cafe. His blue work shirt was already spotted with brown dots, though he was only halfway through his first cup of coffee. Philosophizing, for Gunther, was always a messy business. "One, you can become your parents. Please them. Try to outdo them." He threw a scrawny limb to either side, curled his hands around, as if he had a pretty girl under each arm. "Or, two, rebel. Be your own man. Make their lives a living hell." Gunther scratched his scrubby goatee, smoothed back his ponytail, relaxed into the banquette. He had spoken.

Patrick, being a teacher's kid, had some thoughts of his own on this subject, not necessarily in accord with Gunther's. But he took a sip of coffee and kept his own counsel. Friends, in Peterson's Prairie, were hard to come by for him—let alone best friends. And the kids at Willard County High School who could quote Kafka or Kerouac in one breath and Harmon Killebrew's batting average in the next were limited to a party of one.

It was pointless arguing with him; there was no topic on which Gunther could not, and would not, speak with authority. From women ("girls like it rougher than you'd think") to the most efficient high ("mixing vodka with Gatorade gets you drunk 37 percent faster"), Gunther always had the critical information. If he was occasionally sketchy as to his sources, Patrick lacked both the background and stamina to pin him to the mat. And when he'd try, Gunther would launch into an upward spiral of psychology-physics-sociology-pop culture that would make Patrick's eyeballs ache. "You see," Gunther would screech, popping into the soprano of Eric Idle, his favorite from that Python show, "I've run circles 'round you. Law-jic-ly."

Today's thesis couldn't be easily dismissed. Yes, being a teacher's kid made one suspect. And when your dad had been a teacher, principal, *and* superintendent, it pretty much sealed the deal. And—completely unnecessary—Patrick's mom was the high school office secretary. Education, the Lynches joked, was the family business. Gunther's family's business was running the smaller of the two filling stations in town, Hendrickson's Best Gas. It was their shared sense of irony that had brought the boys together, the superintendent's son with *Mad Magazine* hidden in his science binder and the mechanic's son who was re-reading *The Stranger*.

"Your problem, son," Gunther said, leaning to one side, crushing the invisible girl on his left, "is that you haven't decided which way to go. You're too afraid of alienating the old man to risk doing something dangerous." Since Gunther discovered Camus, alienation was a risk we all had to take. "And, on the other hand," he cozied up to the girl on his right, "you're too terrified of failure to boldly go beyond your dad's achievements out in the real world." *To boldly go.* Camus to Captain Kirk: that was Gunther. "Thus, in essence," he leaned over his coffee cup, took a gulp, "you're rat-fucked."

"Gunnie," Patrick shook his head, "you're so full of shit your eyes are brown."

"They're blue." True, of course; a shocking Norwegian blue. Patrick slurped his coffee. "You're down a quart."

Gunther shifted to one buttock, smirked. In a moment, Patrick discovered why.

"Just a small free sample," Gunther said, "of Hendrickson's Best."

It was Gunther's turn. He leaned back against the corner of his unmade bed, clacking the dice in his cupped hands interminably, as he always did at this stage of the game, to heighten the drama. Bat-o-matic, a fantasy baseball game involving dice, a spinner, and cards with the statistics of Major League players, was Gunther's favorite. After the dice were rolled and the spinner spun, the cards were consulted and a formula followed that only Gunther understood, leading to a triple or a strikeout, a wild pitch or stolen base. It was a slow-paced game, slower than baseball itself. Patrick found it tedious, but it captivated Gunther, combining two of his loves, sports and stats. Patrick indulged his friend only for the pleasure of listening to his play-by-play.

"Well, Jack, we got a real cliff-hanger here at old Wrigley, don't we?" Clackety-clackety-clack. The giant tongue on Gunther's Rolling Stones T-shirt licked the air as he bobbed with the dice. "We sure do, Lou. Bottom of the ninth, and yes-sir-yes-sir-three-bags-full of Cubbies. Two outs, Mets up by three, and..." he shuffled through the players cards "...Paul Popovich ambling out of the dugout to pinch hit." Gunther always opted for obscurity in key situations. If Billy Williams came through in the clutch, where was the glory in that? Just doing his job. But if Popovich...

In more lopsided games, when Patrick's interest flagged long before the ninth inning, Gunther resorted to his rain-delay parody:

Jack: Should he bring in a righty or a southpaw to pitch to the switch-hitting Kessinger?
Lou: I guess it's all relative, as old Al Einstein would say.
Jack: Are you talkin' the general or special theory of relativity, Lou?
Lou: I'm talkin' the 1915 general theory, Jack, wherein Einstein posited that space is curved and light bends around planets like a Mike Cuellar screwball around Reggie Jackson's forty-ouncer.

or

Jack: This one's a real tight-collar job.
Lou: Speaking of collars, that's a snappy tie you're wearing, Jack.

Jack: Thanks, Lou.

Lou: And I like how those pants fit, kinda snug across the thighs.

Jack: Oh, Lou...

And always there was a moment when Gunther would invoke Katie Osterlund. Katie, Queen of Willard County High, the pertest and blondest in a land of pert blondness. It was embarrassing to Patrick, this hopeless crush, but it dated back to elementary school and had grown just as he had grown, unstoppably, unpredictably. That this infatuation was so disconnected from reality, that Katie was smitten with Doug Knutson, broad-shouldered pass-hurler for the Willard County Homesteaders, and that her devotion was manifested every autumn Saturday afternoon as she cheered him from the sidelines, made it worse. That, and Doug being an idiot. "She's your Daisy Buchanan," proclaimed Gunther when they finished *Gatsby* last semester. His friend's literary allusions, offered up for Gunther's self-amusement, generally sailed past Patrick, but this one struck home. The implication that Katie was both unworthy of his worship and forever out of his league stung doubly. Years ago, Gunther fell upon Patrick's object of desire as an essential bit of gamesmanship. At a game's climax, when Patrick would have his moment of indecision—bring in the reliever? pinch-hit for the starter?—Gunther would husk: "Do it, Pat. Do it for Katie."

Finally, Gunther let the dice spill across his stained, gray bedroom carpet. Two sixes. He spun the spinner: ten. He checked the Popovich card. "Back. Way, way back," he said in his high-pitched Jack voice. "Cubbies win. Can you believe it?"

"I can't," Patrick shouted. "Let me see that." He stole the card from Gunther's sweaty fingers, nearly knocking over his lemonade. "I can't tell what the hell this means."

"We've been playing this since we were twelve. I'm not explaining it again."

"Well, this is a fucking stupid game. And there are way too

many ninth-inning grand slams." Patrick glared at the card. "And always for your team."

"Are you impugning my integrity?" Gunther squared his narrow shoulders, centered his watch cap. Mick's tongue stuck out from his chest.

"I'm not playing this again."

"Fine."

"I'm not. I mean it this time."

"Fine. Think of something better. I'm sick of always making the plan, then you blame me for it." Gunther swept the cards, dice, and spinner under his bed and threw himself back onto his carpet, his hands under his head.

Like an old married couple, they'd had this argument countless times. Patrick knew his next line. He could have typed up the whole transcript and printed it out, had they computers and printers in Peterson's Prairie, Minnesota, 1978.

Gunther rolled over to his secondhand record player and placed the needle back on *The Dark Side of the Moon*, an album he was nearly wearing out.

Pink Floyd summed up Gunther neatly: anglophilic, like no other teenage boy in Peterson's Prairie, and angry, like all of them. Patrick was angry, too. At Gunther, for being right. His dime store psychoanalysis at the Full Moon had gotten under Patrick's skin—he *was* alarmingly passive, a failure in both the Honor Society sense and the born-to-be-wild sense. What had he accomplished in his sixteen years? He was a minnow even in the tiny pond of Peterson's Prairie, achieving neither fame nor notoriety. Gunther was weird, true, but Gunther was Gunther. Who was he? His father's son, that's who. His father's son.

Pink Floyd slipped into "Time," their clocks chiming, pulsing. Tock, tock, tock. And as Patrick stared at his best friend's dirty left foot flexing to the metronomic beat, it came to him.

"Gunther," he said, "I have a plan."

Gunther practically skipped down Main Street ahead of Patrick, nearly knocking over Mrs. Johansson, her arms full of groceries. He'd never looked more delighted or amazed. He was always the one with the propositions. Patrick's role was to approve or veto: yes to shooting hoops on the backboard behind Hendrickson's Best; no to shooting squirrels behind the Methodist church; yes to testing bottle rockets in Patrick's backyard; no to testing Newton's Laws of Motion at the abandoned gravel quarry off Rural Route 17.

"This," he cackled at Patrick, "is perfect. For you, perfect. It'd be like me," he spread his arms to encompass downtown Peterson's Prairie, which was two blocks long but their known world, "it'd be like me torching Hendrickson's Best."

Patrick glanced modestly to his left as they passed Knutson's Shop-Rite. Van Kamps Pork 'n' Beans was only thirty-seven cents this week. "Oh, it's not that extreme." He couldn't help grinning. "After all, we don't own the school."

"But what a plan, man." Gunther smacked Patrick's shoulder. "It's more than a plan—it's a *scheme*."

The Scheme had been Patrick's brainchild; that was the vital thing. But, that understood, the details, inevitably, were Gunther's.

"We've gotta case the place first, make a floor plan." Gunther squeezed his eyes shut and rested his head on the steering wheel. "Oh, damn, brain freeze." The Walgreens in the new strip mall on the access highway into Winnipee Falls had the best grape slurpees. And Gunther's mom worked there, so they got them for free. When you figured in the gas, though, it was hardly a bargain, but that wasn't the point. They'd recently graduated from bikes; thanks to Gunther's new license and use of one of the ancient trucks at Hendrickson's Best, they'd magically expanded their universe. Delicacies previously unavailable were now within reach.

"Floor plan? We don't need no stinkin' floor plan."

Gunther snorted. They both were insomniacs addicted to the *Late, Late Movie*. He shook his head.

"Gotta have one."

"I got it all up here, Gunnie." Patrick tapped his temple. "I was raised in that building." Even Gunther couldn't argue that point. Patrick's dad had been a history teacher at the high school when he was born. He and his big sister Erin, now a freshman at the U of M, had had the run of the place when they were little, until Mr. Lynch became principal of Peterson's Prairie Elementary. Saturdays, when their mom was doing the wash, their dad would take them to the empty high school. While Mr. Lynch planned lessons, his children made a playground of his workplace; there was no teacher's desk they hadn't rifled through, no yardstick they hadn't sword fought with. Now Superintendent Lynch was back at the high school, his office next to the principal's. Patrick knew every square inch.

"You've memorized all the outlets? The vents?"

Patrick shrugged. Gunther kept insisting they go in through the roof, though there was no alarm system and a window would be simpler. It was all very *Thomas Crown Affair* in his mind. Which was okay, maybe, except Gunther would expect to play the Steve McQueen part. And what did that leave him—Faye Dunaway?

Gunther leaned against the steering wheel, licking his purple lips. Patrick could tell by the way his buddy ran his hands up and down the wheel that this issue was nonnegotiable. For all his what-the-hell goofy indifference, Gunther was, at bedrock, one stubborn bastard. "Okay," Patrick said, planting his sneakers on the dash, "we make a floor plan first. We can do it Saturday. I'll tell my dad we're doing technical drawing in art class."

Gunther just nodded, slurping at his slurpee and squinting at the Walgreens that would eventually attract a Target discount store that would attract a McDonalds that would attract a Mobil station that would put Hendrickson's Best out of business, and then, finally, a Walmart would thump down like that flatulent foot of God at the end of the Python show, squishing the mall, downtown Peterson's Prairie, and pretty much the town itself. "This," murmured Gunther, "is going to be so great."

Yes, it was only meatloaf, but his mother's meatloaf was excellent. Patrick was still in that late-childhood stage where the choice of dinner could make or ruin his day. He cut himself two thick slices and spooned several spoonfuls of the au gratin potatoes his mother had made especially for him. He felt her approval as he stuffed his mouth with the cheesy potatoes. Before this recent growth spurt she was always picking at him (*Eat, eat*), fretting that he was going to be smallish and thin, like her and Erin, which was fine for a girl—hadn't Erin been adorable in her pom-pom outfit?—but it was harder, she said, for a boy. Since he'd shot up and filled out this school year, she still clung to the possibility of him taking after his father.

"Frank," she snapped at her husband as he reached for the potatoes. "Yours is in the oven. I think it's done." Patrick watched his dad nod, then lumber into the kitchen and return with his baked potato and a stick of margarine. With surgical care he sliced open the spud and administered a pat of margarine to each half. He then helped himself to a single slice of meatloaf and a bowl of green salad. He dosed the salad with a drizzle of low-calorie dressing and looked up at his wife, waving over the meal as if he'd suddenly made it appear. "Very nice, Francis. Dr. Greene would be pleased."

Since Patrick started putting weight on, the focus had shifted to his dad taking it off. Looking at his father, he wouldn't have called him fat, exactly: a broad genial face centered on a huge pair of shoulders, as if his designer had forgotten the neck part; a Gibraltar of chest overlooking a gently sloping gut. Nothing unusual in a male of forty-eight, particularly in Peterson's Prairie, where the '70s fitness craze wasn't even a rumor. The outline of the high school linebacker was still there. But Dr. Greene had sounded the alarm—lower that blood pressure, take off twenty pounds. The Field Marshal had gone to work: no more bratwurst, no more bacon, Frank's beloved cream soda replaced by Tab.

Patrick's mother tossed her son that girlish grin, as if his dad's new health regimen was their little conspiracy. But Patrick just looked down at his plate. His father's bulk was reality at its most basic, a reassuring monument, like Mt. Rushmore or

Stonehenge. Do what you like, it wasn't going anywhere. "So, honey," she chirped, "how did that geometry quiz go today?"

Patrick stabbed his meatloaf. "Okay, I guess."

Before his mother could say You *guess?* his father sighed. "Ah, geometry. My nemesis. My *bête noire.*"

His mother laughed. "You? You were good at geometry. You were like Patrick—good at everything."

His father waved his fork. "Not geometry, Norma. Why do you think I taught history?"

"Now I—Erin and I—we're pluggers." His mother swirled her salad around her bowl. "We plug away. We get the job done, but it doesn't come easily."

"Geometry's not easy," Patrick mumbled through a mouthful of meatloaf.

"Oh, I'm not saying it's easy, honey. But when you apply yourself—"

"Leonardo," interjected his father. "Everything came easy for him. Painting, inventing. Great athlete, too. They say he could bend a metal bar with his bare hands."

"Did Mr. Sheehan like your *Catcher in the Rye* piece?"

Patrick shrugged. "I guess."

"Well, I thought it was very insightful. You're good with words, Pat."

He shrugged again.

"Alexander Hamilton," said his father, lifting his fork, proffering a wedge of tomato to no one in particular, "cranked out four or five of those *Federalist Papers* a week. Thousands and thousands of words—gorgeous prose—almost no revisions. Remarkable. Mozart, too—"

"Frank." Norma gave him her indulgent smile, her cheerleader-who-tackled-the-linebacker smile. Although highly esteemed in the community as an administrator—Dr. Lynch, local farm boy made good—he was ever nostalgic for the classroom. Such history moments were a staple of the Lynch dinner table.

"My point is," Patrick's father set his fork down, "these few geniuses aside, we're all *incrementalists*. We don't learn in sudden epiphanies. We learn," he moved his hands down the table in parallel vertical planes, "step-by-step. Except for the Newtons and Darwins, we're all 'pluggers.' We just plug at different rates in different subjects. Considering—"

"Francis."

Frank put his hands flat on the table and looked at his wife.

"This wouldn't happen to be the rough draft of your presentation to the school board on that new reading program?"

"Perhaps." Frank laughed. "I'm not Mozart. I need practice."

"Speaking of practice," Patrick's mother turned to him, "Miss Sturmblad wants to know if you're going to continue guitar lessons this summer." She waited for her son to respond. "What do you think?"

Patrick wobbled his head side-to-side.

"Is that a 'yes'?"

Patrick deked the last bite of meatloaf across his plate. "I don't know. Maybe."

"Well, she needs to know."

His father nodded. "She's got plans, too, sport."

Patrick found it hard to imagine Miss Sturmblad having plans, stuck as she was on "Tom Dooley" and "Kumbaya," despite her claim of being Bobby Zimmerman's childhood playmate back in Hibbing. She wouldn't know Lou Reed if he bit her on the ass. Which he wouldn't. But this was as directive as his father ever got with him, and it forced his attention. Everyone assumed that Patrick's general disinterest in the world was a response to his dad's expectations. But his father's expectations, if he had any, were a mystery to him. His mother's cheery prodding aside, he was left to his own devices. It was a conflict of interest for Dr. Lynch to inquire too deeply into his children's dealings with their teachers. If his son needed help with his homework, he'd give it. If he wanted to play the guitar, he'd buy it. If the guitar gathered dust in Patrick's closet, so be it.

"Okay." Patrick turned to his dad. "I'll decide."

"And the job at Knutson's," said his mother, "are you still interested in that?"

This was a moment when he really missed Erin. She would've chatter-chatter-chattered throughout dinner with their mother—her dress for the prom, what boy was asking what girl, did they have more Cool Whip?—random and meaningless—irritating—questions, but the spotlight would never have fallen on him. His dad would fill any dead air with a set-piece on the Renaissance or ancient Egypt or the best pedagogy for teaching fractions. A question this uncomfortable—and untimely—would never come up.

He tapped his fork on his plate. "Actually, I was thinking… Gunther said maybe…I could work at—Hendrickson's." Patrick looked at his parents. They looked at each other. There, he'd said it. This was not the week he'd planned to spring this on them, but there it was.

"Hendrickson's?" His mother fought the inflection she gave this word, but her voice rose that judgmental half-step. "Are you sure you don't want to—"

Patrick's father showed a palm to his wife. "No offense, son, but what do you know about cars?"

"Not much. But it'd be pumping gas and stocking and cleaning, mostly. Gunther could teach me stuff."

His mother shook her head.

"What? Gunther's really smart, you know."

"I know." She pursed her lips. "He's got the highest Iowa test scores in the history of Willard County. And the lowest grades in the sophomore class."

"Norma." This was as loud as his father got. But Patrick took no comfort from it, understanding that Dr. Lynch's displeasure came from this singular breach of professional ethics and not its use against his friend.

He turned on his mother. "You've always hated Gunther."

She flushed. "That's not true. Not true at all." She swallowed. "I just don't think he's the…the best influence."

"He's my best friend!"

"What about Charlie Sorenson? You two used to get along so well—"

"In third grade, Mother!" He threw up his hands. "We both liked *fire engines.*"

"Patrick," said his father, the voice of reason. "Your mother and I will discuss it, consider it." His mother let out a bitter sigh that revealed they already had. "You could learn a lot from Fred Hendrickson. The man's a magician with a carburetor. And an honest businessman—never charges a nickel more than he's owed. But I've known him a long time. He's got more temper than any adult you know." His father let that truth linger in the air.

"May I go do my homework?" Patrick asked. Not a request his parents were likely to hear twice, and one they could hardly refuse. *I only said we'd discuss it, Norma,* he heard as he retreated to his room, a voice something like his father's but with a lot less authority.

"A toast," proclaimed Gunther, hoisting his Bovenmyer's beer, "to Patrick's Scheme."

Patrick raised his beer. "To tomorrow."

"May 9, 1978, a day which shall live in infamy."

They clinked longneck bottles and leaned back against the windshield. The windshield was pleasantly warm, as was the hood of the rusty Ford pickup. Dusk was settling over the soybean field off Rural Route 17, the sky gray-pink beyond the stretching flatness. Patrick breathed in the freshly turned soil. "I love that smell. What is that?"

Gunther took a large swallow of his Bovey's, *the beer to pick when you're having six.* "That?" He inhaled. "That's loamy."

"It's—it's what? You made that up." Gunther had a rich invented vocabulary, a personal dictionary. Yesterday was *frajulation.*

"Loamy." Gunther adjusted his watch cap. "Jesus—haven't you read anything? Willa Cather? Rolvaag? Midwestern earth is loamy—everybody knows that."

Gunther seldom oppressed him with his superior knowledge; that was at the core of their friendship. He teased him plenty, called him a Philistine, but the joke was always on Gunther: Can you believe how weird I am? It was that third beer that brought out the edge. He'd heard it in Mr. Hendrickson's voice before: *Gunther, you dumbshit, where'd ya put the oil gaskets?* It scared him more than he'd ever admit. But he'd die before he'd take that job his mother had lined up with Mrs. Johansson, bagging groceries at Knutson's, Doug's family's store.

Patrick swigged his beer, forced a mouthful down. He had no taste for alcohol. Neither of his parents drank; it held no glamour for him. Just one of the factors that kept him outside every clique at WCHS. Nursing a beer alongside Gunther was an occasional price of his friendship, like playing that stupid baseball game.

Gunther didn't look at Patrick, just bobbed his head slightly, pulling at the hairs on his chin, an attitude Patrick read as disdain. "Maybe we should just forget the whole thing tomorrow," Patrick mumbled.

"What?" Gunther jerked his head back, as if Patrick had interrupted a conversation he was having with himself.

Patrick put his beer down on the hood of the truck. "Maybe you could find a smarter partner in crime."

"When, exactly," Gunther waved his Bovenmyer's in befuddlement, "did you start listening to me?"

Though he'd spent countless hours—days, weeks—inside Willard County High, as faculty brat and student, he'd never been on the roof. Only a tall single story, it couldn't have afforded much of a view even in daylight. All Patrick could make out by moonlight was the chain-link backstop, the white lines of the parking lot and the yellow rectangle marked BUS. The original WCHS had come down when Patrick was in kindergarten. The older building—two-story, red brick, built during the booming 1920s—had seemed majestic to him, a big school for big kids. An edifice well worth climbing. This '60s pre-fab job was a disappointing, already-crumbling embarrassment. "Late Prairie School," Dr. Lynch had once described it, as if Frank Lloyd Wright himself had taken part in its design.

Patrick kicked at the tarred, pebbly roof. Somehow he knew he'd wind up playing the girl's part—lookout—in his own scheme. No sign of the county sheriff's car, of course, not at 2:07 a.m. Still, the sheriff was known to cruise by the high school at night this time of year, senior prank season. Through the years, seniors had deposited cows, sheep, and the principal's St. Bernard on this roof. Running into inebriated seniors—not cops—had been Patrick's biggest fear, but Gunther assured him that prank season never started till after prom, next week.

"Shit, shit." Patrick pointed his flashlight toward Gunther's muffled shout. A pair of work boots waggled out of the vent—a large upside-down J—like a chorine in a big Busby Berkeley production number. "Pull me out, pull me out," he shouted. Patrick wrapped his arms around the ankles of Gunther's greasy jeans and tugged. His tool belt was jammed in the curve of the J.

"Harder."

"I'm trying," Patrick grunted. Throwing all his weight backward he freed Gunther, who fell, tool belt jangling, into his lap. Gunther shook himself, wiping under his eyes, smearing the black eyeliner he'd scribbled around his face. Hadn't Cary Grant used it as a cat burglar? Okay, Peter Sellers, then. "You look like a raccoon, Gunnie." Patrick smelled the sour beer on his breath, tried to push him off. "A fucking drunk raccoon."

Gunther rolled over. "I'm not drunk," he mumbled. "Just a little toast beforehand."

"Yeah, a little toasted." Patrick stood, smacking the dust off his jeans. Gunther had mandated black, but jeans and a purple Vikings sweatshirt were the best he could do. "So, what's the problem?"

Gunther sat up, pulled his black watch cap over his forehead. "It's like this," he began, and launched into one of his monologues, this one so technical Patrick was lost from—defibrillator? He wouldn't ask for clarification.

Patrick threw out his hands. "Stop, Gunther. Make this simple. What's the bottom line?"

Gunther took in a deep breath, blew it out. "Bottom line: we go in through the window."

Patrick kicked pebbles at him. "Jesus H. Christ!" He kicked at the roof again. "After all this!" He stalked off.

Gunther stood. "I'm sorry, man. I didn't figure in the—*car.*" He pointed toward a set of headlights turning into the faculty parking lot driveway. "Down."

They fell to their stomachs. Patrick skinned his palms as he hit the roof, pebbles imprinted his face. He fumbled for the flashlight and turned it off. "Seniors?" he stage-whispered. Gunther commando-crept to the roof's edge. Patrick crept after him, pebbles filling the waistband of his jeans. The car crept, too, crackling along the driveway toward the faculty parking lot. A station wagon. Patrick swallowed. Dr. Lynch's. His father had gotten up to use the bathroom and checked on him as he still did sometimes, as if he was an infant whose breathing needed monitoring. Christ! His dad was no fool—technical drawing? He wrote the damn K-12 curriculum. His mother's mac 'n' cheese rose in his gorge. He was going to leave it, along with his dignity and his father's trust, on this roof.

The car stopped just before the parking lot. Patrick held his face in his hands. He heard gears grinding and looked up. The station wagon was backing onto Main Street, heading toward Evergreen. Toward his house.

Gunther sat up and smacked Patrick's side. "Okay, let's move."

Patrick lay prone, head in hands. "I am so, so fucked." He looked at Gunther. "That was my dad."

Gunther laughed. "No way."

"How many olive green station wagons you expect to pull into the high school tonight?"

"One: you're imagining the color; it's too dark to tell. Two: your dad drives a Ford."

"So?"

"That was a Chevy."

Patrick sat up. "How can you tell?"

"Taillights. Chevy's are more…rhomboid."

He was too relieved to press Gunther on terminology. "You sure?"

"Positive. That was some salesman, thought he took the Red Wing exit."

Patrick exhaled. "Man, I was sure that was my dad."

"Well, relax, matey." Gunther bounced some pebbles in his hand. He tossed one at Patrick. "Sorry about the vent. You were right—simpler is better." For all the millions of words he'd heard Gunther expound, this was a first: an apology. Gunther stood. "It's still your scheme. Let's do it your way. I've got the tools." He slapped his tool belt. "You got the pack?"

"*Jawohl.*" Patrick's old Boy Scout pack was a key piece of gear. Into it they would stuff as many student files as he could carry: records of Patrick's mediocrity and of Gunther's brilliance and failure; grades, comments, test scores for the entire sophomore class and as many juniors as would fit. Everything a college would want to know—gone. This wouldn't be another prank, another trivial farewell joke played on the school. School was the joke. The records were locked, of course, but the key to them was in the secretary's desk, lower righthand drawer, under a stack of notepads. *Just a Thought from Norma Lynch.*

Gunther checked the tire iron that anchored the rope around the vent. He trailed the rope to the roof's edge and gave it a good yank. "All set. We leave as we came." After a lucky seventh toss had snagged the tire iron on the vent, they'd scaled the building, Gunther first, more Batman than Thomas Crown, leaving oily boot prints up the wall that would be visible for years to come. "You lead the descent." He held out the rope.

Patrick hesitated. He didn't know why.

Gunther thrust the rope at his chest. "Do it for Katie."

Even in pitch dark, Patrick's fuck you face was discernible.

"Very well," said Gunther, wrapping the rope around his right hand, pacing backward. A final tension check. Uncharacteristic caution, thought Patrick, from his contrite buddy. "*Salud*," said Gunther, eyes wide, before he raced past Patrick in a storm of pebbles, stepping off the roof and into the inky Minnesota night.

Patrick had expected him to rappel the one story slowly, like Spencer Tracy in *The Mountain*. But this time Gunther, whose movements tended toward the lethargic, flung himself in space before Patrick could exercise his veto. He could only watch as the rope snapped taut and Gunther turned, disappearing boots-first toward Dr. Lynch's office window.

Patrick had heard accidents before. He lived at a dangerous four-way stop at the edge of Peterson's Prairie, where town met farm and Buick met tractor. Many a supper was punctuated by the crunch and crinkle of spraying glass, of metal folding into metal. But no sound compared to that of his best friend slicing through his father's office window. Though instantaneous, he heard it in three parts: boots punching a man-sized hole; flesh compacting broken glass; and, moments later, a jagged fragment falling from the window's top, tinkling down onto the pile.

Somehow Patrick thought to grab the flashlight before he, too, leapt from the roof. Though he also remembered to bend his knees he landed hard, biting deep in his tongue. He stuck the flashlight through the semi-circular hole and swirled the light around his father's office, darker than the night. The beam caught shards of glass, shiny, red. Gunther was up hard against Dr. Lynch's desk, one leg straight out, the other underneath him. His black T-shirt was matted to his chest, his watch cap down over one eye, his face striated with blood. Blood was on the floor; Patrick could taste it. Gunther's right arm was bent the wrong way at the elbow, the back of his hand nearly touching his shoulder. He waved his left weakly.

"Gunnie?" was all Patrick could manage.

"Oh, Paddy," said Gunther, shifting on the glass. "I think I'm dying."

Patrick had to buy a suit for the funeral. Even in this extremity his mother was practical, insisting he get navy blue, not the traditional black. Blue he could wear at Christmas and Easter, she'd said as she flitted through the racks at Target, maybe even graduation if he'd done most of his growing. When, she asked, patting down his shoulders, pulling at his sleeves, attempting that embarrassing inseam check, would he wear a black suit again?

Erin had managed to avoid the "freshman fifteen" at the U of M and still fit into her long black dress from senior choir. Her mother, too, wore a black dress, similar length but more sophisticated, that she'd gotten for her twentieth anniversary. When their parents had come back from that anniversary weekend in Minneapolis, they'd laughed, recounting how young everyone thought Norma looked in that dress, how she'd even been carded trying to get a Tom Collins in the Radisson lounge. Patrick couldn't see it at the time—can any boy see his mother as young?—but as they stood shoulder to shoulder now, two trim, pretty blondes, eyes red-rimmed, he was struck by how sisterly Erin and his mother looked. The girlishness, though, was gone from his mother's expression; he appreciated it now in its absence. He doubted he'd ever see it again.

The basement of St. Immaculata's was jammed. All the women, it seemed—ancient Mrs. Jones, his second-grade teacher, helmet-haired Mrs. Johansson, even Miss Sturmblad, who'd delivered "Ave Maria" at the service with her rapid-fire, Joan Baez vibrato—wanted to embrace him, kiss him, weep over him. The men didn't embrace him, of course (male hugging would come to Peterson's Prairie in 1992 with a Robert Bly reading in Winnipee Falls), but they gave slow, double-palmed handshakes and firm hand-and-elbow grips. Ben Carlson, coach of the Willard County Homesteaders, who'd played tackle on the 'steaders next to Patrick's dad, stared at Patrick, swollen-eyed, for a full minute. He'd never known what to make of his friend's unathletic son, couldn't stifle a laugh when Patrick punted a football *behind* himself in gym class. But now he held Patrick's hand between his and stared, eyes filling. "If you…" he began, "…if you grow to be half the man your father was," he pursed his lips, "that'll be twice as much as most men." Patrick nodded dumbly, unsure what to say, unsure he could do the math.

The receiving line snaked to the far side of the basement, till it commingled with the line for the table filled with noodle-bake casseroles. All these people grieved for his father and wanted, sincerely, to comfort his—his family's—grief. But if Patrick could have made them disappear, blinked them away like the girl on *I Dream of Jeannie*, he would have. He wasn't a child; he understood, intellectually, that his dad was upstairs in that big gold box. He believed his mother when she said, calmly, too calmly, that she'd found his father on his office floor Saturday afternoon, that he looked like he was sleeping, that Dr. Greene could do nothing to wake him. But it felt like his dad was away, maybe at the Minnesota Superintendents' Convention, and he'd come back from St. Paul in a few days, refreshed, having schmoozed with colleagues and watched a Twins game, and ask his son, *Did you realize the state capitol was covered with genuine gold leaf?* The people in this basement wanted to share grief. But grief would come later, much later, in periodic, never-ending waves.

Patrick did feel shame. And shame at his shame. No one, of course, spoke of his and Gunther's failed escapade, perpetrated just a week before his father died. Frank Lynch's death made it trivial, no longer worth mentioning. Even before Dr. Lynch's heart attack, in the days between the two events, the boys' abortive caper was melding into WCHS prank lore. Once Gunther's injuries proved to be the bloody-but-superficial kind (except for his right elbow, which, like his old Ford pickup, would forever unexpectedly pop into reverse), the only sub-stantial consequence of The Scheme was the week-long sus-pension meted out by Dr. Lynch.

Typically the principal, Mr. Sheffield, would have handed out the suspensions, but Frank Lynch wasn't one to leave such a thorny task to a subordinate. He insisted on calling Patrick into his office, like any other wayward student, keeping clean, as always, the boundaries between parent and administrator. Dr. Lynch began by detailing the consequences of Patrick's actions: the suspension, which would be part of his permanent record; the bill for damages to the building that would be sent to his home. Patrick looked at the floor. Had it really been covered with broken glass and Gunther's blood Friday night? He looked out through the new window at the girls' gym class playing softball and marveled once again at his father's efficiency. As Dr. Lynch worked his way through the actions-and-consequences boilerplate, Patrick gazed, like many a miscreant before him, at the loon decoy on the shelf above the desk, at the 1974 Superintendent of the Year plaque from the Minnesota Secondary School Administrators Association, objects as familiar as the knickknacks on his bedroom dresser (hadn't he and Erin run around that desk with that wooden bird, trilling loon calls?), somehow different, weightier, from this angle.

The superintendent had stopped speaking. Patrick looked down from the shelves. His father's eyes and mouth were open, his massive torso still. Although Dr. Greene later assured him that there was no cause and effect between The Scheme and his father's heart attack, that Frank's heart condition was a ticking alarm clock set to go off when it did, Patrick looked down from the loon and thought even then: My dad won't survive this conference. Finally, his father said, "Patrick, are you angry at me?" When he didn't respond, his father said, "It must be hard, I know, being the superintendent's son," and bit his lower lip. "I've always tried—" he said. Patrick had never seen pain on his father's face—never recognized it—and he realized, with terror, that this was what his dad looked like when he was about to cry.

Before this could happen, Patrick spewed up his mea culpa. He'd said nothing to his father—or mother—over the weekend. He'd just sat on his bed, stunned. He was so, so sorry, he said now, and found himself crying. He couldn't explain his actions, he said. He had no idea why. Breaking the window, that was a stupid accident. No, he wasn't angry at his father, of course not. It had nothing to do with him.

He felt he'd stumbled on the right words, disassociating his hostile actions toward his father's workplace from his feelings for his father. It had the desired effect, allowing his dad to become Dr. Lynch again, compassionate administrator, dispensing Kleenex to troubled students. But Patrick would recall this moment with a fresh wave of regret when, a few years later, his college girlfriend would maintain, tearfully, after he found his roommate's Lucky Strike boxers underneath her bed, that it had nothing to do with *them*, that it wasn't about Patrick *at all*.

Patrick scanned the crowd over Mrs. Johansson's shoulder as she enfolded him in her fulsome bosom. "We must be strong," she whispered. Mrs. Johansson was, embedding his ribs in her pillowy chest. Katie Osterlund was behind her, wearing the same black choir dress his sister wore. Katie took his hand. "I'm so sorry for your loss, Patrick," she said. She seemed to mean it; no tears were in those bright blue eyes, but sobriety supplanted the chipper giddiness that was her default expression. To touch her, even formally, to hear her say his name, would have been the highlight of most weeks. Their last physical contact, promenading together at a fifth-grade square dance, was a moment he'd often re-lived.

But today, even Katie Osterlund was just part of a crowd. Patrick found himself looking past her, and certainly Doug Knutson behind her, for the one person he had hoped to see in that basement after the service. Gunther had been in the last pew, next to his parents, his face a fright show of Band-Aids and gauze tape. His right arm was in a shoulder-to-wrist cast, frozen at a right angle and slung tight to his body. The strangest thing to Patrick, who expected the medical details, was Gunther's hair, gathered back tightly, glossy on top, naked of the watch cap. Mrs. Hendrickson, mournful even in good times, dabbed at her eyes with a handkerchief. Mr. Hendrickson, in sports coat and tie, looked angry. Gunther, despite the short-sleeved white shirt, blue clip-on tie, and Lon Chaney make-up, looked his old impenetrable self.

Patrick would try to make contact with him, had tried. A few days after their failed scheme, when Patrick called to see how Gunther was, Mrs. Hendrickson said he was resting. After several more calls, Patrick's mother and the Hendricksons would make it clear that it would be best if the boys were apart as much as possible. But no sanctions were necessary; their friendship ended with that leap off the high school roof. No big scene was needed to make it official, no drama like girls would have had, no confrontation filled with blame. Gunther spent more time at Hendrickson's Best. Patrick bagged groceries at Knutson's, then dusted off his guitar. He started a garage band with some other non-athletes, including Charlie Sorenson, who no longer cared for fire engines but now shared with Patrick an abiding passion for the power chords of Judas Priest.

Oddly—odd to Patrick—the two, nearly simultaneous losses of his father and best friend made him less of an outsider at Willard County High. His band played school dances; he joined the debate team. His grades rose sharply. He never became part of the popular group, but he had a social niche, and, briefly, a girlfriend. Katie Osterlund said hello to him in the hallways.

Of course, he and Gunther saw each other. Unavoidable in a school, a town, that small. They guarded one another in gym class basketball games. Gunther sat behind him in a few classes, farther and farther behind as they moved through junior year, as Gunther reflexively sought the back row and Patrick, with decreasing timidity, edged nearer the front. They spoke, awkwardly. Patrick would sometimes glance back at Gunther in class, or as he drove past Hendrickson's Best in his dad's green station wagon, and see him gazing off in the distance, stroking his goatee or pulling down the black watch cap, and wonder at the conversation he was having with himself.

Patrick missed it, the conversation—the monologues—and had no one to tell how much. Missed it more, he sometimes felt, than his father's counsel. At such moments he'd gun the green wagon past Hendrickson's Best, hop on I-94, crank up Judas Priest or Led Zeppelin and cruise past the loamy fields on Route 17, past the burgeoning mall at Winnipee Falls, headed for nowhere, fast as the law would allow.

5

BIT BY BIT

It was a leap year, Patrick suddenly remembered, glaring at the dusty shelves of Marcus Garvey High School's book room. February, which had once seemed so promising—and brief— was endless, a slushy mess in every sense. He stuck his head in the empty space on the middle shelf, between the Malcolm X autobiographies and *The House on Mango Street*, where *at least* ten copies of *Huck Finn* should be. He sneezed, banging his head on the shelf above. "Damn it, Dorie," he muttered, smacking the metal shelf below, stinging his hand. His beloved, forgetful senior colleague, who had helped him write the grant for the "American Dream" unit, had put in the book orders in the fall and come up short. Again. Time for Plan E: an afterschool dash to the Barnes & Noble on Eighty-Second and Broadway, where the Twain selection was generally long and deep. Unlike his checking account.

The book room, inexplicably, was the pride of Marcus Garvey. "Oh, we have a book room," Wally had replied enthusiastically when Patrick had asked what he'd be teaching when they'd hired him seven years ago. That first day he'd followed the vice principal's wide hips down the white-tiled hallway designed in the '50s to ease the conversion from school to hospital in the event of nuclear attack that now provided a convenient white-board for graffiti, doodles, and gang tags. Wally had trooped Patrick up two flights of the fabled Up staircase, stopping before a solid metal door. He twirled through the brass key ring at his belt and unlocked the door slowly, with some ceremony, as was his way. "I'll leave you to peruse the literature," he said, and left.

Patrick had snapped on the bare bulb to find himself surrounded by floor-to-ceiling stacks of yellowed paperbacks in various stages of decrepitude, covered by dust dating from the Eisenhower administration. There had been no need to paw through the stacks as the floor was littered with a fair sampling of book covers: *Bartleby the Scrivener, Silas Marner, The Red Badge of Courage, Great Expectations.* Though Patrick, a Midwesterner and novice teacher, was no authority, he found it difficult to imagine the New York City classroom for which these titles— Civil War melodrama? Travails of the Victorian scribe?—would ever have seemed appropriate. He'd been force-fed a number of these volumes himself back in high school and the experience had nearly killed all native interest in literature.

The book room, he would soon understand, was management's answer to having no syllabus, no state frameworks—no clue—as to what he should be teaching. Marcus Garvey, like many warehouse-sized high schools in New York, had been broken into thematic "mini-schools" in the early '80s. After the federal government told the city to drop dead in the mid-'70s, the chancellor decided to let the hundred flowers bloom: anyone with an idea, a space, and a connection at the DOE central office at 110 Livingston Street, Brooklyn, could jolly well set up a mini-school. The first mini-schools—dedicated to the disciplines of art, math, technology—focused on self-explanatory curricular needs. But as time passed, their themes grew more fanciful, abstruse, even. Patrick had landed in Experiment in Cooperative Learning, a program that had recently lost its director, most of its students, and its way. What it did have was four classrooms at Marcus Garvey, nominal oversight by the principal and vice principal, and access to the book room.

Once it became clear that his first-day tour of Garvey was over and that Mr. Kupczek was never returning to the book room, Patrick braved his dust allergy and began the nasty business of sorting through the novels. But the deeper he got in the stacks, the more dust-filled the air and the more he sneezed, sending ever-larger clouds billowing across the book room. He blew page 217-18 clear out of an ancient copy of *Tess of the D'Urbervilles*, sparing Tess the cruel advances of Alec D'Urberville. Which was more than Hardy ever did for her. It seemed arbitrary which would be the lucky first book to begin his Experiment in Cooperative Learning, but this choice was made simple in one regard: only a single novel had a useable class set. Unfortunately, that novel was Joseph Conrad's *Lord Jim*.

Patrick sat cross-legged on the book covers, rocking, holding his head, sneezing. Why, oh why, this book? He could picture his tortured adolescent self slogging through this novel on his bed back in Peterson's Prairie, counting the pages still left to read, waking to the smell of its musty text, chapter five sodden with drool. What idiot had chosen this? And why? But, as a rookie teacher hopelessly overmatched by his situation must, he made peace with it. Okay: stuffy colonial British story; tea drinking; stiff upper-lips. Ridiculous vocabulary. But: sea disaster (link to *Titanic?*); implicit violence; a fair amount of boozing. And, he further rationalized, wasn't there a certain fitting irony—inspirational, maybe—teaching immigrant kids an English novel by a Polish author writing in his third language?

All rationalizations dissolved in the face of the realities of the Experiment in Cooperative Learning. Cooperative learning, it turned out, involved replacing students seated in neat rows with "participants" slouching on randomly placed sofas. The participants were not required to remove their hats or coats or to address their "facilitators" by other than their first names. Process, not product, was the thing at EICL: We're all co-learners here; no one has the right answer.

EICL was the dumpster program at Marcus Garvey. The Computers for the Future program had a waiting list, as did Math in the Real World. Mothers clutching false addresses lined up outside the Science & Technology Academy on the first day of school, trailing all the way out to the 103rd Street Deli.

Security was called from down the hall when the office doors opened and the line devolved, half queue/half scrum. No such measures were necessary when EICL opened its doors. EICL was for the leftovers: just off the boat, just out of juvie, just out of luck. It was the dumpster program and everyone—parents, students, teachers—knew it. Everyone except Patrick Lynch, desperately clutching his nineteenth-century British novel.

They were, indeed, co-learners at the Experiment in Co-operative Learning. Patrick learned that "homework" was a euphemism. That supplies would be provided by the facilitator. To be aware of the thousand-and-one unseen landmines: don't call Sanji Smith *Mr. Smith,* for example; Sanji never met Mr. Smith Sr., and it will only make Sanji quiet and sullen to remind him of that fact. What did the participants learn? Damn little at first, it seemed to Patrick as he reviewed his failings as an educator on the subway home every afternoon. Not to participate, certainly. But eventually they learned to listen—first to him, then to one another.

It seemed they'd never been read to before. When he began reading long passages of Conrad aloud—of necessity, to bridge the half-dozen language groups in his classes—they whispered, reclined on the sofas in their puffy black parkas—pillows on pillows—in a way Patrick found both rude and distracting. Then he realized they were commenting on his performance: Listen to his voice... Look at his face... That's so *funny.* They had no experience of live performance, even one so modest as his. He certainly wasn't the performer his father had been, reading Dickens to him at length, swelling voice and body as the bloated Mr. Bumble or shrinking to the unctuous Uriah Heep, settling not merely for an English accent but modulating with each change in age, sex, region, class. But, limited as his gifts were, Patrick learned to captivate his captive audience, beginning with, of all books, *Lord Jim.*

He'd thought of his father that morning as he paced his room before first period; he knew this was the moment they would be hooked by the story. Or not. As usual, they strolled into his classroom in twos and threes during the first five minutes of class, bearing bagels, coffee, hot chocolate from the 103rd Street Deli, plopped themselves down on the sofas and began chatting. When Patrick decided there was a quorum, he cleared his throat. So, where is the ship going? he asked them, a token reference to last night's homework. The mandatory fifteen-second pause elapsed. For all the United Nations-wide diversity at EICL, the participants broke neatly in two camps: those with limited English who would love to please their facilitator if only they could, and those whose first language was more or less English who would lose face by raising a hand. When a hand went up from the second camp, it was generally followed by Yo, Patrick, gotta use the bathroom.

Sanji, a member of no group, one of three or four who were actually reading the book, raised his hand. They are on a pilgrimage, he said.

Very good. Where to?

To the holy city of Mecca, Sanji enunciated in his clipped, Anglo-accented English. Where was his family from? Patrick wondered. India by way of Indonesia? Minus the puffy coat and the oversize Timberlands, he could have stepped out of this novel.

Exactly so, said Patrick, launching into the pivotal scene of *Lord Jim*, a scene he'd practiced the night before in his bathroom, listening to the echo of Conrad's words. The title character leans over the *Patna's* railing as the ship founders in the Red Sea squall, the lifeboat below containing the other Europeans, captain and crew, who have already deserted the eight hundred dark-skinned pilgrims in their charge. Jim clings to the railing. *Jump!* the white faces below scream. *The ship began a slow plunge; the rain swept over her like a broken sea...my breath was driven back into my throat,* Jim confesses. *She was going down, down, head first under me...* And Patrick's voice, which had swirled up with the squall, sank to a whisper as the prow of the *Patna* went under. Jim leans, leans, over the railing.

Patrick flicked his eyes up from the page. They were leaning,

leaning toward him from their sofas. Shavonda, an immense girl who took up half of one sofa, sat, mouth agape, like one of his nephews in front of the TV. Then, almost inaudibly, he read: *I had jumped…it seems.*

Silence.

Did he? Shavonda rasped. Did he jump?

Well? Did he? Patrick swiveled his head back and forth, meeting the eyes of each participant. They looked down at their laps, or at one another. Finally, Sanji raised his hand. It was bad practice to keep calling on the same student, Patrick knew, rule number one from Ed School. It discouraged all the others. But, as Lord Jim himself would attest, any port in a storm.

Sanji cleared his throat and sat up as straight as the Salvation Army sofa would allow. He jumped, but he can't admit it, said Sanji. He has lost his honor.

Whoa, bullseye, thought Patrick. But he only said, How so?

He was responsible for all those passengers. He was first mate.

What about the captain? The crew screaming 'jump'?

That doesn't matter, said Sanji. It is Jim's choice. And his honor.

Iz about ree-*spect*, boomed James from a couch in the back. Everyone turned to him. It was the first they'd heard from James, who was tossed into the EICL dumpster a few weeks after school began, released from custody. For what offense, Patrick was never informed. But no one chose to sit next to his muscular, tattooed body. Ree-spect, y'all, said James, thumping his chest twice with a fist.

Yes, James? said Patrick, trying to disguise his surprise, delight, alarm.

He s'posed to be a *man*, James declared, pulling the tiny noun to at least three syllables. But he couldn' do it. He couldn' *do* it. And James slumped back into the couch, glowering, flexing the thin scar that ran from the right corner of his mouth to his chin. It was the first and last literary analysis he would share with his fellow participants; James would disappear suddenly, several weeks hence, slipping once again into the murky depths of the New York State court system.

The bell rang before Patrick had a chance to have James clarify his remarks, which was just as well. But he reflected on them that afternoon on the subway. True, his lesson hadn't touched on the finer points of Conrad's art—his use of the past perfect at Lord Jim's critical moment, for example—but it was the first ride home where Patrick thought, I can do this. I can *do* this. And James was right: Iz about ree-spect. Tomorrow, he would tell the participants he was Mr. Lynch.

Patrick tore off a corner of his bologna sandwich and turned to Dorie, who sat at the head of their lunch table, hunched over her split pea soup. "Would it be...*imprudent* to inquire as to the whereabouts of the rest of the *Huck Finns*?" he over-articulated, smoothing a make-believe mustache, trying to hide just how pissed-off he was. Dorie curled her thin lips defensively, making them disappear. George nearly coughed up his Diet Coke. George loved Patrick's Wally impression. Denise and Naomi looked up from their lunches, always ready for the teacher's lounge floorshow.

"I *told* you we'd finish it next week. Tuesday, you can have all the friggin' copies you want. Capeesh?" Dorie gathered the fingers of one hand together and shook them at Patrick, Brando as a tiny, frizzy-haired Jewish woman from Queens.

"I only need six, Doris, thank you. Six is all I ask." Patrick popped the chunk of bologna sandwich in his mouth, signaling that the controversy was at an end. She'd said nothing to him about the *Huck Finn* copies. But how could he stay mad at Dorie, who wrote the "American Dream" grant with him, who—truth to tell—did the lion's share of the book room reorganization? And to whom, really, he owed his teaching career. It was Dorie, six years ago when the Experiment in Cooperative Learning finally imploded, who insisted to the director of Science & Tech that they snag Patrick. At Science

& Tech, he'd become a real teacher. If not for Dorie, he'd be selling insurance for Susan's father.

"Denise," said Dorie, licking split pea from that almost-missing upper lip, "didn't you hear me tell Patrick—"

"Oh no, Dorie, I'm not going near that mess." Denise poked at the salad in her Tupperware container. "My whole computer lab crashed this morning. Thirty-two bored teenagers staring at blank screens. Ugly, ugly." She shook her head, stabbed some romaine. "I'll worry about my hard drives, you and Mr. Lynch can fight over Mark Twain." She turned to Patrick and flashed that brilliant smile, one of the things he looked forward to at lunch, that got him through the afternoon. And it made him laugh just looking at pale, chickadee-sized Dorie next to big, brown, and beautiful Denise. Odd partners in crime, it seemed at first, though both were city girls (Denise survived the South Bronx) and mothers of teenage sons.

"What is that outfit Maria's wearing today?" Naomi asked.

"Nice segue," said George.

"No, seriously."

"The little bustier under that lacy thing?"

"Where'd she get that, Victoria's Secret?" asked Dorie.

"I hate when my students have better underwear than I do," said Naomi.

"You must hate them all," said George.

"Must work for Abdul," Patrick chimed in. "I found a love note on my floor. Seems he's getting some in Sitkowitz's class."

"No," mumbled Denise, munching lettuce.

"I hate when my students have better sex lives than I do— say nothing, George." Naomi brandished her plasticware.

"Put down the knife," said George.

"It's a spork."

"Put down the spork."

"One of you ladies should speak to Maria," offered Patrick.

The women looked at him in varieties of disbelief.

"I'm serious. Something's going to happen to that girl."

"Already happening, I'm afraid," said Dorie.

"*Hello,*" Naomi said.

Denise shook her head. "Such a smart girl."

"It's the Ramirez Effect," said George.

"The what?" asked Patrick.

George looked at Dorie and Denise. "You remember that girl, seven, eight years ago? What was her name, Ramirez?"

"Anita."

George nodded, yogurt dribbling down his chin. "Anita Ramirez. Sweetest, smartest little girl. And flat as a…a chessboard—"

"A chestboard?" said Naomi.

"—when the year started. A real late bloomer. Then, like magical Barbie, she grew." George put down his yogurt to demonstrate the inflation curve. "Suddenly, she was queen bee. And her grades never recovered. The bigger they got, the more her grades fell—"

"That would make a good story problem for you, George." Patrick lowered his sandwich. "'If x is Juana's cup size, and y her GPA…'"

Denise pointed her fork at Patrick and George. "You boys have no clue what these girls go through. Girl like Maria has grown men doggin' her all over the Heights. Thirty-year-old dealers offering her jewelry—"

"I know, Denise, you're right." Patrick put his hands on the lunch table. "That's why you should talk to her. Or her mother—"

"Who do you think got her that outfit?" said Naomi.

George turned to her. "Maybe you should call, Nomes." He swiped some yogurt from his graying mustache. "After you straighten Maria out, her mom could give you some, you know, tips."

"Spork you, George." Naomi smiled and batted her eyes at George, the big brother she never had. Like Dorie and Denise, Naomi and George were a pairing that shouldn't have worked, but did. George wrote ad copy for twenty years (and remained proud of that famous line from his condom account, "Pleasure dots—for *her*," showing just how sensitive a gay man could be to a woman's needs) before he decided to quit Madison Avenue and teach math to inner-city youth ("And thus canceling," he said, "that reservation in hell"). Naomi, destined for med school, planned to do Teach for America for two years but had stayed for five. Pretty, whip-smart, unhappily unattached, Naomi, all soft curves and hard edges. What did she want? Patrick sometimes wondered. That sharp tongue wound up in his ear one drunken faculty Christmas party, a moment they seemed to have agreed never to acknowledge.

"Why must it always fall on the female faculty?" asked Dorie. "This is a huge problem. And no one expects the men to break up every fight."

"Maybe Betty could do another workshop on self-esteem," Denise said. Guilty laughs all around at the expense of their beleaguered social worker. Patrick looked at his colleagues and marveled once again at how this disparate little group cohered. They'd hit some bumps, to be sure. When the *Daily News* revisited the Yankel Rosenbaum stabbing, Denise and Dorie got into it one lunch period—a chair was overturned, Patrick learned some choice Yiddish phrases—and Denise ate in her room for a week. Occasionally one of George's quips cut unintentionally deep and Naomi lunched at the Golden Dragon for a few days. And Dorie's memory lapses could push Patrick to the edge. But the anger subsided; they worked it out, somehow. They had to: Denise and Dorie had *The Garvey Gazette* to turn out every month; George and Naomi co-taught that math/science unit on bridge-building. And Patrick—he was no New Yorker; conflict-avoidance was in his DNA.

"We *did* have a dress code," said a voice from the nubby red couch against the back wall of the teacher's lounge, behind a *New York Post*, "once upon a time." The voice, impossibly nasal, bearing the heavy imprint of its native Lawn Guyland, belonged, unmistakably, to C. The paper sank to its owner's lap, revealing a face whose features—narrow-spaced eyes, flat nose, cracked lips—seemed to have fallen in on themselves, forming a valley between a jutting chin and ledge-like forehead. A face, reputedly handsome in its youth, that long ago collapsed in disappointment. C turned to a pair of hands clenching an outstretched *Times*. "Didn't we, Sidney?"

"Indeed we did, Jerry," said X, the voice behind the *Times*. "Long pants—no jeans—with belts, for the boys, collared shirts—tucked in, mind you. Girls wore skirts and blouses. No skin. Gym shoes were for gym—"

"No patent leather, I hope," said George.

X allowed the above-the-fold *Times* to crumple down. "We let the Catholics worry about that, George." He didn't smile. The topography of X's face was the opposite of C's: buggy eyes, a long sharp nose pointed accusingly at the world. They also parted company when it came to grooming: whereas C favored the classic comb-over—dark greasy strands raked between furrows of scalp—X's head was topped by a fuzzy salt-and-pepper toupee, like a small middle-aged dog had taken refuge on his head, and died. ("Take off your hat!" X had screamed at a student some years ago. "Take off your wig!" the student had countered, reportedly, a story too good not to be true.)

Though the men on the couch were a contrast in appearance, they shared a bedrock belief: Everything used to be better. They seemed, to Patrick, airlifted from an earlier New York City, one he'd seen on television and in movies back in Minnesota—an Irish, Italian, and Jewish city, one with three baseball teams, with goofy, lovable cops and sophisticated women who shopped Fifth Avenue in white gloves and men who wore dark suits, skinny ties, and hats (not *caps*). Nothing in the past quarter-century had altered their vision of this city: in their New York, Jack Kennedy was president; Mickey Mantle roamed the Yankees' center field; the children were well-dressed, well-behaved, and white. They refused to make concessions to the realities their current students faced. Any deviation from the standards set in the Golden Age was unacceptable, to be railed against. Their every utterance was complaint, their expressions, in repose, dyspeptic. If they'd ever been educators, Patrick thought, they weren't now. They were kid-haters, screamers, so burnt-out that younger staff referred to them only by their nicknames: Crispy and X-tra Crispy. Or, simply, C and X.

"Maybe you could talk to Silverstein about the dress code." C smirked at the lunch table. "He's pretty good about those things." X gurgled in amusement.

A visitor stumbling into the teacher's lounge would have looked C and X over and concluded that these haggard figures were marginal to this system, subs, perhaps, in for the day. The visitor, however, could not have been more mistaken. True, C and X had little to do with teaching and learning, which, the public is led to believe, are the core activities of education. But C was the building's union rep, a job he had inherited from X. If there was a prince of this little city, C was it, and X his trusted adviser.

Now, Patrick was a union man—weren't they all? How could you not be? The union had paid for the crown on his number three molar, the contact lenses he wore. If not for the union, he would have spent this all-too-brief lunch period trying to keep several hundred young people from hurling macaroni-based products at one another in the cafeteria. He was grateful for every benefit, every right collective bargaining had wrung from the system. But at the building level the union was the protector of the most senior and least motivated: Brian Callahan, who insisted on keeping room 117 (the room nearest the exit and, some said, the bars on Amsterdam Avenue) in perpetuity, regardless of how many times younger faculty were forced to shuffle rooms around him; Luisa Maldonado, who refused to go on field trips and would spend the day sipping coffee in the teacher's lounge while a younger colleague was drafted to schlep her class to the aquarium at Coney Island.

C and X reserved the cushiest assignments for themselves. X, having taught math for countless years, now presided over the library, a room with few books and fewer students. C, head of the social studies department when Garvey had been one school, had restyled himself as a reading specialist. Now he tutored one or two students several periods a day in his former office. The other periods he received petitioners, the Callahans and Maldonados, weighing their grievances like a Little Italy don. C fixed his eyes on Patrick and grinned. The scheduling showdown in the library last year, Patrick thought. C would never forgive him that. George had warned him: You take on the king, the king must die.

It had seemed so wonderfully transparent to Patrick, the new schedule, so right. Longer periods, no bells, less time in the hallways with boys grabbing girls, bumping each other, fewer fights. More time teaching and learning. What was there to debate? The lunch table had immediately concurred and nominated him to run it by Silverstein. The principal was uncharacteristically enthusiastic. Great idea, he agreed, should have happened long ago. Silverstein tugged on his bottom lip. But there's that sticky union rule about schedule changes, you know.

Patrick didn't know. And when the lunch table heard that any schedule change had to be approved by a 75 percent vote of the faculty, they were daunted at first. But Dorie rallied them—shamed them—into action, and they worked the hallways of Marcus Garvey like seasoned ward heelers. They called in every chit from every colleague—classes they'd covered, textbooks they'd lent, detention periods they'd taken over—and called on every bit of goodwill the four of them had amassed in their collected years at Garvey. After several weeks of bare-knuckled politicking, George, the self-appointed lunch table "whip," announced that, by his count, they were over the 75 percent mark. Barely.

Silverstein introduced the topic of the new schedule at the faculty meeting; there was no way around that. But he was shrewd about it, Patrick had to concede. Any plan with the principal's imprimatur was DOA with C, X, and the other

Lifers. To them, education was a zero-sum game: anything that helped administration hurt them.

Silverstein looked down at his clipboard. "I'll keep this meeting brief." Despite the tension in the library that afternoon there were smiles and rolled eyes all around. Every faculty meeting began with this promise, but the principal was famously a man of many words. No point summarizing in two sentences when six would suffice. "It has been proposed that our schedule be changed from eight forty-two-minute periods to seven fifty-minute periods. According to union rules, 75 percent of the faculty must consent for the proposal to be adopted. The floor is now open for discussion." Then, to the surprise of all, he sat. Good start, thought Patrick. Kept his fingerprints off it. Deft use of the passive voice.

A phlegm-clearing noise broke from a far corner of the library. All eyes went to X as he rose, smoothing the lapels of his plaid sport coat. "Look, he's entered the '70s," George whispered.

"Shhh," said Patrick.

X stood next to a blackboard he'd wheeled into the library. He was surrounded by antediluvian faculty. Generally, teachers sat grouped according to mini-school, but this issue had divided them into new units of self-interest: generation, department, personality type. The naked blackboard was angled by the window, illuminated dramatically by the southern exposure. X began flipping the board to the other side, but it stuck in mid-revolution. C sprang up, loosened the nut at the side of the board and helped X swing it around.

The backside was covered with numbers. Two grids were at the top of the blackboard; beneath each were sets of equations, some connected by serpentine arrows in blue, green, and pink chalk.

"It seems simple, at first, this new schedule," said X, arching his fingertips, rocking up on his toes at *simple*. "And practical. Fewer periods, less moving around. We talked about it at Garvey way back in the '60s. Some of you remember the '60s." He paused, giving that grimace of a smile. "Or maybe not." A few chuckles from the Lifers. That place in Patrick's sternum tightened. He expected the numbers from X, the old math teacher. But not the rhetorical flourishes—setting up the straw man, the attempt at humor. Patrick leaned back next to George; the perpetual smirk was gone from the former ad man.

X led the faculty down his yellow brick road of figures and squiggles. Patrick's eyes glazed as they had in sophomore algebra. An occasional phrase popped out at him: *not a minute more for lunchtime; blood from a stone.* Patrick surveyed the faculty. Peggy O'Malley, the PE teacher, was nodding, vacant-eyed, the way Susan had when she dragged him to her accountant to help with her taxes. Susan had bobbed her head while Lonnie Appelbaum prattled on about the new 508(b) exemption she could *probably* take, if she wanted to. "You have no idea what Lonnie was talking about, do you?" Patrick had asked on the subway home. Susan shrugged. "You'll visit me in prison, right?"

Two tables to his left, Laura Steiner was bent forward, eyes narrowed. How he'd worked Laura Steiner! He'd made a special trip after school to the art room, where he found the stocky art teacher sponging up papier-mâché paste. She was nervous, as always, that any change would be bad for the art program; art was always the first to go. C had already gotten to her and convinced Laura that the period axed from the schedule would be hers. "Do you know what the market is for unemployed art teachers?" she'd asked Patrick, pulling at her spattered smock. "Oh, Laura," he'd said, leaning against the wall like a high school jock, "the Garvey art program is famous." He deepened his voice. "They wouldn't dare cut it." Laura looked up at him, perhaps recalling their dancing to "Inna Godda Daveeda"—the long version—at the faculty Christmas bacchanal. She brushed her bangs with the back of her hand. A streak of wheat paste crossed her forehead. "You don't think?" she said.

At lunch the next day, Patrick assured George that Laura was "in the bag." George shook his head. "You are such a whore," he laughed. "I love it."

But George wasn't laughing now. Nor was Dorie, who shot Patrick a squinty, lipless glance. By the number of times he thrust up on his toes, it was clear X was reaching the climax of his presentation. Finally, he circled a large number eight in pink chalk. "In the end," X said, "it comes down to this number. Eight more minutes. That's the additional, unpaid teaching time the administration wants from us every week. That is what this new schedule would mean." X slapped the chalk down in the chalk tray, smacked the pink dust from his hands, and sat next to C. An alarming number of Patrick's colleagues, young and old, from every department and mini-school, were nodding their heads.

"Thank you, Mr. Greenblatt," said Silverstein, with practiced even-handedness. He looked over his faculty. "Anyone else?"

Patrick turned to George, who gave him the thumbs-up. Patrick stood. "I have a confession to make: I got Cs in high school algebra." He rubbed his chin. "Good thing I teach English." Dorie, planted among the Lifers, let her lips re-emerge in encouragement. Laura Steiner, sitting in the back with the other "specialty subjects," smiled politely but continued pulling on her right sleeve. "However, I've examined the new schedule backwards, forwards, and sideways and I don't see any extra teaching time in it." Faculty eyes went to X, who sat expressionless. He shook his head; the little terrier on top bristled. "But I won't argue that point. I yield to Mr. Greenblatt's computational expertise." Patrick waved toward the blackboard. "Let's assume that we might teach an additional eight minutes a *week*. Is that really a deal-breaker?" He wheeled to his right, putting his face as close as he dared up to Phil Sitkowitz's ashy jowls. "Mr. Sitkowitz, how often have you said that you never have enough time to finish your chem labs? Wouldn't fifty minutes make all the difference?" Actually, Phil's every complaint stemmed from his inability to keep teenagers at bay for forty-two minutes, but he'd hardly voice that in this setting. Panicked at being singled out, he wobbled his head about his shoulders, an uneasy compromise between a shake and a nod.

Patrick pointed toward the specialty subjects table. "And Ms. Steiner. Just as you get an entire class deeply engaged in an art project, it's time to clean up. Am I right?" He gave her his most boyish grin. She smiled and nodded and let go her sleeve. "And Betty." He dropped his voice and turned to the round, sweet-faced social worker at his left. Betty Goldberg was always Betty. "We have so many kids with special needs. How much would they benefit from fewer passing periods, fewer transitions?" Betty mouthed up at him, "You're right."

Patrick stood tall, spreading his arms to embrace his colleagues. "We're educators. The public may think we keep banker's hours, but we know better." Those who had nodded for X were nodding for him. A soft *huzzah* from George. "We didn't become teachers because the hours were short. Or for the pay." Laughs all around, even from the Lifers. "We're here for our students, for what works for them." He offered his palms to his audience. "I know this faculty. And I don't see us letting eight minutes a week stand in the way of something so good for our kids."

Patrick sat. George leaned forward, clapped him on the shoulders. "Home run," he said in his ear. Denise and Naomi beamed. Silverstein stood, tapping his clipboard. He said, "Well—"

"Young man," a nasal trumpet sounded from the back window, "how *dare* you?" There C stood, his face red, jabbing a finger at Patrick. "How dare you lecture this faculty about what teaching time means?" C strode over to Patrick, an arm's length away, shaking. Would C strike him? "When you were in kindergarten, some members of this faculty spent what you now refer to as your 'prep period' down in the cafeteria, breaking up food fights or doing clerical work in the office." C's hands went to his hips. "My first year at Garvey, starting teaching salary was four thousand, three hundred and seventy-six dollars a year. Pregnant women were laid off. Healthcare was non-existent. Principals could demand to review lesson plans."

C took a few steps away from Patrick, addressing the Lifers.

"Some of us marched in '68 when the mayor decentralized the schools and we nearly had race riots. Marched in the snow with Al Shanker." Graying heads dipped in reverence as C invoked the patron saint of public school teachers. C whirled back to Patrick. "So do not lecture us, young man, on what teaching time means, snickering at eight unpaid minutes. We know what teaching time means. We also know that nothing has ever been given to teachers. We fought for it. And we'll be damned if we'll give it back," his voice fell to a husky whisper, "bit by bit."

"Two votes," Patrick told Susan that night. "Two measly votes."

"Seventy-five percent is a tall hill to climb, baby," Susan said, putting her book on her nightstand, rolling onto his side of the bed. She threw an arm across his torso and squeezed.

"Laura Steiner. I'll bet she lost her nerve and went with C."

"Steiner. Isn't she the chubby art teacher? The one with the crush on you?" Susan poked him in the ribs.

"She doesn't have a crush on me." He looked at her. "And she's not *that* chubby."

"Sure," she said, and bit his shoulder.

No one could jolly him out of his public school teacher funks like Susan. But not that night. Patrick looked up at Chauncey, asleep except for his tail, thrashing like a spastic metronome. "Two fucking votes," he muttered.

"Honey, you did a terrific job. Everybody said so, right?" Susan sat up, patted his chest. "Look how close you came. You'll get it next time."

Patrick slumped into his pillow. "That's just it. There won't be a next time." He closed his eyes. "There is no next time."

6

IF ONLY THE CZAR

February ended at last, as February must, even in New York. The sooty slush melted, and March showered heavily, sweeping the flotsam down Broadway. April, opening with a humid, southeasterly breeze, tried to finish the job, hustling the remaining debris uptown. It was finally, fully spring. Manhattan heaved its windows open, breathed deeply. Time for spring cleaning, time to take stock.

No one was readier for stocktaking than the new mayor of New York City. He began by asking the chancellor of public schools a simple question: How many employees do you have in the public school system? After a brief interval, the chancellor gave a simple reply: I can't tell you. Exactly. He was happy to give an estimate, a ballpark figure, an educated guess if the mayor liked.

The mayor didn't like. This being New York, it got personal. The mayor was a native New Yorker, bluff, Italian, a former prosecutor who'd tackled organized crime. The chancellor was a small, tidy Hispanic gentleman, imported from San Francisco. In another city this issue might have been addressed as an accounting problem, a question of antiquated technology. Here, it became a test of manhood and orientation. The *Post* gleefully quoted the mayor as calling the chancellor a "fussy little man," referring to his San Francisco roots so often one imagined him preening on the lead float of the Gay Pride parade, bearing enough fruit to make Carmen Miranda envious.

The chancellor, unaccustomed to this level of political fisticuffs, refused to respond in kind, instead issuing a

MacArthur-like pronouncement that he would begin a comprehensive tour of the schools, a personal inventory of the system. He declined to state whether or not he'd be counting employees.

The chancellor was coming! He was on his way! Rumors had bounced through the white-tiled halls of Marcus Garvey all week—He's down at the deli, he's getting a knish—but now he was really almost there!

Silverstein had called an emergency faculty meeting the week before. "I'll make this brief," he began. The chancellor was going to make an "unannounced" visit. Marcus Garvey would be putting its "best foot forward." Displaying Garvey's best foot, the principal clarified, would entail a Herculean cleansing of classrooms, detagging the hallways and papering them with a Potemkin village of hastily assigned interdisciplinary art projects. "Do we have to kiss his ring?" brayed a nasal voice in the back. "No, Jerry, we don't," said Silverstein, tapping his clipboard. "Or anything else."

"I don't want to put on a dog-and-pony show for the chancellor," Patrick whined to Susan the night before the "unannounced" visit. "I want him to see my broken bookshelves, my cracked walls, my missing desks."

"If only the czar knew," moaned Susan, a willowy babushka in a J. Crew nightgown. She plumped her pillow, thumbed forward in *Aspects of Modern Social Work*. "If only he knew how we suffer."

"Well, exactly. I want him to see what we produce, given the circumstances. But I want him to note the circumstances."

"Fair enough. But there's always that other possibility." She shut her book in her lap.

"Yes?"

Susan took his cheeks in hand. "That the czar knows, *bubeleh*." She squeezed. "And he doesn't give a shit."

This possibility weighed heavily on Patrick's mind the next morning when Kupczek rapped on his open door. "Excuse me," Patrick told his second period, breaking away from their discussion of the final chapter of *Huck Finn*—waist deep in the Big Muddy. He was graciously excused.

"He's downstairs, Mr. Lynch," Wally panted, "touring the Computer School." Kupczek, red-faced, was sucking in the thick April air as if he'd taken the stairs two at a time. Patrick could almost see himself in the vice principal's shiny forehead. "Next he's going through Visual Arts, then Engineering, then here." He patted his cuff along his damp brow. "The chancellor has his entourage with him, so we'll just take him through a brief observation of a few classes. Mr. Holbrook's first." George was a nut at the lunch table, but his math classes were crisp, well-paced, precise. "Then yours, if you'll permit." Patrick nodded. "I've taken the liberty of closing the door to Mr. Sitkowitz's lab." Beneath the mustache, his I-am-the-walrus grin. Patrick looked off down the hall; no one had less respect for Sitkowitz than he, but it was creepy being pulled inside one of Kupczek's jokes. "The chancellor will most likely come through here toward the end of this period. Then back to his palace in Brooklyn." He raised his eyebrows. "Good luck."

Patrick faced his second period class. "It seems we may have a little visit from the chancellor." Sly glances all around. "We'll just keep discussing Mr. Twain." Second period wasn't buying Lynch's understatement. Not after a week of subtle reminders and implicit threats: It would be a good thing to take *Huck Finn* home tonight and actually read chapter thirty-four; a pop quiz on the Fugitive Slave Act isn't an impossibility. Patrick welcomed—yes, craved—the chance to show the chancellor and his posse room 234 in all its dilapidation. But he wanted his students to shine. Look, Mr. Chancellor-with-your-car-and-driver-blocking-traffic-on-103rd, look at the Afghan girls sitting in folding chairs borrowed for your visit, look at the hole in the back window, look at the clock that's correct twice a day, look at the outdated textbooks with covers missing, that begin on page seventeen. But, for the love of God *listen*, Mr. Chancellor, listen to Maria's emerging Latina feminism as she critiques Aunt Polly's parenting, listen to Jamar compare

Malcolm and Dred Scott and Nigger Jim, listen even to Julio, whose apartment in Washington Heights contains not a single written word, who is semi-literate in three languages, who would kill himself sooner than admit to his classmates that he tried, really tried, to read the first three pages of chapter thirty-four of a novel that could just as well be in Arabic. Listen, Mr. Chancellor, then imagine what we *could* do. Then go back and do battle with the mayor over things that matter.

Second period wanted to look good too. Some classes—fourth period, fuggedaboutit—had no pride. But second period, even Abdul, sat up a little straighter when Silverstein flitted through. They didn't want to be caught caring, but they did. It was important, however, to let them think they were "getting over" on the system. Mr. Lynch could rag on them—study, study, study, there's a test tomorrow; it's not magic; come prepared and you'll see results—till the No. 2 Express ran crosstown. Jamar, Angela, Hegira aside, he was talkin' to himself. Ah, but take a copy of that same test, crumple it up a little, find a sneaker in the Lost and Found and make some dusty shoe prints on it, leave it under Abdul's desk for him to *find* the day before the exam. *Now* they would spend the evening doing what Patrick had wanted all along. Patrick tried not to smile at their smugness as he handed out the tests; Tom Sawyer himself would have been proud. (One could get too clever with these strategies, Patrick discovered his first year teaching. He'd planted a ten-spot in the text of an ever-sleeping student, then plucked the book off his desk, opened it, and waved the sawbuck in front of the class. "You never know what treasures you'll find in a book," he crowed, then watched helplessly as they dismembered a complete class set, pages swirling to the floor like so many autumn leaves.)

Patrick had only one reason to doubt that second period would rise to the occasion, and he was resting in the back, face pressed against the editing table. It was a delicate thing, getting Josh's cooperation. Patrick was at enormous disadvantage with the chancellor downstairs, a disadvantage Josh was pleased to exploit. It was too loud, Josh complained, when the jackhammers started up on Columbus Avenue. Patrick closed the windows. The classroom grew clammy. It was one of those spring days in Manhattan where the temperature spikes to the mid 80s, a teasing foretaste of July, lovely weather for lolling on a blanket in Central Park with your honey; it was not great weather to be in a second floor classroom with thirty-six perspiring teenagers above a baking blacktop. Too hot, Josh moaned, flipping his head back and forth on the editing table. Patrick opened the windows. The breeze caught the door, which slammed, rattling in its frame. Patrick propped it open with a wastebasket.

On your typical April morning, second period would have welcomed the diversion of watching the intrepid Mr. Lynch being jerked around like a well-hooked trout. But an unusual number of them had taken their teacher's counsel and struggled through Twain's wry nineteenth-century prose, and they were, damn it, gonna strut their stuff before the chancellor. Angela and Maria rolled their eyes at Josh's interjections. "Shut up," muttered the ever-pleasant Jamar. And even Abdul, who was happy to play tag-team with Josh when it struck his fancy, swiveled back and said, "Why you gotta be so stupid all the time?"

Josh was building, building. Patrick knew it would come, what he was building toward, just a question of timing. Could he nurse him past the chancellor's visit? The stress of the occasion might be more than Josh could handle. And, after last Wednesday's failed "tutorial," all bets were off.

The afterschool session with Josh had been Wally's bright idea. This particular brainstorm came out of a command performance for Josh's mother in the vice principal's office two weeks before.

"What you don't seem to understand, Mr. Lynch," she'd barked at him from an opposing chair angled at the far side of Wally's desk, "is that Joshua's a *gifted* dyslexic." Ah, Patrick wanted to say, that would account for the Lynch Is A Foggat he'd found scrawled across his blackboard that morning. Such fine prose so cruelly twisted.

But he kept his powder dry, flicking a look at Wally, who was drowsing behind his desk, evaluating a hangnail. "Joshua is frustrated," Dr. Mishkin continued, forcing Patrick back to her pained expression. "We were up all night working on his *Huck Finn* essay. And, yes, sometimes he expresses his frustration inappropriately." She cleared her throat. "Which I have discussed with him. But he has *special needs*. And none of the accommodations in his Ed Plan has been enacted in your classroom." She unfisted her hands and placed them atop a folder the thickness of the Manhattan Yellow Pages.

Summoning compassion for a troubled student—even an irritating one—was never difficult for Patrick. And the sight of a parent's broad face contracting with distress would normally have wrung his heart. *Julio's father in jail again, Mr. Lynch. We gonna be evicted. I know he oughtta be doin' his homework, but he won' lissen to me. If you could only help him.* Patrick melted at such entreaties, a total softie. But the tortured mother was never a solidly built NYU professor ("Well, adjunct," said Dorie) and the unseen father a Columbia Sovietologist. ("Though I never hear him on NPR anymore," said Dorie. "That whole Berlin Wall thing really hit him hard.") Upper West Side lefties, whose colleagues sent their kids to first-tier prep schools, they prided themselves on being public school holdouts. But they never imagined their son getting the same attention as the other thirty-five students in my second period, thought Patrick.

Still, he almost felt sorry for her. Was it only a year or two ago she'd watched Josh recite his Torah portion so perfectly, not a single stumble or hesitation? Her son, the tallest and handsomest boy in his Hebrew school class, proud and manly in his navy blue suit, his yarmulke neatly pinned to his wavy hair. Was this the same boy, she must be wondering, with his amber dreadlocks, his pants slipping down his ass, who had embraced this rap culture, this culture that was at once so misogynistic and anti-Semitic that it couldn't really be interpreted as anything but a repudiation of everything that was *her*? Yes, Patrick could have felt some compassion. If only she hadn't insisted on reducing this timeless mother-son drama to an educational issue. She was mad as hell, and she was going to make it his problem. She was going to leave with a piece of his hide.

"Might I suggest..." Kupczek's voice entered the room slowly, as if it had traveled from a far-off place and needed rest, its appearance so unexpected that Dr. Mishkin's expression changed from rage to surprise. "Might I suggest that this situation is not entirely...*intractable*?" Patrick had grown used to Wally's Dickensian circumlocutions, but those new to him were always disarmed by this man who looked like the former gym teacher he was ("Mr. Cup-check") but spoke like Mr. Micawber. Wally leaned over his desk, brushed his mustache with his fingertips. "It seems that Joshua might benefit from some additional tutoring. Perhaps he and Mr. Lynch could find some mutually advantageous time to meet—during a study period, or after school." He looked at Dr. Mishkin, then Patrick. Dr. Mishkin's large features fell into something like satisfaction. The Kupczek grin peeped from under the stash. Peace in Our Time, once again.

And it was thus that Patrick found himself sitting at his editing table with Josh at 3:30 the following Wednesday afternoon, holding Josh's dissection of Twain, *Nigger Huck*.

A siren had wailed down 103rd Street as Patrick bent over the essay, chin in hand. Josh, reclined in his chair at sixty degrees, was playing with his X cap, trying to find the most rakish backwards angle. Satisfied at last, he smoothed down the front of his T-shirt, which bore the do-ragged and belligerent visage of St. Tupac, exhorting his public to KEEP IT REAL. Softly but insistently one heard the taptaptap of the basketball Josh's buddies were dribbling down at the end of the hall. Moments earlier they'd been dribbling it in the doorway, until Patrick had been forced to shoo them down toward the exit, which he did firmly but with some restraint, mindful of how such a situation could turn on you, of how Wally, in a similar circumstance, had yelled, *Gentlemen, hold your balls.* And they had.

Dr. Mishkin was right about one thing: her son was damn smart. Most of what Josh had handed in this year was dashed off and under-written. The only pieces he'd spent time on were angry, painfully derivative, the anger imported from the South Bronx. But this essay was really strong—well-organized and -argued, with a command of standard English few students, regardless of ethnicity or class, had these days. True, the first draft had been blue-penciled to a fare-thee-well by Dr. Mishkin, or possibly by her husband, the other Dr. Mishkin, but the editing was largely mechanical, a poignant parental attempt to unscramble the workings of a mind so badly miswired. The thinking and prose were clearly, and impressively, Josh's.

Patrick looked up. Josh had his eyes fixed on the doorway. Patrick assessed his possible first moves. Don't be too complimentary, that was the main thing. Patrick leaned back in his chair. Casual. Like they were gettin' together for a coupl'a beers. "Josh, you know, you got some stuff in here." He patted the essay. "Some stuff that's kinda—*interesting.*" Josh's eyes were trained on the doorway like a hungry dog's on its bowl when it's being filled. Was the room empty? Patrick wondered. Was he talking to himself? Did he need this? Only the vision of a second conference with Wally and Dr. Mishkin, perhaps both Drs. Mishkin, prodded him on. "Actually, it's more than interesting. Some of the issues you raise about Huck Finn are really *important.*"

Josh favored him with a glance but managed not to move his head nor disturb the angle of his body. "Yo, my moms made me write it."

Patrick picked up the essay. "What you said on page three, 'Nigger Jim is the archetype of the helpless slave'—archetype, good word—'incapable of independent action in his own self-interest.' That's pretty provocative. Could you tell me more about that?" *Joshua requires significant amounts of "wait time"* said his Ed Plan. He waited. The fluorescent lights buzzed.

Taptaptap from down the hall. He leaned in, elbows on the table. "Are you saying Jim's incapable of action, or is it just a matter of independence?"

Josh shook his dreads and shifted to an angle slightly less obtuse. "Twain's a stone racist, and I ain't gonna say anymore 'bout dat," he mumbled. His eyes went back to the doorway. Taptaptap. Yo, Lynch, this audience is over.

Patrick had hoped this essay was a breakthrough, that they could actually talk. But Josh was only willing to drop his persona on paper; he wouldn't cop to having written in his mother('s) tongue. Had he really said *dat?* No doubt Josh scrutinized Black Entertainment Television with the same intensity his scholarly forebears had invested in the Talmud—he had the particulars down—but occasionally he slipped and sounded like he was auditioning for the road show of *Porgy and Bess.*

Patrick ran his hand over his hair, noting the lack of follicles at the corners, how, even at this relatively tender age, he was replicating his father's Nixonian balding pattern. Cynical, Susan had called him recently. Had he lost his patience, his passion? Had he become one of *them?* He thrust his head back and cocked it in an attitude of disbelief. "Oh, come off it, Josh. You don't think I'm gonna buy this *bull* about Mark Twain being a racist? For its time, *Huckleberry Finn* was fiercely pro-Black. You say right here," Patrick flicked open the essay, "right here on page four that Clemens practically adopted a Black boy named Jimmy and put him through school."

"Yeah, and he ripped-off his African dialect and style and painted him white and renamed him Huck and made a million dollars!" Josh had thrown himself forward, halfway across the little round table. His eyes blazed, his dreadlocks shivered. "Just like Elvis and Chuck Berry."

A smile at this point would be fatal, but it was hard to tamp down. Patrick puckered his lips slightly and scratched at his chin. "You've got a long way to go to convince me about Twain…but this Elvis connection…I'll have to *think* about that." Josh settled back some, but his elbows were on his knees now and he looked straight at Patrick, eyebrows animated. Patrick leaned back—had to stay cool—which would be difficult, his cheeks feeling flushed, that tight thrill in his chest. A familiar sensation but somehow distant. How long since he'd cracked a nut this tough?

Patrick evaluated the various avenues before him. Josh sat motionless, anticipatory. The tapping down the hall had gotten closer, louder, and the dribbler had added a more insistent crossover—tataTAP—but Josh seemed not to notice. Patrick sniffed, pulled on his nose. He threw out a hand dramatically. "Let's just say…let's just *entertain the idea* that Twain was doing something radical here. Perhaps he was so fascinated by African-American culture that he wanted to create a white character who *inhabited* those qualities, that style. A character who scorns white bourgeois values—a bold and spirited traitor to his race!"

Patrick let this sink in. Josh's eyes showed nothing, or, rather, too much, as if he were trying to make a long and complex series of calculations and all the circuits were full. Seven years of teaching experience told Patrick to let this sit, but that feeling in his chest drove him on. He spoke gently, almost a whisper. "Can you imagine why someone, Twain, Huck—anyone—would make such a choice?"

Josh sat open-mouthed, slack-jawed. His lips, surrounded by that pale and wispy facial hair, took on an unusual shape, the shape of a question. Then it came—tataTAP, tataTAP. Louder and louder, right outside the door. And laughter: soft, off-hand, derisive.

Josh shot up from the table with such speed, the unfolding of his long limbs requiring such effort, that his chair flew out, skidding halfway to the wall behind him. "Yo, dis is *wack*," he shouted. Laughter, tataTAP. "Dis is *wack*."

Patrick couldn't help flinching when the chair smacked the floor, but he'd seen and heard much worse and quickly pulled himself in. "Hey, Josh, take it easy. Have a seat, let's talk."

Josh backpedaled, stumbling over his chair, kicking it away.

"I'm gone, man. I'm outta here." Then he was, in fact, leaving. Too much was leaving with him. Patrick stood and raised his voice as he never did in class. "Josh, this is not going to get your mother off your back!"

Josh whipped around, his dreadlocks flailing about his skull. "Or yours! Which is what this is all about. My mother." He jabbed an index finger at Patrick. "You, Kupczek, you're all so intimidated by *Dr. Mishkin.* She just might yank out one of the last white kids in this school. That's what this is all about." They stared at each other, Patrick afraid to blink and lose him. "You're all so pathetic."

Patrick cupped his hands in front of his chest, weaving a loose basket there. It held Josh for a moment, but not long enough for Patrick to fashion a counter to Josh's claims. And, if he'd had longer, would it have mattered?

Someone in the hall, perhaps Abdul, said, "Yo, J-man, les go, a'ight?" and Josh was out, greeted by laughter and hand slapping and that fancy dribbling. Patrick listened to their sounds recede until all he heard was the buzzing of his lights and the basketball's echoing tataTAP: inyourFACE, Lynch, it said, inyourFACE.

Patrick felt his neck tensing as he waited for the chancellor to enter his classroom. Down boy, he told himself. Just another day at the office. He loosened his tie, the one Susan gave him for his birthday, with the Marxes—Groucho and Karl—on it. *That's the most ridiculous thing I ever hoid,* Groucho says to Karl. Patrick's little joke for the day, chancellor be damned. He'd left scarface Emily Dickinson up, too, though he knew he'd get flak from Silverstein.

"So," Mr. Lynch growled at second period, "what's up with that ending?"

"Made no sense," said Jamar.

"Yeah," said Angela, "why do they risk Jim's life after that big trip down the river?"

"And all for some stupid little play Tom wants to be making out of Jim's escape," said Maria.

"Good point, Maria. Many critics have wondered about that." Julio clapped toward Maria. "Julio?" Julio froze when Patrick spoke. "What do you think?"

Julio scratched an elbow. "That Maria's right."

Second period laughed.

"Yes, smart girl. We're all in agreement on that," Patrick said. Maria tilted her head, patted her hair. "But why does Jim go along with it?"

Julio shrugged.

"Yo, that nigga's crazy," said Abdul.

Mr. Lynch gave him the death stare, reserved for special occasions, such as violating the class's sacred vow to only use the n-word in context, with quotes around it. They'd spent the better part of a tough week discussing the history of that epithet, processing Twain's 219 uses of it in his novel.

"Sorry," said Abdul.

Mr. Lynch looked away from Abdul, apology accepted. "Hemingway called *Huck Finn* the 'Great American Novel.' Did Twain mess it up? Why this choice at the end?"

Josh lifted his head off the editing table, periscoping it around, as if tuning in to a familiar frequency. The teacher flop-sweat started up under Patrick's pits, beneath his tie. *Why would anyone make that choice?* He'd said it again. Damn. Why would anyone make *that* choice? Josh looked him full in the face, dreads twitching, ready for action. He stood. If he flips the editing table again, Patrick thought, he'll take out Hegira's girls in those folding chairs.

Josh looked over Patrick's shoulder. Patrick glanced down: Jamar, Abdul, Maria, Angela—all of second period—was looking over his shoulder. Mr. Lynch twisted his head toward the door.

The chancellor was a little man, as the mayor had so memorably noted, but he was one of those small men who, like rice, puff up under pressure. He seemed to fill the doorway in his broad-shouldered charcoal suit. He took a few steps into room 234, followed by Silverstein and the entourage. Mr. Lynch nodded at the chancellor. The chancellor, arms folded across his chest, nodded back. Silverstein glanced at the teacher, then past him with thinly veiled fear, the expression he wore when a faculty meeting promised to run to riot. Patrick remembered that he was in the midst of a student's psychotic break.

"So, Josh," Mr. Lynch said, cool, so cool, as if the second most important man in New York City weren't watching, "what are your thoughts on the ending of *Huckleberry Finn?* Did Twain lose his nerve?"

Josh looked at Mr. Lynch, then the chancellor, then Silverstein, then his classmates. He licked his lips, tugged at his T-shirt, which featured an orgasmic Jimi Hendrix gripping the head of his phallic guitar. Josh looked down at the editing table, seeming to forget why he was standing. He looked up. He opened his mouth.

What would come out? Patrick wondered—the latest in ghetto profanity? His Torah portion? What?

"Well," said Josh, clearing his throat, "first you have to consider Twain's audience." He stood a little straighter. "He wanted to appeal to the quote unquote liberal northerners. They wanted an enlightened view of race relations. But he didn't want to alienate his broader audience, who wanted a, wanted a—" He glanced at the window, the meshwork over the hole. He was quoting himself, of course, highlights from his masterwork, *Nigger Huck*, but he'd lost the thread. He looked back at Patrick. Those blank eyes again. Please, prayed Patrick, don't let the table hit those girls. You saved them from the Russians, Lord. "—who wanted a funny sequel to *Tom Sawyer.*" Josh swallowed. "And then there was a deadline to face. He had to pay for that monster house he was building in Hartford. And there was Mrs. Twain. And the little Twainses." He let himself grin. Inside that furry frame was a lovely smile.

Everyone laughed appreciatively.

"Thank you, Josh. Interesting viewpoint, well stated," said Mr. Lynch.

Josh sat.

"Thank you, Mr. Lynch," said Silverstein. Patrick twisted back: the chancellor, hands stuffed in pockets, nodding, grinning. *This* was his school system. Silverstein beaming, monumental relief spreading across his face. *This* was his school. And, thought Patrick, if a public school teacher could ask for a raise, *this* would be that moment.

Mr. Lynch turned back to his class. They heard the chancellor and his crew sweep down the Down staircase. The slice-and-dice of Twain continued, the entire class jazzed by the chancellor's appearance. A forest of hands in Patrick's face; everyone wanted a piece of the action.

Everyone but Josh. As soon as the dignitaries left room 234, he slumped to the editing table, spent by his examination of *Huck Finn*. Mr. Lynch patrolled the room, up and down the aisles, hurling questions, demanding better conclusions, stronger evidence. Soon they heard engines starting up, doors slamming. Patrick strolled to the window, caught the taillights of the chancellor's convoy as it sped down 103rd Street, flags flying, home to Brooklyn.

Patrick pirouetted back to his class. He looked at his watch: seven minutes left. Time to pull it all together. He put those two fingers to his mouth.

Abdul leaned back in his desk, stroked the hair above his upper lip. "Thank you, Pro*fessa'* Mishkin," he stage-whispered. Julio giggled.

Josh twitched. He took a deep breath, filling with air, the slumbering beast within aroused. He mumbled into his hands, something, Patrick thought, about being sick, and needing a bathroom pass.

It was Mr. Lynch's policy—ironclad—not to allow students out during the last ten minutes of class, lest they begin packing up and checking out after the first thirty minutes. But why not let Josh go this once? He'd just made the teacher, the principal, the chancellor—New York City—look good. His mother would be *kvelling*. Let him have his meltdown in the boys' room. For once, he'd earned it.

From his desk in the back, opposite the editing table, Patrick plucked the wooden slat into which the art teacher had burned BATHROOM, 234 and laid it next to Josh's head. Mr. Lynch turned back to the class. "Jamar," he said, "having completed *Huck Finn*, knowing what you now know about the author and his era, what would you say to Mr. Clemens if he sat here among us?"

Those bright eyes sparkled as Jamar adjusted his Malcolm glasses, pleased to be giving the summation for this long unit. He leaned forward in his seat. "Sam, I'd say—may I call you Sam?"

Angela turned to Maria. "Jamar is too funny."

"Sam, I'd say—" The bathroom pass whizzed past Patrick's right ear, bounced off Julio's desk, and skidded down the aisle.

"I said, I'm fucking *sick* of this *class*."

The erstwhile Twain scholar stood in front of the editing table, shaking, dreadlocks doing the merengue on his forehead. Damn, thought Patrick, almost made it. He'd already begun crafting the replay for Susan. *You should have seen the look on the chancellor's face. And Silverstein! Jesus!* Sarcastic musings aside, nothing aroused his significant other more than his tales of one man's triumph over the indifferent System. He was going to get so lucky tonight.

But that thought-bubble popped as Angela handed the bathroom pass to him, disgust on her face. Maria was shaking her head, that black crest bobbing. Even Hegira, ever-placid, narrowed her eyes and stiffened on her folding chair. And Jamar—sweet Jamar—was livid, those chubby cheeks tightening, that plump bottom lip disappearing. In his relief over the chancellor's coming and going, Patrick had missed just how ripped second period was at Josh. He'd wasted their time yet again and, worse, stolen their thunder in front of the chancellor. Isn't that just how it goes? Jamar's disappointed eyes said. We do the work and white boy gets the goodies.

No one was happy now except Abdul, smirking at the rise he'd gotten from his quip, and Julio, grinning behind him. Josh, who so longed to be Black, got redder by the moment. He'd been caught tap dancing for The Man, had outed himself as the professors' kid. All that hard-earned street cred, down the drain.

Josh and Mr. Lynch glared at one another. Second period watched, and waited. Patrick patted his palm with the bathroom pass. Too late for that method of disposal. A Black kid using the n-word was survivable. The f-word, if not directed at someone, was finessable. Hurling a piece of wood at the teacher, however, was automatic. Patrick reached in his pocket for the slip to the principal's office, pre-filled out with Josh's name.

Mr. Lynch thrust the slip out toward Josh. "To Mr. Kupzcek. Now."

Josh stroked Jimi Hendrix, who stroked his guitar. He jerked his head back and laughed. The breeze kicked up through the meshwork; *Huck Finn* rustled on desks. An edge of Emily Dickinson's shawl broke free and flapped. Josh strode to Mr. Lynch, stopped, and snatched the slip from his fingers. The boy nodded, smiling. "Now," said Mr. Lynch. It had to be his idea.

Josh ambled to the door. Mr. Lynch escorted him, hurrying him along. Josh made sure to kick the wastebasket on his way out, freeing the door. Patrick caught it, watched Josh through the doorway. Then he pivoted toward his class and flicked the door closed, the matador flourishing his cape, turning his back on the bull.

The breeze kicked up. Patrick regretted his grand gesture; he paused for the slam.

I HATE THIS FU— he heard and then something less than a slam, with no rattling afterward. A muffled crunch he heard, the sound of the middle distal interphalangeal joint disjointed, the flexor digitorum profundus severed, the radial digital artery and nerves, disconnected. And then a thin, high noise, no human noise, the sound the deer made when his grandfather had goaded him into going hunting up north, and Patrick, trembling, had only grazed the creature's head above the eye.

Patrick turned. The door quivered; a bright red line ran down the bottom of the jamb. Above it, stuffed in the latch plate, was the upper two-thirds of Josh Mishkin's finger. His right middle finger, pointing up.

7

TEACHER SOLITAIRE

So this, 65 Court Street, Brooklyn, Room 337, was solitary
confinement? Patrick gripped the Styrofoam cup, put the
tepid coffee to his lips. Four white windowless walls, a scarred
brown table, several ripped vinyl-covered chairs, a wall clock,
a plastic plant. Not a great deal larger than the bedroom he
shared with Susan, disappointing for a place whose legend
figured so prominently in New York City teacher mythology.
He'd heard the stories since his first hesitant steps into a city
school: the middle-aged Spanish teacher caught practicing
Latin cognates on a pantless protégé in the teacher's lounge
bathroom; the bearded geek from the Computer School who'd
lost his cool and hurled a keyboard at a boy, fracturing an arm.
What happened to them? Patrick asked. The old-timer would
shrug, laugh. Put 'em in solitary. Then transferred to another
district, where their file wouldn't follow them. *Tabula rasa.* Patrick would give a sidewise glance over his peanut butter and
jelly sandwich, wanting to appear neither too credulous nor
ignorant. Now he was in that mythic place, part purgatory, part
holding pen.

It was 9:23, like always on a Monday morning, but then it
was twenty-four past, twenty-five. At least the clock worked
here. Now it was 11:13. In forty-seven minutes it would be
lunchtime. Or what he told himself should be lunchtime;
Patrick felt certain they wouldn't check. They never check,
Silverstein had said.

"Don't worry, Patrick," said his principal. "It's just for a
couple weeks. Let things cool down. Then due process will
happen." Life occurred in the passive voice in Silverstein's

world. Surely a job at the CIA awaited him. "And you'll be paid to shuffle papers." He tried to smile. "Practically a vacation." Patrick looked away from the clock, over to the poster tacked to the left of the door, above the plastic plant. A pretty blonde teacher sat at her desk, a rainbow of smiling school-children clustered around her. Beneath the beaming group: *Teaching Changes Lives.*

He took a deep breath, let it go, and fingered an essay on top of a tall stack of citywide English exams. Grading this year's citywide writing test was, apparently, the paper he'd be shuffling to earn his keep in solitary. A short, voluminous secretary, half-glasses resting on her bosom-shelf, had plopped down the stack on the brown table, handed him a rubric for evaluation, and left the room without explanation. Patrick thumbed through the stack and read the rubric. The secretary came back after the second hand swept around the clock a few times. "You're an English teacher, yes?" The simple affirmative came to Patrick's lips, then stalled. Last week, *yes* would have sufficed: yes, he had a masters in English Lit; yes, he'd taught English for seven years; yes, the directory at Marcus Garvey said Patrick Lynch, room 234, English and AmStud 10. The secretary stared down at him, first with the tired indifference of all Board of Ed employees, then with annoyance, then disdain. She knows my story, thought Patrick. They all know my story.

The morning after "the incident," as Silverstein would forever call it, Patrick had taken the subway to school, like always. Most New Yorkers considered the subway a necessary evil, but for Patrick it was still the urban adventure ride at some edgy theme park. He loved the shapes, sizes, colors of the riders, so different from his native land, where brown eyes put you in a suspect minority. He loved to eavesdrop on the conversations, soak up the accents, guess at the language groups. Was that Vietnamese? Thai? He was even intrigued by the scratches on metal and plastic that had replaced an earlier generation of graffiti. The casual tagging of city and school was an irritant, dogs lifting their legs, marking territory. But etching yourself into the subway car seemed different, spoke of a desperation to communicate, however feebly. He tried to remember that urge in his classroom.

The first year in New York, he'd been moved by how sad, how exhausted, most of the riders looked. Some even closed their eyes standing up, hugging the poles, chests rising and falling in the slow evenness of sleep. He'd become one of those riders, he realized with a jolt, when he opened his eyes one late afternoon and found himself in the South Bronx, having ridden far past his stop, off the island. The station was empty, eerie, devoid of commercial activity at a time when the rest of the city bustled.

But that morning, after the incident, Patrick counted himself lucky to have found a seat, a place to hunker down and avoid thinking about what awaited him at school. He looked at shoes: the polished Florsheims and sexy pumps of young office workers, the sneakers and Timberlands of teenagers. The jostling of the train was comforting. He looked up at a row of commuters, hands outstretched, all holding the *Post*. The image struck him as comical until he took in the headline, repeated in triplicate: *Student Gives Teacher the Finger*. Beneath the headline, a picture of Marcus Garvey High School.

Patrick looked furtively around the train. Was his picture in the paper? Was his face on page three, something cribbed from the *Garvey Gazette*, maybe that snapshot of him at the urban garden project, pointing his shovel at the student photographer in mock menace? He imagined the row of *Post*s crumpling to the readers' laps. You. You are the teacher to whom the finger was given. Now a phalanx of outraged citizens, they'd point at him with their own accusing fingers, wagging them until the entire car was focused on this monster, the one who slammed doors on the digits of innocent students. Just look at him with that shovel. Why do they let people like that teach our children?

The secretary stood, staring. Surely she had read the story. She had that condemnatory expression he'd envisioned on the faces of his fellow straphangers. She knew his type; for years she'd doled out busywork to teachers who'd betrayed the public's sacred trust. Her arms were crossed under her bosom. She was waiting for his confession. Solitary broke them all, eventually.

She plucked her half-glasses off her bosom and plopped them on her nose. She scanned a piece of paper. The secretary looked down at him, over her glasses, with a face that could only be achieved by a lifetime at the Board of Ed. "You *are* an English teacher," she repeated, now as a statement.

Patrick nodded.

She exhaled heavily and left.

He took a sip of his coffee, now cold. She was not going to beat him.

He'd done battle with the Board of Ed before, seven years ago, when his very first teacher payday came and went without a paycheck. Everyone in the Experiment in Cooperative Learning got paid but the new guy. Snafu at Court Street, Human Resources, Kupzcek had said. Happens all the time. Then he shook his head gravely. But don't call. Never call. He looked Patrick in the eye, imparting an eternal truth: You must speak to them in person.

The last bell rang that Friday at 3:00 and Patrick was out the door. He caught the No. 3 train, pushed his way onto the No. 7 at Times Square, and was dumped off at Court Street, Brooklyn. He entered the Board of Education building at 3:47, sweaty, braced for his encounter with Them. Half an hour's wait in line gained him the information that he must talk to Pedagogical Personnel, third floor. This reassured him somewhat; he'd been there before, procuring his teaching license.

But, no, the lady at Personnel said, we can't help you. You need Payroll, fifth floor.

No, the man at Payroll said, can't do a thing for you.

But you're Payroll, Patrick pleaded. You can't pay me?

Not without a file number, the man said, looking up from his computer screen.

File number? Patrick shook his head.

The man pointed at his screen. Far as Board of Ed is concerned, you don't exist.

But I do exist. I've already taught two weeks. Patrick swallowed. Two really hard weeks.

I understand, the man from Payroll said, palms lifted. You need to talk to Pedagogical Personnel.

Been there, Patrick said.

Hmmm. The man frowned. Technical Support, then. Fourth floor.

We're closed, the woman at Technical Support said and pointed to the clock: 4:50.

You're not open till five? Patrick said, sounding whiny even to himself.

Friday, the woman answered, as if that made everything clear. She pushed her unfinished sandwich into a bag, slipped on her shoes. Try us on Monday. Have a good weekend, she said.

Not bloody likely, he thought. But he was back at Court Street on Monday after school. And Tuesday, and on several other afternoons over the next pay period. The answers were always the same: another department, another floor. On the Wednesday before the next payday, Patrick got angry, raising his voice at a small Asian woman in Licensure. Someone, he nearly screamed—a Minnesotan scream—had to know where his file number was. They gave him a license, he had to have a file number.

The woman, possibly his mother's age, remained calm, like his mother. She leaned toward him, across her desk. Her expression was confidential. After 3:30, she said softly, nobody's here except for us temps. We don't know where anything is. We're not authorized to take any actions. She looked to either side and so did Patrick, noticing for the first time how many desks were empty. We answer phones, we file. She looked around again. When someone needs something, we send them to another department. She shrugged apologetically. Until five o'clock.

Things were getting desperate. He might not exist to the Board of Ed, but he was very real to his roommate, who was large and terse and only interested in when, not how, Patrick produced his share of the rent. My mother, Patrick thought. She, of course, would front him the money. And she'd laugh, former high school secretary that she was. I was the bureaucracy in Peterson's Prairie, she'd chirp. Never thought you'd miss that, huh?

Patrick held his face in his hands. Hit up his widowed mother for rent money? No, he'd play guitar in the subway first. Beg.

At last, he went to Silverstein. Ah, the Board of Ed, the principal sighed. Sometimes you have to get tough with them. There's a story I heard, he began. Here goes my prep period, thought Patrick. The story, perhaps apocryphal, Silverstein conceded, involved a teacher, unpaid for months, who finally went up to the controller's office at Court Street, pulled out a pistol, and said Nobody leaves till I get my motherfucking check. Patrick scarcely knew Silverstein at this point and his head snapped back at an administrator laying the mofo on him. He'd only heard his father say shit once, and only after he'd hammered a thumb. Go right to the controller, Silverstein said. No gun, he chuckled.

Patrick did as instructed. He nodded his way past the security guard, who by now assumed Patrick worked for the Board of Ed, strode onto the elevator, punched seven. He whisked by the woman who sat at the desk with the Office of the Controller plaque. It was 4:45; she was a temp. He wove through a maze of empty desks, stopped before a darkened room. A pale blue light reflected off the open door. Patrick peered around the edge.

The room was lined with computer monitors, glowing blue. Behind one monitor sat a tiny, tonsured man in a wrinkled white shirt and gray suit pants. His face was but a few inches from the computer screen; he moved it back and forth, scanning figures.

Patrick tapped on the door and cleared his throat. Excuse me?

The little man kept scanning, a full minute it seemed to Patrick.

You can't be in here, he said calmly, without turning.

I'm sorry. Patrick cleared his throat again. I'm sorry, but no one else can help me.

Leave your name with my secretary—

She's a temp, Patrick said, with more edge than intended.

The man turned. He wore a green bow tie and thick glasses that reflected the blue of the monitors. He looked Patrick up and down. My *secretary* will be here Monday. Come back Monday—

With the broomstick, thought Patrick. But he only said, Look, before he caught himself.

The blue lenses took in the doorway behind Patrick, located a nearby phone. Maybe Silverstein's tale of the teacher packing heat was true.

Sir, Patrick said. I'm a first-year teacher. I don't have desks. I don't have enough paper, or pens, or books. And I've been teaching—trying to teach—for a month, and I've got next to zero in my checking account. And my rent's due. He swallowed away that hard place that was building in his throat. And I just want to get paid…for my work.

The controller leaned back in his chair. He turned to his screen.

That's it? wondered Patrick. Class dismissed?

What did you say your name is? the controller said.

Patrick Lynch.

The controller tapped rapid-fire at the keyboard. He waited, drumming on his desk. Ha! he shouted. Look at this. He waved Patrick over, pointed to his screen.

Patrick hesitated, but the controller waved more emphatically. Patrick stepped into the room, leaned over the controller's shoulder, peered at the screen. *Patrick Linch, File Number 100328.*

User error! crowed the controller, jabbing his finger at the screen. It wasn't the system, he clarified, as if that brought great comfort to him and should to Patrick also.

He corrected the typo. Well, Patrick Lynch-with-a-*y*, stop by your school secretary tomorrow at 10:00 a.m. and she will give you a check for a full month's pay. He stuck out his hand. It was small, moist. With the apologies of the New York City Board of Education, the controller said, pumping Patrick's hand with surprising vigor. All square?

Patrick could finally see his eyes, huge behind the thick lenses. Thank you, sir. That's great.

The little man leaned back in his chair, his head hammocked in his hands. Anything else? he said with the casual tone of a fixer. They didn't call him the controller for nothing.

Else? Patrick's mind raced. He almost laughed. Well, he thought, some new textbooks would be nice. But he just shook his head and backed out of the room.

The controller returned to his controls, his eyes glowing blue.

Patrick checked the clock: 2:45. He slipped the final exam of the day from the tall, somewhat diminished pile on the brown table. He glanced at the top of the paper. Let's see what Carmelita Fuentes had to say about that article on the Gettysburg Address. *Now let me tell you something about Abe Lincoln,* her essay began. Patrick looked around the empty room, smiling. The voice of this girl was so vivid, he could see her. She was sitting here next to him, waving her hand in front of his face, passing judgment on our fourteenth president as she would on school lunch. You see what they serving yesterday? Let me tell you something—it *nasty.* Patrick read on as the essayist dismissed the Emancipation Proclamation with a finger snap and a head roll. *Everybody say Lincoln free all the slaves. But NO! he only free slaves in the South. And that's the onnest truth if you want to know. Even tho he's Lincoln he's still a politishun. Just like them all.* True enough, Patrick laughed. Amen.

Patrick checked the rubric. Level 5: Does the writer display a thorough understanding of the role of tone and audience in persuasive writing? No. Level 4: Does the writer demonstrate command of paragraph and sentence structure, the use of evidence in supporting a single clear thesis? No, no. Level 3: Does the writer have fundamental control of grammar, spelling, and punctuation? No, no, and no. Level 2:

He slapped Abe Lincoln down on the stack of unevaluated tests. Why did they always ask the wrong questions? Why did the rubric capture none of this girl's aptitude or enthusiasm? Why not:

Does the writer display passion for this subject? Yes.

Does the writer appreciate the connection between history and her life? Yes.

Does the writer show evidence of having paid attention in a history class of thirty-five students, taught by an apathetic man with a degree in Phys Ed, seated next to a big girl with a sharp nail file who promised to *mess her up* after school? *Yes.*

Patrick scratched his head. The wrong questions. He snapped a half moon of Styrofoam off the rim of his cup.

"Did you see the student leave your classroom, Mr. Lynch? Were you aware that he was still in your doorway?" Officer Rodriguez had scribbled the replies in his notepad as quickly as Patrick gave them. "Before he threw the bathroom pass at you, Mr. Lynch, did the student threaten you?" Scribble, scribble. "Did he threaten you afterwards?" Scribble. "What did you say to him when you sent him to Mr. Kupczek's office?"

Silverstein sat at his desk, chewing his lower lip. Patrick sat in the chair you sat in when you were called into the principal's office. How many times had Josh sat in this seat? And Raul Rodriguez, how odd in this role. Not the jovial figure on the street corner after school, in front of the 103rd Street Deli, munching on a bagel, wiping cream cheese from his lips. Good afternoon, Mr. Lynch, he'd nod. Top o' the day, officer, Patrick always responded, with a little salute, acknowledging their comradeship, that they were actors in the same drama, costumed, staying in character for the teenagers streaming by, making that uneasy transition from student to juvenile pedestrian. Patrick would duck into the deli and pop out with his after-school coffee, sometimes with a cup for Raul—black, three sugars.

Raul had two kids, Rosa and Enrique, at P.S. 205 in Queens. His wife was a bookkeeper at an auto parts store. He was always worrying, even as he licked the cream cheese from his lips, about the buttons of his uniform that pushed over his belt. But who can find time for the gym, you know? he'd say, examining Patrick, effortlessly lanky in his khakis and corduroy sport coat. It's easier when you don't have kids. You got no idea, he'd grin. Just wait.

Patrick looked at Silverstein, hands folded on his desk, doing his best to appear sanguine. He couldn't be happy—that future superintendency the staff always joked about must have seemed tangible when the chancellor left Garvey. "You might want to have Mr. Roselli here," Silverstein said before Officer Rodriguez showed up. C? Patrick thought. Why would he want C there? Silverstein paused. "He *is* your union rep. He might be useful to you." Patrick nodded. "And a lawyer. Though I don't think that's necessary yet, no charges have been filed." Charges? Patrick stared at his principal. Silverstein examined his knuckles, coughed. "The Mishkins mentioned something about assault."

"You met with Josh Mishkin after school last week, Mr. Lynch?" It was almost funny—almost—Raul in his cop-show persona. Was he holding in his gut? "One of your students," he fingered his notes, "Abdul Phillips, said he heard you and Josh arguing loudly. Some noise, maybe a desk knocked over. Then Josh ran outta your room. Is that correct? Can you tell me about that?"

He'd interviewed second period! Patrick glared at Silverstein. Odd, he hadn't mentioned that. Patrick left school yesterday thinking he'd witnessed a random, bloody—all right, horrifying—accident. He returned to an episode of *NYPD Blue*. Or worse, *Rashomon*. He knew how it went: Who started this fight? Who took Jamar's bus pass? Thirty-five witnesses, thirty-five stories. Never any bottom to it. Dorie was the best at it: I'm leaving the room for two minutes, she'd tell them, and when I come back, I expect to see the missing money, watch, bracelet on my desk, no questions asked. She'd stand in the hall for a couple minutes, listen to the turmoil within, then enter her classroom to find the missing quantity on her desk, some boy in the back holding his nose, some girl drying tears. There was no truth to be found, just street justice.

Questions and answers, questions and answers. He wasn't prepared for this inquisition. Picking up the pieces, he'd prepared for that. The class may be traumatized, Susan said, prepping him, slipping into social worker mode. The kids who've been abused at home, and those Afghan girls, they might be post-stressy for a bit. Let them talk to Betty, if they need to; let her do her grief thing. And Josh's parents, whatever they want from you, give. You've seen blood in your classroom before, Patrick, you know what to do. She caressed his cheek and smiled. Strange how his skill in dealing with these situations was the touchstone of their romance.

But he didn't know how to deal, not with this. Raul Rodriguez looked down from his pad, revolver bulging at his hip. Surely he always wore it, but Patrick never took it in before. And what was he telling his uniformed pal from the street corner? He was babbling. It was like recounting a film you'd seen. Not *Rashomon*, not *To Sir With Love*—the movie that'd inspired him into this mess. No. Something B-grade. An unusually violent "Afterschool Special." *Josh grabbed the office pass from him and walked through the door. He was gone. Patrick turned and touched, just touched, the door. Then the slightest flick…it seemed.* And then the wind, the wind through the windows he'd opened because Josh said it was too hot.

"Are you finished?"

He almost laughed, looking up, expecting to see Raul Rodriguez and his bulging holster but instead seeing the Board of Ed secretary—bulging. She looked peeved, the secretary did, as she jabbed an index finger at the stack of essays before him. But Patrick didn't laugh—restraining impulses was a specialty where he came from—and good thing, too: this woman didn't come from the land of self-control and the size of her forearms told him that when she slapped you, you stayed slapped.

Before he could answer her question, she seized the stack and thumbed through it, shaking her head at the unfinished portion. She looked down at him through narrowed eyes, no doubt taking his measure: so lazy and so randomly violent? Another Bernie Goetz. These skinny, milquetoast-y white boys, when they snap, they snap. She turned and walked out, still shaking her head.

He was alone again, alone with the plastic plant and the perky blonde teacher and her multi-hued moppets. She was an Audrey, Patrick decided. Clueless Audrey. Yes, they're so cute and freckled and pig-tailed now. But they grow up and come back as teenagers, armed with anger and sarcasm and malice, armed with—arms. Audrey just kept smiling, along with her adorable students, too busy changing lives to listen. One of them, Audrey, he thought, maybe that boy on the end with the dimples and mischievous grin, will attack you some fine day and they'll charge you—*you*—with assault. And that fine day, Audrey—

"You can leave now." The secretary had a fresh look of concern on her face and it occurred to Patrick that he'd been railing at Audrey aloud. The secretary shook her head. This one was falling apart fast. She placed the clipboard in front of him, with the timesheet he'd signed at 8:00 this morning. The clock read 2:57; he'd keep school hours even with no school.

"Sign 3:00," she said. Patrick did as he was told. "You can go home now."

He handed her the clipboard, afraid to move.

"Go home, Mr. . . ." The secretary fixed her glasses on the end of her nose and peered down at the clipboard. ". . .Lynch." She looked at him over her glasses. Her face was weary, but, he suddenly saw, not unkind. "Go home."

8

YOU CAN'T GO HOME

Home? When he'd left their apartment that morning, he'd called back to Susan, "I'm leaving—" but swallowed the reflexive "for work" or "for school." For what was he leaving? Even now that he'd been there, he couldn't say. And "home," so linked—forever linked—to school in his mind, home, like school, always a constant, was now, like school, not. Susan had bounded out of the bathroom, fresh from the shower, a towel gathered at her chest, another round her hair. Susan, towel-wrapped, always an arresting sight, in better times cause for being late for homeroom. "Have a—" she said and filled the space with a peck to his mouth. She wasn't the optimist his mother had been, who, the week after his father's funeral, could still send him off with a "…good day in school," as if the notion of days being variable, in school or out, still had currency.

"You're wearing *that*?" Susan asked. He'd almost made it out the door.

"What?" Patrick had jerked around, smoothing down his shirt. "I should iron it?"

"You look like you're going to a ballgame. With the guys." She'd looked him up and down. But not like she used to. Like his mother.

"No one cares what I wear…there," he'd mumbled, running a hand through his uncombed hair. He was speaking to his mother. And he was fourteen.

Now, catching bits of himself in the mirror behind the single malts, his face pale dough in the darkness of Marty's Bar, he saw what she saw. The collar of his shirt, a lime green polo his mother sent him for a long-ago birthday, was wrinkled, the left side curling toward his unshaven chin. He looked down at his jeans, one of the knees worn through, a scrim of loose threads. He looked up. Why, yes, Marty, he would have another Guinness. Good man, Marty. Good listener, asked no embarrassing questions. Just nodded that ginger-colored head and pulled the best pint in Brooklyn with those massive freckled forearms. Never asked why Happy Hour started at 3:17 every day for the past two weeks. Never asked why Patrick always drank Guinness as he choked down the bitter stuff. Never asked where he was coming from or going to. No unanswerable questions about home or work. No evaluations of wardrobe.

Who was it that said *Life looks better through the bottom of a glass?* Patrick mused. Byron? His old buddy Gunther? Gunther quoting Byron? Patrick had never been one to find solace, or great pleasure, really, in potent liquids. But he was beginning to see the point. The pint.

He scanned down the bar at Marty's regulars. Definitely not the young after-work crowd. Instead, cheeks, noses, rear ends told of long hours logged on a barstool. The regulars, three elderly men and Dolores, a woman impersonating young middle-age, nodded at Patrick, then looked up at the antique black-and-white screen above the gin collection, where the Mets had runners at the corners. The protocols here were different than any he'd learned in Manhattan singles bars, where drinking was a means to an end, alcohol a device to grease the social skids. At Marty's, drinking was an end. The end, judging by Izzy, the wizened gent trembling three stools down, who stood a greater chance of toppling schnozz-first into his bourbon-on-the-rocks than the Mets did of bringing Bonilla home from third.

But Patrick wasn't there to make judgments. Far from it— this was a darkened land of no-judgments. Outside, the city radiated heat from stone, steel, and nine million striving New Yorkers. He'd never been one of them, could never be, not if he lived here the rest of his days. But in the cool, smoky dark of Marty's, they were a fraternity, sorority, family. No, family was too extreme, even after two pints. Community—yes—Marty

had made a community of sorts. With its own rules, its own silent understandings. Rule number one: never question anyone's
reason for being here. Marty set a foamy glass of stout before
Patrick. Three, Patrick had decided, was his limit. Enough to go
gently, toddling to the No. 7 train with a lethean buzz, but not
to stumble from his barstool. Rule number two: no sloppiness.
All the regulars achieved a boozy equilibrium and maintained
it. Even Izzy in his spotted tie and rumpled suit reached a level
of sustained instability and held it improbably.

Patrick sipped the foam off his Guinness. When he'd first
entered Marty's, after his second day in solitary, Patrick paused
when Marty asked, What'll it be? He'd never considered what
to drink on a Tuesday at 3:17—not since college. Patrick heard
himself say pint of Guinness and Marty nodded as if that
had been the right answer. Guinness had been Grandfather
Lynch's drink. His beer-drinking, pipe-smoking, deer-hunting
grandfather had driven to Irish St. Paul for his supply; none of
the Scandinavians in Peterson's Prairie would have gone near it.
Patrick kept ordering it, despite himself, smacking at its earthy
leatheriness. By his third day at Marty's he'd acquired a taste for
it. Or maybe it was just genetic memory kicking in.

Delores offered him one of her Pall Malls. He took it,
smoking being another sacrament at Marty's. Delores had red
hair and nails, violet eye shadow, and a black skirt that pulled
well above her knees. Delores, he saw as she leaned in to give
him a light, was never going to see sixty-five again.

Patrick said thanks and blew a plume of smoke out a corner
of his mouth, a Bogartism that reminded him of his college
days, the last time he smoked regularly. He'd been a smoker
as he was a drinker, something he engaged in as the setting
required. Never truly an addict, he'd stopped altogether when
he and Susan, never a smoker, became a couple. She was trying
to be supportive through his present ordeal, but this new beer-
iness and smokiness were more than she could abide.

Following his first session at Marty's, he'd left at seven,
caught the train at Court Street, picked up a six-pack and TV

dinner at University Market, and indulged in a bachelor meal. Susan had a staff meeting Tuesday nights at the shelter and could never say when she'd be home. The interns from Columbia and NYU went out for coffee after the meeting, plotting strategy against the new mayor's assault on the welfare state.

Susan had found him in a soggy heap on her couch, nothing but bones remaining of his Hungry Man chicken dinner with X-tra peach cobbler, the third open can of Bud, half-empty, spilling onto the tray. She'd taken pity on him that night, clearing his bachelor detritus, stripping him down to his shorts, bringing him a pillow and letting him sleep it off on the couch. But the next evening, coming home from the shelter to find him in her bed, reeking of tobacco and hops, Susan decamped to the couch. Patrick took the hint. Miraculous enough she'd chosen him to share her bed in the first place, best not to risk changing her mind. He made a point of showering, gargling, changing into fresh clothes, putting his smoky work clothes in the hamper.

Late one night he felt an elbow to the ribs.

"I can't sleep like this," Susan said.

He felt another jab. He rolled over.

"You smell like a brewery."

He was waking. "I'm sorry," he mumbled. "Brush my teeth again." He sat up.

"I can smell it through your pores." She plopped his pillow in his lap. "I can't sleep like this." Susan put her head down. He sat on the edge of the bed, holding his pillow. Chauncey lifted his whiskers off his paws, blinked at him.

"Sorry," Susan said.

Sorrow—pity—thought Patrick, swallowing a mouthful of his third Guinness, was the best he could summon from Susan now. He found himself in the scotch line-up again, smoothing down that cowlick on the crown of his head.

"Pat," she'd sighed at him this morning, surveying the ruins of her boyfriend in the doorway. "Pat. I know this is hard. Really hard. But it's going to blow over." Susan had stuck one hand in the pocket of her Indian print summer dress, the other adjusting those arty glasses, the better to scrutinize. "What you wore last week—your school clothes—that was just right. You're a teacher, you want to look like one." She crossed her arms, cocked a hip. "And you gotta impress Brunhilde, right?" The Board of Ed secretary, whose actual name he'd never know, was the one remaining source of levity in their household. Where once he'd regaled his sweetheart with classroom tales, recreating student monologues in Nuyorican, he now depicted the BOE secretary, her officious movements and mountainous dimensions.

But he wasn't feeling comical just then; he felt like one of her homeless women, being job-counseled. She was trying to be helpful, he knew, keep it light. Susan was trying hard. The night after she'd woken him up with the rib-jab, she'd roused him again, taking him in her mouth so tenderly he wasn't sure, at first, if he was awake. In the past few nearly passion-free months, he'd sometimes woken, sweaty and stiff, confused then embarrassed to realize he'd been sex-dreaming about the woman sleeping next to him. Yes, he'd dreamt of getting it on with movie stars, unavailable colleagues, his Sunday school teacher. Who hadn't? He'd dreamt of his exes. But dreaming of the woman sleeping mere inches from him—his lover, ostensibly—was a new low on the manhood scale. And now that he was clearly awake, his most intimate wish fulfilled, he was unable to enjoy. It felt ministrative, unsexy. A kinky *Aspect of Modern Social Work*. Even in his grogginess he was aware of her generosity, the gift of it, given his current unappealing state. But it was no use: alcohol, fatigue, anxiety. He remained soft until Susan—game girl that she was, and not unskilled—gave up. He bent down to reciprocate but found her, and her cat, softly snoring.

Susan was throwing all her moves at him—smart, tough, cute, sexy—like a stand-up working a listless crowd and he wanted to appreciate the effort. It was more interest than she'd shown in a long while. But as he stood at the door of their—Susan's—apartment, he couldn't lose the feeling that she was ashamed of him, that she couldn't bear the thought of her man going out in the world this way. All this advice-giving, coping-instruction. It wasn't that he couldn't take counsel from a female; he'd grown up on it. Like most men, he'd been raised in a matriarchy. Dr. Lynch had the title, *but*. Patrick could take direction. Where did it leave him, though, the older man, the allegedly streetwise one?

He missed that sparkle in Susan's eye when her preppy friends repeated *seven* after he told them how many years he'd been teaching in the city, when she heard that tone of awe that he'd made it past the Teach for America phase they were familiar with, the résumé-building stage, one, two, three years, just long enough to make law school sound fun, or, maybe, if you were creative, gather enough local color to write that Young White Idealist Touches Troubled Ghetto Hearts screen-play. In those moments he'd had a glimmer of achievement, of having answered, in a small way, that question Gunther had tossed at him years ago, like a grenade in his lap, about who he'd be—rebel or star. Those moments, when he allowed a scintilla of pride to seep in, he felt he'd been a bit of both: going somewhere his dad wouldn't and, possibly, couldn't go.

"This—situation—will be resolved, Pat, you know it will," Susan said, taking in his sneakers, his third best pair. Lawn-mowing shoes, his dad would have called them. "But, till then, you can't look like you're giving in." She leaned forward, uncurled his collar, frowned as it sprang back up. He couldn't help noticing her odd tone, the Silversteinian passivity. How his dilemma would resolve itself. Why was everyone else so certain of the outcome? Were they being naïve or humoring him? Or was it just entertaining, watching him stumble over the cliff?

Patrick couldn't keep himself from flipping the paper open across the bar top, peeling the Band-Aid off to check the sticky sore. There he was again: the *Post*, second piece on the Op/ Eds, page seventeen.

"Blackboard Jumble"
While reading and math scores across the city plunge, in-school violent crime rates rise, and the best young teachers flee to the suburbs, the mayor huffs and puffs at the chancellor, who scurries about his Livingston Street house of straw, daring the mayor to blow it away.

True enough, but hardly news. He scanned down to the money shot:

Even on the Upper West Side, in one of the city's premier "mini-schools," a young teacher was removed from his duties for attempting to keep order in his classroom. Ironically, the chancellor himself was in the classroom moments before a tragic accident occurred involving a student who physically threatened the teacher.

Patrick turned to his barmates. Look, Marty, everybody, something perverse in him wanted to say, I'm famous. Infamous, whatever. Made my mark, passed the Gunther-test. The TV erupted, the drinkers glanced up: Segui scoring from first on a single and a two-base error; Vizcaino thrown out over-sliding third; extra innings. Cheers, groans. Dolores ordered another vodka stinger in celebration.

Made his mark. Patrick stroked the hair above the knuckle on his left middle finger. He could hear Miss Sturmblad, his high school guitar teacher, chiding him to get that middle finger flush on the string: This is Appalachian folk, Pat, not the Delta blues. He closed his eyes and saw Josh's finger stuck in the door latch, pointing skyward. *Student Gives Teacher the Finger.* He shivered the image away, took a gulp of Guinness.

What did it say when your only defender was the *Post*? How many lunch periods had he spent laughing with George about the headlines C and X held in front of them? Congressmen and hookers, the mayor in drag. And the *Times*, which he read religiously and quoted frequently to his students as an example of all journalism could be, had recused itself, perhaps because Leonard Mishkin, noted Sovietologist and Josh's dad, had written editorials in the mid-'80s on *perestroika* and *glasnost*. The

Paper of Record made only an oblique reference to "the incident," opining that even "the physical presence of the chancellor" couldn't guarantee "the safety of our students." Patrick slapped the *Post* closed. It was the anonymity of Marty's, of course, that was its sole charm. No one he knew would ever venture into it; that had brought him here in the first place. None of the regulars seemed to recognize him from that crazed picture in the paper. He thought he saw a glint of recognition in Marty's eyes with that first, What'll it be, but that was just bartender craft, making everyone feel like a regular.

Ironically, the *Post* photo was so unlike Patrick that almost no one recognized him from it. "A simple mug shot would've sufficed," Susan teased when she saw it, then put her hand over her mouth and muttered, "Sorry," when she caught his reaction.

He could picture the moment, a snapshot in his head. Yo, Mr. Lynch, ovah hee-ah, bellowed Javier, a skinny kid working part-time as the *Garvey Gazette*'s ace photographer and full-time on an underfed mustache. Patrick had looked up from the hole he was digging on that warm October afternoon with the only expression possible: disgust. No one had asked his opinion on the Urban Garden Day, a day he'd planned for a review of independent and subordinate clauses. This outing was another one of Sitkowitz's babies—anything to get away from actual teaching. The man showed so many "science" films (*Krakatoa, East of Java* was a favorite, though he taught nothing about volcanoes and Krakatoa was, still, west of Java) that George Holbrook called him Mr. DeMille.

Dorie Rosenfeld, all five feet of her, was on the far side of this fifty-by-thirty plot of stone, weeds, and glass, trying to stop Abdul from committing unnatural acts on Julio with the business end of a hoe. She looked over for backup just in time to catch Patrick's disgust immortalized. Dorie rolled her eyes and yelled, "You can do better, Mr. Lynch." Javier nodded behind his camera. Everyone was looking now. They loved it when teachers broke character with each other, joking or arguing like kids. They'd never forget the day Sitkowitz got so agitated at Mr. Holbrook he dropped a test tube filled with silver nitrate, creating a permanent stain the shape of Italy on the floor of his lab.

When Javier strolled over with his camera, Patrick was showing Angela and Maria how to use your heel to force a shovel into solid earth. And having a rough go of it. This soil, surrounded by ten-foot fencing topped by razor wire, was tougher than Minnesotan soil. He kept striking something hard, a bottle or can tossed down from one of the aged high-rises surrounding the lot. Maria, who'd declined the shovel in deference to her long magenta nails, was peering over Angela's shoulder, stifling a laugh that came out a sneeze. Which made Angela Wong, culturally unable to disrespect a teacher, giggle.

"You're the farm boy, Lynch," shouted Dorie. "Show us how it's done."

Doris Rosenfeld of Queens couldn't have guessed at the nerve she'd struck. She knew Patrick was pissed at being out of his classroom, that he'd grumbled all week in the teacher's lounge about it. But though she was Patrick's best faculty friend, his comrade in the trenches, she didn't know much about his life before teaching. And her knowledge about the Midwest was strictly literary; she imagined Patrick's upbringing as a quirky but benign mix of *Main Street* and *Lake Woebegone Days*. She couldn't know the saga of the Lynches losing the family homestead in the Depression, of his Guinness-drinking grandfather eking out a living at Anderson's Hardware, his father's escape via football scholarship to the U of M, how his son would grow up a townie, alienated from the land, having his face washed with snow after school by *real* farm boys. It would've been too much to expect her to know all that, to know that he'd been almost as much an outsider in his own small town as in Manhattan.

It *was* true, nevertheless. And somehow this history, overlaid with having his teaching plans confounded once again, his two best students choking back laughter at his inability to make a dent in this island's soil (no wonder the natives sold it so cheap), and the entire ninth grade witnessing his frustration, was too much.

Patrick stopped digging. Sweat dripped from his chin and onto the denim work shirt he'd worn, with jeans, for the occasion. He looked up: at Dorie, who was smiling, gathering that bushy frizz off her shoulders; at Sitkowitz, glancing up from the clipboard that held no lesson plan; at Abdul and Julio, who'd stopped throwing dirt to enjoy his humiliation. Patrick was naked—out of his element and out of uniform—stripped of his essential Mr. Lynch-ness. He gripped the shovel tighter, felt himself flush. It was a first-year feeling, back to the Experiment in Cooperative Learning: I don't know what I'm doing and I'm doing it in public.

Patrick had, as Abdul would've delicately put it, Lost His Shit.

He screwed up his mouth, bulged his eyes. He took a step toward Javier, raised the shovel chest-high, and thrust it at the camera like a draftee in bayonet practice. Click. The photo that would appear on page six of the *Garvey Gazette* and on page 3 of the *Post* (Javier's first credit!): Charles Manson goes gardening.

It wasn't the first time Patrick had gone postal in front of students. Controlled madness—both in the angry and crazy sense—was an indispensable arrow in his teaching quiver. He'd learned early on that once kids thought they'd figured you out, that all your moves were predictable, you were dead in the water. So he scheduled a yearly mini-fit in mid-to-late February. Throw it earlier and you lost credibility, any later and nobody cared. You had to find that sweet spot—February 23rd, say—where the class had bonded with you, wanted your good opinion of them, but before hormonal drift made you a springtime sideshow. The script went something like:

Mr. Lynch
(red-faced, veins popping)
I cannot BELIEVE that I gave this class an entire WEEK'S notice

*before the grammar exam and no one (pauses)—NO ONE—came
in for extra help. (Clomps to teacher's desk, snatches pile of tests)
And LOOK at these grades. (Brandishes tests at class: Does this
refresh your memory?) THREE people passed this test (Looks away
from Angela, Maria, Jamar, who are embarrassed). You think this is
FUNNY? (Looks at Julio, who grins, foolishly) YOU think this is
FUNNY? (Makes Julio look him in the eye: Do I have to call your
abuela again?) I don't know WHAT to say to this class anymore.
(Pauses. Eyes mist.) I'm...I'm...speechless. (Sighs heavily, throws
tests in trash, stalks out the door.)*

Then Patrick would stroll down the hallway, straighten his
tie, smooth back his hair, get a sip from the water fountain. If
he'd timed it right, a mixture of fear and embarrassment would
greet him when he returned to the classroom, once again his
calm, professorial self. And he'd have a new advantage the rest
of the year: nobody could be certain when he'd go off again
and nobody wanted to see it. One year he re-entered his classroom to scattered applause and knew he'd waited too long for
this particular performance.

But he never got to give that speech this year; the shovel
episode made it impossible. The shovel episode and Josh. For
just as Patrick had looked over his students and colleagues and
determined that this situation could be rescued, it took a turn
for the worse. Patrick was about to re-claim his Lynch-ness,
lift the shovel high and proclaim, *Once more unto the breach* or
God for Harry! England and St. George! in the soaring tenor of Sir
Laurence Olivier. His students, unfamiliar with the body of Sir
Laurence's work (or Shakespeare's), would roll their eyes—Mr.
Lynch's so wack—his colleagues would laugh and say, There
goes Lynch again, and he'd be where he wanted to be, the only
place *to* be: out in front of the parade. This, however, was the
moment Josh dug up, of all things, a horseshoe. Leave it to
Josh to discover the urban garden's earlier purpose, as a police
livery during Teddy Roosevelt's reign as commissioner.

"Yo," shrieked Josh, tossing those pale dreads, "I'm the

win-nah." As soon as he had everyone's eyes on him, he hurled the rusty horseshoe over his shoulder, clearing the razor wire and smashing a second story window. The moment was transformed: Sitkowitz dropped his clipboard and declared the Urban Garden Day completed; Dorie supervised the gathering of the tools and hustled the kids back to Garvey; George, always full of charm and cash, made nice with the building super and left compensation for the shattered window, keeping the cops out of it.

Josh had saved Patrick, it seemed at first, erased Mr. Lynch's breakdown moment and replaced it with his own. When the photo appeared in the next *Garvey Gazette*, everyone seemed to remember that instant as Patrick had meant to re-frame it: sheer goofiness. Grinning kids stopped him in the hallway, begging him to autograph the picture. Dorie clipped it out, tacked it to the faculty lounge bulletin board and added the caption *Can You Dig It?*, beneath which George added *Would you buy a used shovel from this man?* Someone else—C, probably—scrawled the ominous *Lynch, digging himself deeper.*

This last caption was prophetic. When he saw Josh's mom clomping out of Silverstein's office the following week, the displeasure on her formidable square face told Patrick all he wished not to know. Dr. Mishkin hurried by him in the hallway, the padded shoulders of her black pantsuit brushing his arm. Silverstein waved him into his office.

The principal sat on a corner of his desk, tapping a pen against his knee. For once, he cut to the chase. "I know this garden thing wasn't your trip." Silverstein shrugged it away. He hated outings of all kinds. Hard to justify to parents, things always went wrong. No argument there: on Patrick's first field trip in New York, to MOMA, two of his students got into a scuffle in front of the Impressionists and an errant punch came inches from busting a black hole in *Starry Night.* "And what happened with Josh Mishkin certainly wasn't your fault." He thumbed the pen, clickety-clickety-click. "But—word to the wise—that mom's got you in her sights." He shook his head.

"Don't know why. Maybe it's just your class is the toughest."
Silverstein forced a smile. "That's how it goes sometimes." Patrick nodded, accepting the implicit compliment. "But, as you know, we don't get many…families like the Mishkins. Between you and me, a real *shmerts* in the *tokhes*." Another smile, like a gas pain. "Still, we'd hate to lose them to Collegiate."

Patrick's Yiddish was rusty, but he got the gist. Dr. Mishkin had come to put the horseshoe mishap to rest. Certainly she would have paid for the window—gladly paid—under *normal* circumstances. But, clearly, the trip had gotten out of hand (see photo) and set her son, predictably (see his Ed Plan), off. Silverstein finessed it, offering to pay for the window out of the Principal's Fund (Don't ask, advised George, where *that* comes from) and sending Dr. Mishkin away with the promise of a future meeting involving all the major players in her son's school career. The principal, as ever, told him more than was necessary, but the bottom line would've fit on a car bumper: Don't Piss That Woman Off.

And thus was set the template, the *leitmotif*, for the year: a student who wouldn't be educated and a mother who couldn't be pleased. Josh became the pebble in Patrick's shoe that he felt with every step. He could never discipline him like any other student; too much was at risk. The more he waltzed around him, the more respect he lost with second period. Patrick never felt on top of his game with that class, with any of his classes, really, knowing they'd witnessed him at his most unhinged. Or what he'd once thought was his most unhinged. He could see it in their faces, a look he hadn't seen since his first years: You're never in control, Mr. Lynch, not really. Josh had frozen that moment in the garden more surely than Javier's snapshot.

And that made him angry. Not pretend angry, not performance angry, real angry. Childish-adolescent angry. The persona, the rep he'd spent tough years building, day-by-day, period-by-period—poof—gone. That Patrick's moment of insanity wasn't Josh's fault, that blaming him revealed a latent immaturity in Patrick's character, just made him angrier. Don'tcha just wanna smack a kid sometimes? his big sister Erin once asked their dad at the dinner table. Don'tcha, Daddy? Well, honey, Dr. Lynch laughed, I feel that way sometimes. But, he said, spreading Parkay over Wonder Bread, you can't do that. Can't lose your temper with kids. When you let yourself get angry at a student, even if you're right, you've lost. You're a grown-up playing their game, and you can't win.

Patrick could feel it still, his fingers tightening around that shovel, his knuckles getting whiter. And he could feel his fingertips cupping the frayed edge of his classroom door, flicking—flinging?—it back toward the frame. Word choice, he told his students, over and over, it all comes down to word choice. Especially the verb.

The bar exploded. Izzy slipped from his stool, stood, and clapped. Delores spilled her vodka stinger. The replay: Carrasco throws a fastball down the middle; Bonilla hits a walk-off grand slam. Mets win. Patrick snorted to himself. An ending only Gunther would have scripted.

"Another Guinness?" asked Marty, lifting those ginger eyebrows. Patrick shook him off regretfully, like Carrasco leery of throwing that full count change-up to Bonilla. Marty slapped a bar rag down and smiled. "No? I'm buyin'."

Patrick looked over Marty's shoulder and saw himself, his angry, shameful, unshaven self, shaking his head in the mirror.

"Hold on," Susan had said in the doorway that morning. "I'll get your khakis and blue button-down. I just washed 'em." And she was down the hall to their bedroom.

"No. Thanks," he called to her. "I'll be late."

She turned back to him. "For what, honey?" She pushed her glasses up her nose. "For what will you be late?"

"Thanks," he heard himself say. Then again, louder, so Marty could hear him over the post-game buzz. "Thanks."

Marty swung around. Patrick pointed at his empty glass and nodded. Marty nodded back.

9

THE RUBBER ROOM

He was in his classroom, second period. The clock read 9:23. Angela Wong stood at her desk, reciting the "Preamble to the Constitution." Abdul and Maria were in the back-left corner, making out. Julio was pirouetting down the center aisle in a tutu and Mets cap. Josh was atop the crumbling bookshelves, channeling Tupac, digits gang-splayed, thrusting the stump of his middle right finger at the teacher. And from the back wall, Emily Dickinson, Josh's booty girl, chimed in. *Because I could not stop for death*, she chanted, flexing the Frankenstein scar on her cheek. *For death! For death! Yo!* shouted Josh, dreads twirling. At the editing table, dark-suited Malcolm X dealt seven-card stud to white-suited Mark Twain and the Afghan girls. "Deuces wild. Two raise limit." He snapped a hole card in front of Hegira. She lifted a corner. "Don't cheat the Black man," he growled at her.

And then the bell rang. And rang and rang and rang and rang. Patrick twisted on the couch, hit his head on the wooden corner. The ringing continued. He groped for the phone on the end table, knocked it over, heard it hit some empties. "Shit," he heard himself say. He found the phone cord among the beer cans, reeled in the receiver. "Hallo?" he managed. He sounded drunk.

A long pause. Vocal music, opera, maybe, in the background. "Hello…may I speak to Patrick Lynch?" a nasal tenor asked.

"This is him–he," Patrick mumbled.

"Patrick, this is Jerry Roselli."

"Yeah?" Who the hell was Jerry Roselli? Patrick waited for the man to launch into his *spiel* about the life insurance he needed or the marketing survey that would only take three minutes of his time.

"From Garvey. Your building rep."

He almost said *C* aloud, but he wasn't *that* drunk. "Oh, sure. Hey, Jerry." Patrick sat up, wiped the drool from his mouth. "Uh, what's up?"

"Are you all right?"

"I'm, I'm fine."

"Jesus, you sound drunk."

"No, I was just...resting." He sounded very drunk.

"Not that I blame you. The Mishkin boy, what a *putz*. Hang on a second." The aria in the background softened. Patrick fumbled for his remote. He'd fallen asleep during *Law*, now Sam Waterston was bringing *Order*. Or was it the other way around? "We *all* must be held accountable for our actions," Sam lectured the jury, far too loudly. Patrick muted him.

"The Mishkin kid, he's back in school," said C. "Wears a white glove on his hand, like he's Michael Jackson." He took a sip of something, smacked his lips. "Oh yeah, he's bad," C gurgled, pleased at his ten-year-old pop reference.

"Is Josh okay?" He had to ask.

"Okay? Yeah, I guess he's okay. Never play the violin again." Patrick winced. C took a sip. "But if that kid gets any Blacker, gonna give himself sickle cell anemia." C coughed up that nasal, hiccupy laugh. He waited for Patrick to join him, as if he were X and they were in the teacher's lounge.

"Anyway," C continued, "been tryin' to expedite this matter for you. But the BOE, you know, it's the KGB. Had to twist arms to find out where you are."

"I'm at Court Street."

"Yeah, got you in solitary. So I heard."

"Evaluating citywides."

"Stop. They can't do that anymore. Can't make you do *bubkes*. Far as the UFT is concerned, you're still assigned to Garvey." Patrick felt queasy. And not just from the junk food and six-pack that had been his dinner. Suddenly he was in C's little office; he was one of *them*, making his grievance. *They can't change my room, Jerry. I've been in 117 since 1973. I can't take the kids on the field trip to Natural History, Jerry. You know my phlebitis.*

Patrick sat up straighter on the couch. "I don't care about that, Jerry. I just want back in my classroom."

"Of course."

"I want to teach."

"Of course you do."

"It was an accident." He'd said it. The first time to anyone.

"No doubt. Cops dropped it right away."

Everything the man said made him feel sicker, dirtier. But he couldn't hang up yet. C had information. "What happens now, Jerry?"

"What have they told you?"

"Nothing."

"That's what they do. Make you sweat." C took a sip. Puccini played softly behind him. *Madama Butterfly*, the only opera Patrick knew. Helene, his old college flame, had forced-marched him through the libretto before dragging him to the Met. She listened to her father's scratchy LP with tears in her eyes, but Patrick was unmoved. Basically the story of an unassertive lover getting dumped. Which, it occurred too late, should have been foreshadowing enough. "Our guy does an investigation. Their guy does an investigation," said C. "Then you get a 3020-A."

"A what?"

"A formal hearing. Could be a while. High-profile case, family's got juice. That story in the *Post* didn't help. And how the hell did they get a hold of that picture? You look like Charles Manson."

Patrick knew. Javier: every man has his price.

"Anyway," said C, "Silverstein's stonewalling me. He'd like to drag things out, look like he's doing his job. For once. And the Mishkins want their pound of flesh." C snorted. "Sorry— bad choice of words."

Patrick had been holding his breath. He let it all out. "Jerry, what's the bottom line? How long is this going to take?"

"Honestly, it's hard to say. Could be a couple weeks. Could be a couple months. Or more." Ice and glass tinkled. Madama Butterfly was discovering she'd been dumped, pissed-off Japanese girl bellowing Italian. "But it's only time. What's a few minutes, here or there?"

The fucking schedule debate. When would he let it go? "For Chrissakes, Jerry—"

That nasal laugh. "I know, I know. I'm an asshole, right? But I'm your asshole now."

An image Patrick fought to erase.

"And you need an asshole in my job. But it's all right, Mr. Lynch, I can be a gracious winner." C slurped his drink. "You just didn't understand: It's us or them. They win or we win. But I think you're beginning to see the light." He waited for Patrick to agree. "Oh—the thing I meant to tell you," he blurted, finally, as if he'd forgotten his sole purpose for calling. "My source at the BOE says you're being reassigned."

"Reassigned?"

"That's what they call it now, a 'reassignment center.' You know, a Rubber Room."

"A Rubber Room?" He didn't know. He didn't want to know.

"It's what they're doing now. No more solitary. They're coming after us, Mr. Lynch, this new administration. In big numbers. Ed Reform they call it." He hacked up "reform" like Chauncey clearing one of his fur balls. "Got these rooms scattered across the city, nobody knows how many." He took a sip, allowed Patrick to envision his new internment. "They were gonna stick you in a room in Flatbush, but my guy at the BOE owes me big-time. I got you a spot in Chelsea. Better commute, nice coffee shop across the street." This is what he'd called for. This, and the humbling.

Con onor muore, sang Madama Butterfly, falling on the ancestral blade. See? Helene had choked, misty-eyed, she'd rather die than live dishonorably. Isn't that beautiful? Now Patrick felt something in his gut lurch downward, hit something sharp. His throat was dry, but he swallowed hard. "Thanks, Jerry."

C waited for Madama Butterfly to finish expiring. "Hey, I'm your rep. Solidarity forever." He smacked those cracked lips. "In the meantime, keep your pecker up, kid. You're still getting paid." Ice rolled around his glass. "And pull yourself together. We have just begun to fight."

Die yuppie scum! his eyes screamed. Patrick didn't see him coming through the drizzle till the last second, when the yellow delivery truck swerved at him and the driver bared his teeth. A front tire caught the edge of a filthy puddle, spraying him head to toe. Patrick swiped bilge from his face and shook his fist at the truck as it blew through a red light at Seventh and Twenty-Fifth. He looked down at himself, a Jackson Pollock done in Manhattan sluice-water. It was the trench coat, of course. The trench coat opened to reveal the Harris Tweed, a cast-off of Susan's dad. That and the paisley tie peeping above, smartly re-knotted by Susan. "Daddy always insists: the worse you feel, the better you should look," she said, burying the knot beneath his Adam's apple. Things were surely headed south when the budding socialist started quoting from the book of Chairman Dad.

But this was where her class background came in handy; it was pointless arguing that he knew better. C had said they could call him for the hearing at any time. Had to be prepared. Had to look like a teacher.

He was still smearing the filth on his garments when he reached the fifth floor of a red brick building on Seventh and Twenty-Sixth and opened the Rubber Room door. Patrick got into a line that ended with a young woman holding a clipboard, working hard on a wad of gum. She asked for name, rank, serial number. "You're late," she said.

Patrick looked at his watch: 8:04. "I was here at 8:00," he protested. "I was in line." He swept his hand behind him to show her, but he was the only one there.

"You don't want to make a habit of it. They'll bring it up at your hearing." Patrick flinched. She shrugged. "Whatever. Sign out's at three." She jerked a thumb behind her. "Have a seat."

So this was the Rubber Room: the width of a classroom and

maybe three times deeper, fluorescent lights, several blinking, mud-grey carpet redolent of mold. Naked off-white walls crying for paint. Chairs, mostly filled, were grouped at tables in threes and fours. Forty or fifty bodies altogether, Patrick estimated, with a teacher's skill at headcounts. The inmates evaluated him as he walked the center aisle, looking up from and then down at their crossword puzzles, spy novels, knitting. A few did double-takes as Patrick took off the spattered trench coat, loosened the paisley tie, aware of how he was violating the dress code, which seemed to be Laundromat-wear: coffee-stained sweatpants and Rangers jerseys, cream cheese on the cuffs. It was the junior high caf: what group would have you?

In the far-right corner was a cluster of chairs, several empty. Patrick settled into a seat opposite a fiftyish guy, jeans and a black sweatshirt, big mustache, graying soul patch and ponytail, pawing through the *Village Voice*. Faculty poet, thought Patrick, safe bet.

"That's Louie's seat," said the poet behind his paper.

Patrick moved over.

"That's Stan's." The poet peered over his *Voice*. He spoke with the hoarseness of weightlifters and movers, men who'd logged time grunting. "They're getting coffee."

Patrick moved again. "I didn't realize there was assigned seating." He'd meant to sound jocular but heard the edge that came from sitting in a damp room in wet tweed.

The poet lowered his *Voice*. "It's very territorial here. Couple guys got into a Thrilla in Manila last week over a corner seat. Quite a show." He shook his head. "Nothing like a bunch of caged teachers without their classrooms. Creatures of habit, teachers." The poet offered his hand. "I'm Ralph." He nodded. "And you're new. Nice suit."

Patrick flushed and swiped at his grime-speckled tie. "My girlfriend—"

"Say no more. Gotta look good for the first day of school." He stroked the soul patch. "And you never know when you'll get that sudden job interview."

Patrick smiled an insider smile. "Exactly." He gave Ralph his hand. "Patrick."

"There's a bathroom in the back, Patrick, but it's nasty. Nick's across Seventh has good coffee, and he lets teachers use his facilities. Lunch is at 12:00. Fifty minutes, live it up."

With that, Ralph hoisted his *Voice* and Patrick dared ask no questions. He looked around the Rubber Room. It had the atmosphere of a late-night bus terminal: travelers slumped in their chairs, vacant-eyed, waiting for the vehicle that would take them somewhere else. But the stasis was deeper here; nothing was coming to whisk you away. Slowly, pockets of activity sprang up: a middle-aged woman with flowing dress and waist-length hair set up an easel and began painting from an oil palette; a young man with a shaved head and hoop earring began juggling three, four, five oranges; a small group practiced tai chi; a petite red-headed woman, barely old enough to teach, stood, burst into tears, and ran to the bathroom. She came back in a few minutes, dabbing her eyes with tissues, sat, then repeated the cycle a few minutes later.

Patrick noted that the groupings were largely by age and, disconcertingly, by race. The one exception was a group of seven or eight who seemed to be holding a book discussion in the back. When Patrick visited the nasty bathroom, he leaned in to see what they were discussing. The Bible.

Two men brushed by, bearing coffee. "Medium, black, two sugars," said a thin balding man, well over six feet, handing coffee to Ralph. "Nick was out of cinnamon swirls," said the other, half a foot shorter, a gut that obscured his belt. Both men wore T-shirts, jeans, sneakers and two-day beards. Both were pasty white, as if they'd evolved in this cave. Ralph introduced Stan, the skinny one, and Louie, his portly partner.

"You look familiar," said Stan, shaking his hand. "You teach in Brooklyn?"

Ralph looked sharply at Stan. It appeared he'd breached some Rubber Room etiquette.

"No," said Patrick, "Upper West Side. District 3."

Stan widened his eyes at Louie, who smiled. District 3 had more than its share of boutique programs for the children of white professionals, all, by definition, gifted and talented. Patrick had gotten that knowing look before.

"Marcus Garvey," Patrick offered, giving up more than he'd intended, but unwilling to be so easily dismissed.

The three men gave small but appreciative nods. Silverstein had upgraded Garvey considerably, but it had a tougher rep in the '70s and early '80s. There had been a shooting, back in the day.

"Nice suit," said Louie.

"Not a suit, technically," said Stan.

"His girlfriend made him wear it," said Ralph behind his *Voice.*

"I heard that," said Stan, grinning.

"You wore that," said Louie.

"I did," Stan admitted, "first day."

"You were expecting a call from your lawyer."

"Still am." All three laughed. Patrick joined them; he'd been accepted. But he was also unsettled by what their laughter implied.

"I see the Weeper's started already," said Ralph, looking off to the corner where the red-headed woman stood, clearing her nose into a clump of tissues. Louie and Stan nodded and snorted. "Little redhead over there's gone through a forest of Kleenex," Ralph explained. "Used to have a boyfriend here."

"A tragic Rubber Room romance," said Louie.

"They started off holding hands," Ralph continued. "Then nuzzling."

"Not that we were watching," offered Stan.

"Then," said Ralph, folding his paper, "they started bringing things in."

"Things?" asked Patrick, relieved to have the focus off him.

"*Furnishings*," said Stan. "Couple sleeping bags, a floor lamp, radio. A little fridge."

Patrick was smiling, shaking his head.

"Yeah," said Ralph, "a regular love nest back in that corner."

"And the *sounds* from back there," Stan chortled.

"A real moaner, that girl," said Louie. "Wouldn't guess to look at her now."

"What happened?" Patrick watched her clear a cheek with a sleeve.

"One Monday morning," Ralph looked at Stan, "two months ago?" Stan nodded. "We show up, the love nest's gone. Red's over there with her tissues. Been weepin' ever since."

"Where's the boyfriend?"

Ralph shrugged. "Had his hearing." The men looked down at their coffees, brought back to the Dostoyevskian purpose of this place, a realm of appearance and disappearance.

But Nick's caffeine revived the trio, and they resumed the task of introducing the rookie to the Rubber Room cast of characters. To the Scribbler, who'd filled a stack of legal pads with ink, his long fingers forever squeezing a fountain pen, his round glasses and chin whiskers inches from his prose; to the Artiste, she of the flowing skirts, who'd filled as many canvases with idyllic scenes of Swiss lakes and mountains; to the Juggler, who'd entertained the Rubber Roomers by keeping a veritable fruit salad aloft, amazing all with the growing quantity and variety of airborne produce, most of which he'd eat as the afternoon progressed. "Though you'll notice how no one sits near him now," Louie observed. Apparently, during the earlier stages of mastery, a particularly tricky banana-behind-the-back maneuver had gone awry, said fruit escaping the Juggler's orbit, making a not-so-still life of the Artiste's Matterhorn landscape. The hippyish Artiste revealed the less pacific side of her nature, suggesting where the Juggler could put his banana, and the man from Human Resources at the BOE was called in to restore relative order.

The trio delighted in the recounting, but, as the morning wore on, it became clear to Patrick that such episodes were rare and served the same purpose fist fights and rodent rodeos did for his students: welcome diversions from unremitting tedium.

Anything to distract the inmates from acknowledging who they were and what they were doing there. This accounted for the odd, backwards introductions in the Rubber Room, where you learned more about who someone was inside the room than outside. Outside information begged the question all sought to avoid, the penitentiary question: What're you in for?

And thus it was only after a grease-laden lunch at Nick's that Patrick discovered Ralph wasn't a poet, not even a teacher, but a custodian. As were Louie and Stan.

"I thought everybody here was a teacher," Patrick said, swallowing the last of his overcooked cheeseburger, trying to sound casual. Custodians were another life form, far scarier than any teacher. Theirs was a union even more legendary than the UFT, with work rules undreamed of by pedagogues. They, for example, were only required to sweep classrooms every *other* day. A standard initially shocking to Patrick, raised among spotless Scandinavians, that left the floor of 234 looking like the bottom of a birdcage by the afternoon of "sweep days." Head custodians, like Ralph and Stan, were Dukes of Earl, with substantial "maintenance allowances" for their buildings, to be dispensed at their discretion. Patrick had heard of one head custodian who spent his afternoons, at the city's expense, fishing off his boat in New York harbor. And Patrick gathered that some financial sleight-of-hand had been Ralph's undoing, as Louie muttered something about "fiscal impropriety" as they haggled over the lunch tab.

"No," said Louie, "there's all sorts in the Rubber Room. A few principals, a few secretaries. That old grey-haired woman knitting that long green scarf? She's a lunch lady." Patrick laughed, trying to imagine her offense. And who she planned to choke with that scarf, well over four feet and growing. Louie raised a palm. "Truly. Word is some girl sassed her in the lunch line. 'What is this shit?' or something. Granny pelted her with meatballs from her big slotted spoon."

"Assault with a deadly side dish," said Stan, looking up from the *Post* crossword.

"We all got our breaking point," said Louie, brandishing a french fry.

Ralph turned to Patrick. "If you see Louie with a broom in his hands, run."

Louie thrust his fry at Ralph. "Never touched him. I just made a suggestion—"

"To his vice principal," Ralph clarified.

"It was ill-timed," Louie conceded.

"*Wait.*" Stan set the crossword down, his brows high. The lunch counter at Nick's took notice. "You're him." Patrick felt the cheeseburger spin. Stan tapped his newspaper. "You're *Student Gives Teacher the Finger.*" There was awe in Stan's voice and respect in his eyes. He looked intently at Patrick, searching for what he had missed, as if he'd suddenly discovered he was lunching with Al Pacino or, better yet, John Gotti, and not just another defrocked employee of the New York City school system. Louie and Ralph, too, gazed at him anew. The lunch counter crowd, many of them Rubber Roomers, checked out Patrick the way New Yorkers do the famous, wanting to appear cool, indifferent, but also wanting a celebrity to add to their list. *Never guess who I saw gettin' a chili dog at Gray's Papaya. No, I'm sure it was him. Got the ninety-nine-cent special...*

Patrick looked down at his plate, crumpled his napkin on it. He was cornered again. "It was an accident," he insisted, the second time in fifteen hours. When had the world become a confessional? Bless me Jerry, bless me Stan.

"Hey," said Louie, eyes bright, spreading his hands wide, "you did what you hadda do."

"Kid was givin' you lip—threatening you—in fronna the, what? The chancellor, right?" Ralph croaked.

Stan gripped his newspaper. "And he...he pulled something on you, right? And he threw it—"

Patrick tried to halt this narrative several times, but it was useless. The trio was enjoying their recreation of the events of April 7th too much to be disappointed with the truth. And his attempts to interject reality, "It wasn't like that," "No, really," were waved away. They would brook no diminishment of the drama. To dismiss the whole thing as a gruesome, strange accident was like hearing Dillinger explain that it was just a misunderstanding with the bank teller. And the ATM was broken...

It was that damned *Post* article, again, that had put these images in their heads, replaying the scene as less Mr. Lynch, room 234, and more Wyatt Earp, OK Corral. But hadn't Patrick himself taught lessons on the power of mismatching text and image—the cruel Hun, the evil Jap, "Remember the *Maine!*"—creating a synthesis, a counter-narrative more powerful, more indelible than fact? It wasn't much of a leap from the terrified, shovel-wielding teacher of Javier's snapshot (with its overtones of homesteader defending his turf from the savages) to a picture of the defenseless teacher surrounded in his classroom, the hurled bathroom pass transformed to a switchblade sprung open. Impossible to penetrate this scenario, with so many layers of media behind it, to explain that he'd faced as much danger that day as the Lunch Lady had at her Waterloo, nothing between her and the adolescent hordes save meatballs.

"I woulda defenestrated the kid," said Louie.

"You woulda reamed him with your mighty push broom," said Ralph.

"I...I," was all Patrick could manage, swirling a straw faster and faster through the remains of his large Coke. The sweaty Coke cup slipped in his hand, brown water and ice cascading onto Susan's father's twill Brooks Brothers trousers. He felt every pair of eyes in Nick's on him. He felt the Coke soaking his boxers. Patrick grabbed at the napkin dispenser, emptied it. "Excuse me," he muttered to the trio and elbowed his way past the lunch counter to the unisex bathroom, which, of course, was occupied. Patrick stood and waited, swiping at his damp crotch with a fistful of napkins. Eventually the Scribbler emerged, pen behind his ear, legal pad under his arm.

Patrick squinted at the madman in the bathroom mirror. His collar and tie were filthy, but he knew that. Since the nasty facilities at the Rubber Room were mirrorless, the forehead stippled with dried gutter-water was a surprise. As was the hair, so neatly combed when he left his apartment, now popping out at angles from his scalp, the cowlick in back set free. More disturbing were the permanent changes—the darkening grooves under his eyes, the hairline retreating at the corners—intimations of early middle age. If this was the man Susan saw, her recent lack of sexual interest and indifference to matrimony were no puzzle.

He checked his watch; five minutes left in his lunch break. Couldn't risk being late twice on his first day. Susan's dad's pants were drier but the boxers were saturated with icy Coke. He plucked off his newly shined dress shoes and slid off the pants, laying them across the toilet lid. He yanked his blue and white striped boxers down his long thin legs and began wringing his underwear over the sink. He managed to induce a thin trickle of Coke but couldn't imagine putting them back on, like putting on a wet bathing suit. He'd go commando—who would know?

The door cracked open. A wispy redhead poked in. The Weeper. Her eyes skimmed up and down him, pausing a beat at his hairy crotch, at his iced-down, retracted manhood, to which he thrust the ball of damp boxer. She didn't cry out, or cry, as he might have expected. Just a giggle and a "sorry" as she punched the door closed. Weird. Locking the door, Patrick remembered: she was the Moaner before she was the Weeper.

He ripped some paper towels from the dispenser, wrapped them around his boxers and stuffed the soggy bundle down to the bottom of the wire trash basket. After tucking and zipping himself carefully into Susan's father's slacks, he took a last look at the madman in the mirror. He washed his hands, wiped the muck from his forehead, tried to smooth down his hair. Put on your teacher face, Patrick, he told himself. It's all acting. It always has been. Then he squared his shoulders and flung himself out into the lunch crowd, assuming as much dignity as a man with cola-colored seepage outlining his privates can.

10

WHAT DO YOU NEED?

Patrick was lost. He'd taken a right out of the Rubber Room, as he had at 3:03 for the past two weeks and headed downtown for the subway uptown. But then he found himself wandering Chelsea, puzzling over the incongruous businesses—Middle Eastern specialty foods, *Comidas Chinas y Criollas*—that had so charmed his Midwestern eyes on first landing in New York. But now, his back against the hot rough brick of Chelsea Dental, perspiring in the bright May sun, he was as dislocated as any tourist. But he wasn't a tourist. Five or six years ago a Japanese family pondering their map of Things To Do In Manhattan had pleaded his help and he'd effortlessly given sets of directions to places they might want to go, estimated how long it would take, detailed what buses and trains went where. To them, he was a New Yorker. And Patrick, for the first time, had felt like one.

But now the polyglot businesses of the city left him feeling at once everywhere and nowhere. Panic filled him as desperately as when his mother had left his three-year-old self in the frozen food aisle at Knutson's Shop-Rite and he'd peered down the endless frigid row, gripping a pebbly bag of frozen peas, howling till she trotted around the corner clutching a jar of peanut butter. Could you really be lost on a small island with streets as gridded as the aisles at Knutson's?

A slim, fuzzy-bearded young man bearing a green backpack seemed to want to answer that question. "Are you all right, sir?" he asked. Patrick glared at him, but all he got back was a concerned squint. "I mean," said the young man, gently, "do you need to talk?" It was then Patrick realized he'd been talking to himself again, something he'd never done before but that had lately become a habit. Patrick, he'd hear Susan calling from the kitchen as he ranted to himself in the bathroom, were you asking me something? The young man—an NYU psych major?—lowered his brows and waited. "No, I'm fine," Patrick insisted, and the man said "Okay, have a good day then," and ambled off in search of other addled, mumbling pedagogues.

Is this it? Patrick wondered, clutching hot brick. Had he already succumbed to that Rubber Room fever where you lost your identity and took on a new one, no longer a person but a persona? He'd only been there two weeks, but Patrick feared he'd joined the Artiste, the Weeper, the Juggler in Ralph's Rubber Room lineup. (The Mumbler?) Even on his second day he'd arrived to knowing glances, the men looking with admiration and puzzlement at the teacher-desperado dressed like a stockbroker, the women looking with—amusement? Had the Weeper spread the word to the female Rubber Roomers, what she couldn't help noticing in his diminished, chilled state? Mr. Toughguy, she must've giggled to her sisters-in-crime, *Student Gives Teacher the Finger*, he's not all that. Dillinger packs a derringer.

After his first day had begun so badly, Patrick kept to himself. Day two he'd walked the center aisle after signing in, nodding awkwardly to the trio of custodians, who returned cool nods. (Had he paid for his lunch at Nick's?) A few bearded, middle-aged white guys, the ones who became teachers in the '60s to avoid the draft, raised fists shoulder-high. "Hang in there, man," said one.

Choosing a spot near the Juggler would ensure some privacy, he figured. Ralph had been right, of course, about the territorial nature of teachers. Back at Garvey, George and Sitkowitz had nearly come to blows when George reserved the program's lone VCR during one of Sitkowitz's film festivals. The Rubber Room was the schoolhouse distilled: a chair or a table misappropriated risked blood spilt. Rubber Roomers chose their areas carefully and stayed put. Patrick noticed that the Juggler, whose affect was mild, his focus serene, had the right rear corner to himself. Apparently, though his skills had become impressive, no one had forgotten the incident between the bald-headed fruit tosser and the Artiste. Patrick spotted an empty chair six feet up the right wall from the Juggler and staked his claim.

In the ensuing days, Patrick had sought to bring some order, some meaning, to his tumbling existence. Incarceration, he reasoned, could be an opportunity, couldn't it? Stone walls do not a prison make. If the Artiste and the Juggler could polish their skills, so he could he. The Rubber Room, he decided, was his chance to finally tackle the classic literature people assumed he'd already read. That weighty, faded copy of *Remembrance of Things Past*, for instance, had long called out from his shelves. He'd taught lessons on Proust and memory. He'd used Proust to impress women over cocktails, once dismissing a colleague as "a mama's boy, like Proust." Ha, ha, ha. And his date, who'd never read *Remembrance,* smiled at his erudition. But a tincture of shame crossed his cheek as he turned away: Proust was a challenge he'd avoided in college as being too long, intimidating, and, well, French. Now it would be his penitential ritual to sip a large dark roast from Nick's as he burrowed into *Swann's Way*, his toasted butter bagel aromatic as any madeleine.

And, in the Rubber Room, Proust proved a defense more formidable than the Juggler. The few inmates who were tempted to engage him on their way to the bathroom, intrigued by his legend, took a glance at the title of his book and kept moving. What did that say about his fellow educators? But what repelled most eventually drew the Scribbler, moth-like, to the flame of the world's most irrepressible scribbler.

"Pardon me?" he said, bending down. The Scribbler held a legal pad between a rolled-up cuff of his blue denim shirt and his unbuttoned black vest. Whiskers, not quite a goatee but more than a shaving error, curled off his chin. An ink smudge underlined one of his little round lenses. "You're reading Proust?"

"Uh, yes," Patrick admitted, looking at the faded photo of the author, ready to apologize for his pretension. Susan had chuckled when she saw what he was taking for Rubber Room reading. He excused it; she didn't laugh much these days. And he'd used up her remaining goodwill negotiating his wardrobe back to khakis and a button-down, open at the throat.

The Scribbler pushed his round spectacles up his sharp nose, adding a smudge between his eyes. Trotsky with a tiny blue bindi. "Is that the Moncrieff translation or the Enright revision?"

Patrick scrutinized the cover and shrugged, as if he'd found the book on the subway. "I'm not sure. To tell the truth, it's something on my shelves from college that I never really finished." He gave a weak grin. "Though somehow I passed the test."

The Scribbler was uninterested in Patrick's college career. He slid a plastic chair over the moldy carpet and sat, leaky fountain pen in hand, half-filled legal pad in his lap.

"You read French?"

"A little." Patrick shook his head. "Not really."

"Moncrieff really screwed with Proust, beginning with the title." Patrick nodded absently. He didn't want to encourage this guy, the kind of guy who would get pedantic with a pedant. "*Remembrance of Things Past*, that's Shakespeare, of course. Sonnet 30." He paused. "But you know that, being an English teacher."

Patrick grimaced.

"I'm sorry," the Scribbler inched forward, "but you're the closest thing to a celebrity we have here." His features rearranged into what would have been, in someone less intense, a smile. "*Student Gives—*"

"—*Teacher the Finger*," Patrick snorted. His epitaph, clearly.

"Not a classic New York headline." The Scribbler put a hand to his chin. "Not *Ford to City* or *Headless Body in Topless Bar*, but memorable. B+."

Patrick thumbed back to his place in Proust. He had vowed

long ago not to endure the bloviations of clueless males—always men—with no social skills but full agendas. Men in authority—professors, principals—had to be endured. But guys like the Scribbler, no way. He looked down at Proust, who gazed up with an expression that mixed *hauteur* and *ennui* and several other Gallic attitudes Patrick had forgotten since high school French. Marcel dared the reader to open his book. And Patrick—against all his Midwestern upbringing—did. He waited for the Scribbler to move on.

He didn't.

The Scribbler offered his hand. "I'm sorry, Arnold Westerfield." Patrick had to shake it. "I hate to keep you from Proust—even that translation—but I was wondering if I could interview you." Patrick frowned. "For my book." He gestured over to his table in the opposite corner, where legal pads and library tomes sat in yard-high stacks.

"Me?" Patrick peered around. "What's your book about?"

"Here. This place." He waved his pen in a circle above his head. "The Rubber Room." Patrick looked puzzled. "Nobody knows about this place. Secret as any gulag."

Patrick laughed.

"Well, did you know about it?"

Patrick shrugged. "I'd heard rumors."

"Exactly. And you're a teacher." He jabbed the air with his leaky pen. "That's how they control it—us." He slid his chair closer. Patrick nudged his chair back, glancing at the Juggler, who'd just added two mangos to his Ferris wheel of fruit. "There are over a million students in the New York City school system, eighty thousand teachers. If it were a state, it'd be the ninth largest." He looked down at his pad. "A budget bigger than NASA's, twice the GDP of Bolivia."

Patrick eyed Proust. His *chapeau* fell over his forehead, his mustache drooped. He could use an absinthe.

"But here's my point." He waited for Patrick to look up. "There are three other rooms like this that I've uncovered. I know there are more. Maybe forty-five teachers, on average,

per room. A hundred-fifty, two hundred teachers on full sala-
ries, with benefits. Add in the cost of warehousing these teachers, paying their subs, that's—" he tapped his pad "—fifteen,
twenty million a year. And growing by the month."

"Twenty million? How do they hide that?" He was the kind
of guy you wanted to argue with, even if you agreed. Especially
if you agreed.

"How do you hide water in the ocean? Twenty million,
that's a lot of textbooks, test tubes, art supplies. But it's only
.25 percent of the overall budget. The Pentagon spends more
on toilet seats."

"But the press reports that."

"You know what the press reports. The *Post* wants titillating
random violence. Then moves on. The *Times*—" he pulled on
his chin whiskers. "The *Times* pays liberal lip service. Oh, these
poor kids; oh, these overworked teachers. But"—he jabbed the
pen at Patrick—"when it's Leonard Mishkin's kid..."

Patrick winced. The Scribbler had done his homework.

"I've gone to the press," he continued. "Their business is
selling papers. They take care of their own." He dropped his
voice, leaned in. "You and I, we're here for the same reason.
You tangled with the wrong kid." He didn't wait for Patrick
to agree. "I...I tried to blow the whistle on my principal. A
racist, vindictive martinet." The Scribbler's eyes went a little
unfocused at the recollection, but he didn't elaborate. Patrick
would have to take his word for it. Or read the book. "That's
why we're here. It benefits the powers-that-be to quarantine
us."

Patrick smiled. "So, we're a bunch of Jean Valjeans here in
the Rubber Room?" Not an apt analogy, but it drew an actual
grin from the Scribbler. If pressed, however, Patrick was on
thin ice; Hugo was even farther afield than Proust. But Susan
had dragged him to *Les Miz*. Broadway CliffsNotes.

"God, no!" The Scribbler slapped his legal pad. "That
chubby janitor you had lunch with?" He nodded toward Louie,
dozing next to Stan, who was working a crossword puzzle. "He

threatened to kill his vice principal. The tall one next to him embezzled thousands from his school. They belong in prison." He turned, waved to the front of the room. "The old lady stabbing that scarf with those needles? Madame Defarge? Should be in Bellevue." Fellow inmates were turning to look at them. The Scribbler hunkered down. "There are plenty of people here who shouldn't be within miles of children. But that's what makes this place so...insidious. You stick the whistleblowers, the enemies of the state in with the crazies and the crooks. Willy-nilly. Really clever, *realpolitik*-wise. How can you tell who's who?"

How can you tell? Patrick wondered, scrutinizing the Scribbler, who was smart, well-informed, and about to launch into his theory of what transpired on the grassy knoll. There was much in what he said that made sense to Patrick, that confirmed all he knew. Comforting in some weird way. Until you took in the paranoid tone and noticed how his left eye narrowed whenever he said *them*.

And yet, it wasn't the Scribbler's paranoia or Marxist analysis that had Patrick shambling downtown at 3:12, aimless, appearing more inebriated than after a pint-fest at Marty's. No, it was his parting shot as Patrick dismissed him—with Minnesota niceness—insisting that he'd *think* about being interviewed. He just wasn't ready to discuss the whole ordeal right now. But, he added as a sop, maybe not a bad idea; it would help him prepare for his hearing.

"Oh," sniffed the Scribbler, who, though no great discerner of social cues, had clearly received enough brush-offs to recognize even a polite one, "you needn't worry. You have plenty of time for *that*."

The bleat of an aggravated taxi driver brought Patrick back to consciousness. He slapped on the hood, a yard away from his left hip. The turbaned driver flipped him the bird. Patrick flipped back. The driver jammed the gear shift into park and Patrick was jolted by the notion that he was about to duke it out with Hegira's dad. Didn't he drive a cab when he wasn't

working in his smoke shop? But just as suddenly he realized
that this man, of course, was a Sikh, not a Muslim, that he'd
met Hegira's father—balding, no headwear—and, besides,
Patrick was jaywalking and the driver, whoever, of whatever
nationality or faith, had the right of way.

He gave the cabbie an awkward *salaam* and dashed across
Ninth Avenue, receiving several syncopated honks along the
way. He'd seen a deer once, caught in the middle of traffic
on the Tappan Zee Bridge, weave around cars and trucks and
buses. He had to keep driving past the terrified beast, even as
it reared up on its hind legs alongside him. Against all odds,
Patrick made it across Ninth Avenue and kept running, south
by southeast, dodging pedestrians, veering into the ungridded
streets of the Village.

Ninth became Hudson and it occurred to him that he was
near the White Horse Tavern, where certainly no one would
look askance at an early afternoon Guinness. He'd only been
there once, a pilgrimage he made his first year in New York
when he was still trying to convince his soon-to-be ex, Helene,
that he wasn't just a lowly schoolteacher, that he had a touch
of the poet. And he was young and desperate enough to convince himself that drinking on Dylan Thomas's barstool would
yield some cosmic benefit, that some of the Welshman's genius
would rub off from his ass resting on that sacred space.

The Village businesses—bistros, leather shops—whirred by.
For all his sweaty jogging, he hadn't come to the White Horse
yet and that Alice-in-Wonderland feeling he got in the Village
took hold, that no streets matched up, that he'd have to run
twice as fast to stay in the same place. It seemed he'd crossed
West Twelfth several times, that he now stood—soaked,
breathless—at the corner of West Twelfth and West Twelfth.
But perhaps it was for the best: Helene had been unimpressed
by his backside's brush with greatness at the White Horse and
he'd promised his current girlfriend that the 3:00 happy hours
were over, now that he was settled in a Rubber Room proper
and away from his routine at Marty's. He'd promised himself,

too, that he'd take care of himself, eat better, cut down on the alcohol. Pull yourself together, kid, C had told him. We have just begun to fight.

He stood rooted at the corner of Twelfth and Twelfth, bent at the waist, hands on his damp middle, gulping the dense May air. He wiped his hands on his khaki pants, now aware that, in his despair, he'd left Proust, key to his self-reclamation, back by the Juggler's corner. *Three years*, the Scribbler said. His magnum opus, the work that would bring the Board of Ed to its knees, had been three years in the making. "And your story," he'd concluded, rising as he lowered his voice, "*Student Gives*, could be the final chapter." He paused deliberately. "Think about it."

Patrick had thought about it. The more he thought the more he felt the color leave his face, his pale Irish skin so devoid of pigment even the Scribbler noticed. The Juggler dropped an orange that rolled to the Scribbler's feet.

The Scribbler had kicked it back and sat. "Your building rep didn't tell you?"

Patrick heard C's nasal tenor: Could be a couple months. Or more. He hadn't asked how much more. He didn't want to know.

"The mediators meet once a month per case. The average case meets," he glanced at his pad, "twenty or thirty times." The Scribbler was inscrutable, but had Patrick detected the Scribbler's pleasure, some schadenfreude at Patrick's stunned silence? Payback for his indifference to the Scribbler's grand project? Here they'd sat, blithely swapping literary analogies, when, as the Scribbler knew well, the only relevant parallel was *Bleak House*, Jarndyce v. Jarndyce, on a scale undreamt of by even Dickens's vast imagination.

"But," the Scribbler added, "it can end faster. Some people settle with a fine." He shrugged away any sense of comfort. "Win or lose, you're damaged goods." Then he reached over and patted Proust's weary face: *À la recherche du temps perdu*. He stood, took several steps toward his workstation, stopped. He turned back, pointing the leaky pen at Patrick. "Time: it's only lost if you let them take it from you," he said, squeezing closed his left eye.

Patrick assessed the damage: six bucks a fucking pound. His mother would have had a conniption. Not that scallops were available at any price in Peterson's Prairie, or that his mother would have known what to do with them. Not unless there was a recipe in *Ladies Home Journal* for "Easy Scallop Loaf."

He pushed the fork down on a scallop. It pushed back, way beyond rubbery. And browner than any scallop should ever be. He scattered the scallops around the pan, added another splash of the white wine, as if that would save them. Patrick replenished his glass with the ultra-dry Pouilly-Fuissé the fishmonger at Citarella guaranteed would "impress the little lady." He flicked one of the brown buttons across the pan, past the capers and garlic shards and onto the floor. He took a gulp of the chardonnay, perfect complement to carbonized bay scallops.

Chauncey leapt down from his perch atop the refrigerator, pounced on the bouncing scallop and began masticating. It took some effort for him to gum it down, his ancient head bobbing with each chew, gagging as he swallowed. Patrick knew he'd find it in a stewy puddle somewhere, probably inside his dress shoes, where he'd found Chauncey's latest fur ball.

For a moment the gagging got so loud it seemed possible that Chauncey's next chew might be his last. Which would be one positive outcome to this evening. Patrick unwound the dish towel from around his right hand and inspected the four red furrows across the back of it, now swelling. Chauncey licked the extra virgin olive oil off the floor and blinked at Patrick, smiling, smirking. Patrick fought the image—so palpable, so satisfying—of taking a quick step and sending Chauncey soaring across the room.

Patrick had felt giddy—brilliant!—when it struck him on the corner of West Twelfth and West Twelfth that this was their anniversary—well, one of them—that it was eighteen months to the day that he'd moved his few, humble possessions into

Susan's condo. Susan had made elegant dinners for the six-month and one-year celebrations. But that was then, before her love affair with the women's shelter, before Josh Mishkin plunged him into the sinkhole of the Rubber Room. Clearly, she'd forgotten. It was an opportunity. He'd surprise her this time, with the grand gesture that could change everything, a romantic turbocharge.

But he'd fumbled the pacing of this meal, beginning with his sister calling from St. Paul as he was grating carrot into the salad. Their relationship had been distant through the years—birthday and Christmas presents for his twin nephews—but they'd reconnected since he'd let her in on his current crisis. Erin, whom he'd dismissed in high school as pretty and empty-headed, had emerged in adulthood as an ER nurse in the Hennepin County hospital and über-competent mother-of-two, as the voice of reason, of wisdom, even. Yes, public education in New York City was a puzzle, but severed digits didn't faze her.

"Ah," was all she said when he described the dinner he was whipping up.

"What?" he said, defensive, like they were kids.

"No," she laughed, "it's great, amazing. Especially with all the stuff you've got going on."

"What, then?" He began chopping walnuts, smaller than necessary, for the raspberry-walnut vinaigrette.

"Oh, it's just," she sighed a maternal sigh, their mother's sigh, "these little 'anniversaries' go away. And once you're planning parties for twelve four-year-olds, no one remembers the dog ever had a birthday. But," he could hear her wave the thought away, "all the more reason to enjoy them while you can."

She rang off with the chipperness she shared, cell-deep, with their mother, but the end of the call brought him back to earth. Damn. He'd absent-mindedly dressed the salad he'd been saving for the last moment. He took a sip of wine and popped in the cassette of *More Sinatra Hits*, his favorite musical pick-me-up.

I am so aw-f'ly mis-un-der-stood/ so lady be good/ to me…

He sang with Frank, poorly. He danced even worse. But nothing blended carefree optimism and melancholy like Sinatra's voice. Your baby left you? Frank shrugged. Been there, brother. Lost your job? Have another scotch, crooned Ol' Blue Eyes. Fly with him!

Patrick's spirits rebounded back to that moment on Twelfth and Twelfth when, gasping for breath, he'd convinced himself to disregard the Scribbler's nasty revelation. Who knew how long he'd be in the Rubber Room? Who made the Scribbler God? It was their anniversary, damn it. Celebrate!

He'd hopped the No. 1 train at Christopher Street and headed to the uptown Citarella's on Seventy-Fifth and Broadway, where he'd long admired the gleaming seafood in the window, sprawled across sparkling beds of ice, displayed like necklaces at Tiffany's. The sea scallops he'd fantasized about on the train would require a small loan to finance, but the fishmonger rhapsodized over the bay scallops—more affordable—and how sweet, how beautifully they'd sauté. You spread 'em on a little linguine, he said, find the right wine. Doesn't have to be pricey, just right for the meal—and her. And then he winked, a wink that assured that the meal itself would be an erotic adventure, let alone what happened once the scallops were a memory and the wine bottle empty.

But after Erin's call, his trio with Frank and Sammy on "I've Got the World on a String" and that third glass of chardonnay, Patrick lost all sense of time. *Temps perdu* that no amount of searching could find. Sauté for two to three minutes, the man said. Five, tops. Start the linguine first. All about timing.

At 6:45, he'd panicked. He heard their down-the-hall neighbor, Ashley, and her Pomeranian, Mr. Paws, going for their evening walk. And he heard Susan, who never got home before seven on a Wednesday, greet them. Susan always came home famished and he'd envisioned the main course plated, dramatically, as she came in the door. The girls were chatting down by the elevator. Mr. Paws yapped his two-minute warning; Ashley wouldn't risk him peeing in the hallway again. Patrick lit the candles, arranged the baguette slices in the breadbasket, shifted the single red rose that leaned in its skinny vase. He turned on the gas under the pre-heated water in the pasta pot.

Now was the moment: Frank was launching into the pop-opera of "My Way"; Nelson Riddle's horns were building; the water was boiling. He tossed the linguine fini into the pot, hit the timer. He waited as long as he dared, then eased the gleaming scallops in with the sautéed garlic and capers, giving the *mélange* a loving swirl with the long wooden spoon.

Ashley yelped. New Yorkers famously ignore the cries of the imperiled, but no Minnesota boy could disregard a lady's scream. Patrick ran to the hallway, where he didn't find Susan, but Ashley, with Mr. Paws straining at the leash wrapped around one of her legs, snarling at an Irish setter twice his size. The setter's owner, an elegant elderly woman who lived one floor up, heaved on her dog's leash.

"Are you okay?" Patrick yelled down the hall.

"Yes," Ashley laughed as the old woman yanked her dog into the elevator and Mr. Paws unwound himself from her leg.

"Enjoy your walk then," Patrick hollered, turning to the door and finding Chauncey in the hallway, blinking, shaking his head as if wakened from a deep sleep. "Chauncey, inside, fella." Patrick nudged the lumpish body with his foot. Chauncey rolled on his back. "C'mon, boy." Patrick could feel the scallops hardening, the linguine softening. The cat wouldn't budge. Patrick tried to pick him up, closer than his allergies allowed, but could gain no purchase beneath the fur and fat. He knelt and tried to scoop him up like a football, nose to nose. He sneezed and Chauncey recoiled, hissing and raking a paw over Patrick's right hand. Patrick cursed and dropped him, and the cat scampered down the hallway with surprising speed. "Get back here," he yelled. He examined the back of his hand, where four red rivulets ran. "You waste of fur."

Leave him, was his first thought, but it would kill the occasion if Susan came home to find her—their—aged baby abandoned, wandering the hallway. Back in Darien, in Susan's girlhood, Chauncey once went missing and Susan had cried for two days imagining him dead. The trauma was deep; she still went looking for him if he napped under their bed. Susan was a model of calm and rationality regarding everything but her pet. Patrick raced toward Chauncey and the cat ran past him—when had he ever run?—to the other end of the hallway. They repeated this routine several times, revealing the playfulness Susan always insisted was one of Chauncey's many charms.

The timer was beeping; Patrick ran to rescue the meal. Chauncey trotted after him and bound up to the counter, onto the refrigerator. Patrick turned off the gas, threw the linguine into the colander. The steam cleared to reveal a total loss: the six-dollars-a-pound scallops were vulcanized, the pasta glutinous. The back of his hand stung. He rinsed it in cold water and wrapped a dish towel around it. Patrick poured himself more chardonnay, added a splash to the skillet, flicked a scallop to the floor. Chauncey pounced, chewed, hacked.

"Whoa, what a day!" Susan called out, opening the door. "You won't believe what happened at the board meeting—" she set her purse down on the couch, looked up. Susan was even lovelier than usual, pale cheeks flushed from the heat of the day, her lithe figure draped in his favorite sky blue summer dress. Just as he'd envisioned her. Somehow, this made it worse.

"Hey, what's the occasion?" She gestured toward the candles, the rose. Patrick smiled weakly. Chauncey licked the floor and blinked up in kittenish innocence.

"Our anniversary?" He'd meant it to sound celebratory, not *j'accuse*.

"Next week? No?" She looked at the white board that was their makeshift events calendar. Today said Board Meeting in her lovely prep school script. Underneath it—next Wednesday—Susan had drawn a heart with an arrow through it.

He felt that last thread tethering him to reality snap. "Yes," he sighed, "next week. It is."

"Hey, makes it more of a surprise." Susan was a social worker; her first impulse was rescue.

Patrick would not be rescued. "It was," he grumbled, lifting the skillet over the sink, spooning the scallops into the disposal. He hit the disposal button and listened to his romantic dream ground up. But Frank would have none of it: to the moon or bust.

Susan peered into the sink and gave his cheek a wary kiss. "What was for dinner?"

"Scallops," he looked at the flaccid mound in the colander, "over linguine."

"Oh, honey, my favorite." She poured herself some chardonnay, noting the vintage and the less-than-half remaining. "What happened?"

"Your cat. Happened."

"Chauncey?" She gurgled some wine, covered her mouth. "Ruined dinner?" Chauncey circled his spot on the couch, plopped down.

"Mr. Paws got in a fight…Chauncey got in the hallway…" he waved his wrapped hand. "I tried to—"

"What happened to your hand?"

Patrick unwrapped it.

Susan gasped. "Oh, Pat. Chauncey did that?" She looked doubtful, despite the evidence. Perhaps he'd cut himself in four parallel lines. "Did you put iodine on that?"

He nodded. Better to die of infection than have that argument.

Susan fetched large Band-Aids and iodine from the bathroom and played Florence Nightingale with his right hand. She sat on the couch next to her cat, took hold of his puffy head. "You bad boy," she said in that baby voice reserved for her pet. "It's weird. He never scratches, you know."

"Well, he does now," Patrick muttered, dumping the linguine into the disposal.

My God! She was like one of those mothers of demon spawn who were convinced their children were angels. Oh, he never does that at home, Mr. Lynch.

"I've only seen him scratch when he's really hungry." She pinned Chauncey's ears back. "But you fed him, right?"

Patrick looked at Susan, then Chauncey. Then at the refrigerator where, for the first time, he saw her note: PAT—REMEMBER CAT FOOD. THX. S. He closed his eyes. He saw Chauncey pouncing on that scallop, wolfing it down. Fall on your sword, Patrick, he told himself. Surrender, simple. Simple, but impossible. His account at the Bank of Apology was overdrawn.

"I was going to get some after dinner." Lame. Dog-ate-my-homework lame. Mr. Lynch would have laughed him out of class.

"You got scallops but not cat food?"

The words were judgmental, sure, but her tone left room for negotiation. He could have said "fancy that" and chuckled and run out and come back with the cat food and some pad Thai and listened to Susan reenact the drama of the women's shelter board meeting. Peace—romance, even—might still ensue. He'd defused a thousand tenser classroom moments with less. In better times he would have done just that. But they were way past better times.

"Yes," he said, drying the colander with the bloody dish towel, "I got the scallops first. They don't have cat food at Citarella's." Especially, he wanted to add, not five-pound bags of organic, ash-and-phosphate-free kibble, hand-crafted in Southern France by Capuchin nuns for the delicate kidneys of aged felines.

"I appreciate the effort, Pat. I do. The scallops and the rose. The wine." It wasn't her words that grated but the delivery, the slow over-enunciation. The pause before "wine." Yes, he'd had a couple glasses while he was cooking. So what? Didn't every chef in France? "But we've talked about this. We agreed you were going to help take care of Chauncey." The two, Susan and her cat, stared at him, Susan patting Chauncey's head so it bobbed in agreement with the hard bargain they'd struck.

"And I have." His fourteen-year-old voice again. I did take out the garbage, Mom.

"Yes, you've changed the litter. Twice."

"And I've gotten cat food."

"But the wrong kind. Twice."

He leaned against the sink, folding his arms across his chest. "The right kind's eight bucks a bag."

"So what? I pay for it." Wrong answer.

He pointed his chin at Chauncey. "And he ruined a pound of scallops."

"Is this really about money, Pat? Or Chauncey? I'm sorry about dinner, and that he scratched you, but this all feels really passive-aggressive."

"Jesus," he said, rolling his eyes. She knew he couldn't endure the therapy-speak. Still, she was only wrong about the passive part.

"It's like you don't value what I value."

"How can you say—"

"I'm not saying you don't have good values. You do, obviously. I'm saying you don't value the things that are important to me. Like my work at the shelter."

"I support that. Don't I always have dinner when you—"

"Yes, and you're always pissy about it." She stroked her cat. "And you neglect Chauncey."

"Because I got the wrong cat food?"

"You can't go out for Tylenol for a feverish child and come back with cough syrup and say, 'Well, at least I got some medicine.'"

"Susan, this is a cat we're talking about, not a child."

"It's all part of the same cloth. It's a...continuum."

"A continuum?"

"A continuum of *nurture*." Chapter two, *Aspects of Modern Social Work*.

"Are you saying I'm not nurturing?"

"No, of course you're nurturing. You're a teacher." Patrick studied his wounded hand. Susan tugged at her neckline. She had to finish her point. "But it's neglectful."

That hot, spinning sensation, like everyone at Nick's was staring, clutched him. "Susan, it was an accident."

It took a moment. "Oh God, Pat. You think I don't know that? Really?"

He'd succeeded: now she was just angry.

"And does everything have to be about Josh? Does everything about us have to be displaced onto him?"

It was this last bit of therapy-speak that did it. "Well," he unfolded his arms, windmilled his bandaged hand, "we all can't afford special cat food. And pâté. And…and…" he thrust his good hand at her, "…Gucci glasses."

Susan pushed up her glasses, her eyes misted. He knew she hated to cry, especially when she was angry. It's what *girls* did. She looked down at Chauncey. "I thought you loved these glasses."

"I do, I do." He wasn't too far gone to know he'd gone too far. The designer glasses were her one public extravagance. She didn't own a car, or expensive clothes or jewelry. It was cruel, going after her softest spot this way. Much crueler than finding fault with, say, her small breasts—which he also loved—the glasses were her choice, her signature. "I do," he whispered. He wanted to sit next to her, hold her.

She took Chauncey in her lap. She was crying now.

"Susan, I'm sorry."

"God, Patrick, what is your fucking problem? What do you want from me?" Susan wiped her cheeks with the backs of her hands. "What do you need?"

She said it without irony, looking him square in the face. Seeming to forget that it was his classic classroom question, a running joke between them. That they'd asked each other that question and giggled a thousand times.

Stop messing around. Get back to work. Leave her alone. Keep writing, reading, studying. Stop! These commands were easily deflected with shrugs, shakes, snorts, sneers, Who me's? and the ever-popular, unanswerable double negative, I didn' do nothin'. He'd stumbled upon his magical mantra with James, he of the scars and self-inflicted gang tattoos, back in Experiment in Cooperative Learning. James was once again leaving off pretending to read or write or think and returning to what came naturally, intimidating the world, when Patrick choked back Stop, knock it off, get to work, and out of his mouth fell, James, what do you need?

The question stunned James. And Patrick shivered at the possibility—the probability—that James had never heard this question before. The boy's face hung dumbly, his pumped-up body slack, like a kitten hanging from its mother's mouth. Did he understand the question? Were the answers so manifold— Where does the universe end?—that to begin would suck him into a black hole of neediness?

Nothin', James mumbled, resuming his personal failed experiment in cooperative learning.

With students less deprived, or with greater access to their wants, the answers flashed across their faces: What do I need, Mr. Lynch? What do I *need?* I need breakfast, a father, my cavities filled, to fill someone's cavities, to be loved, feared, respected, paid attention to, or, even, educated. But no teenager could say these words (except for the boys who asked Mr. Lynch if he was going to finish that bagel on his desk). They, like James, would be frozen long enough for Mr. L to say, casually, Okay then, let's get back to learning. And that magical question inoculated him—for the class period, at least—from further harm. Not even a student as disordered as James would make trouble for a man who had just inquired about his needs.

But now, with his would-be fiancée staring at him red-eyed through those funky frames, the full weight of that question pressed on him. It left him as speechless as it had James and every child he'd ever asked.

Susan nudged Chauncey off her lap. She removed her glasses, then leaned down and dried her face with the hem of her dress. When she looked up at him, she was swollen-eyed but contained. "I think you should leave," she said.

Only then did he realize how long he'd been fearing this request, expecting it. Would he cry now?

"Go for a walk," she clarified.

He nodded, exhaled.

"I'll feed myself," she said. "And Chauncey."

He grabbed his wallet and keys. "Come back when you're sane," he heard as he closed the door.

It was dusk and getting brisk, the city cooling off as it never would after a hot summer day. Patrick walked downtown on Amsterdam, the street filling with Columbia and Barnard students looking for food, drink, love. He thought to gather himself at the Hungarian Pastry Shop on 110th, a favorite haunt, but was held by the gravitational pull of the Cathedral of St. John the Divine across the street. Susan, a default Episcopalian, had dragged him there last Easter and he'd been surprised by the hippie charm within the immense Gothic walls.

He paused to ponder once again the Peace Fountain in the garden beside the cathedral: the Archangel Michael wielding his sword astride a smiling sun, a smiling moon; huge crab claws stretching out beneath, one claw pinching Satan's dangling head. Around the whole mess a herd of giraffe gamboled. He'd found it bizarre and vaguely disturbing when Susan showed it to him. What Episcopal bishop signed off on this Xanadu on the Upper West Side? What was he on? And where, Patrick mused, could he get some?

A peace fountain that's violent and waterless, he'd asked Susan, what gives? She pointed to the plaque below:

Peace Fountain celebrates the triumph of Good over Evil, and sets before us the world's opposing forces—violence and harmony, light and darkness, life and death—which God reconciles in his peace.

It's all from the Book of Revelation, she said. Don't you Catholics read your Bible? And she'd poked his ribs, knowing that "lapsed" didn't begin to cover the kind of Catholic he was.

The images were now oddly soothing, more tumultuous than the tumult in his head. Now it made sense, perhaps the way stimulants helped hyperactive kids, speeding the world up to their normal pace. He stood before the sculpture until the light faded and the floodlights came on, throwing a sinister cast over the grinning moon. A soft clucking came out of the garden and a pair of peacocks strutted from behind the fountain, thrusting their heads forward with each step. Patrick half-expected a unicorn to emerge from the shadows. The peacock keeper herded the pair back to a shed behind the fountain, leaving him alone with the angel and Satan and the giraffes. Patrick took this as his sign to leave.

He hung out at the pastry shop until he finished the *Times*, relieved to find himself not in it. Then he zigged over to Broadway and headed further downtown until it occurred how close he was to Garvey on 103rd and to running into his— former?—students. The summer after his disastrous first year at Experiment in Cooperative Learning, Patrick had avoided coming within a three-block radius of his school building. He'd be strolling Broadway with Helene and hit 106th and be squeezing her hand, feeling tightness in his chest, pain in his stomach. That sensation hit him now, the terror that he might run into Abdul or Julio or, heaven forbid, Josh, kids for whom the phrase "school night" had little meaning.

Patrick feared running into his colleagues, too. Didn't Naomi live on 105th? Her first year at Science & Tech she'd thrown a Halloween party, memorable for the justice she did to a French maid outfit. The rest of them dressed to type as well: George a dandyish Oscar Wilde, Patrick as Tom Sawyer, complete with whitewash bucket and brush. Always-upbeat Denise and feisty Dorie came as Glinda and the Wicked Witch of the West. But such easy camaraderie was a thing of the past; since the day of the Incident, he'd only spoken to Dorie, and then only briefly. The Rubber Room was a disease no teacher wanted to catch.

"They've got this sweet young thing just out of Bank Street covering your class," Dorie had said. "Very deer-in-the-headlights. I'm sure Abdul's having her for lunch."

"And Maria for dessert."

Neither of them laughed.

"I check on your room to see it's not trashed," Dorie said. No small favor. At EICL he'd missed one Friday and his students threw the used paperbacks he'd bought for their classroom library out the window and onto the blacktop three stories below, where they remained all weekend in the rain.

"Thanks."

No mention of Josh, his missing middle digit. He'd heard Dorie's raspy breathing from her springtime hay fever. "Patrick," she said, "I'm sorry."

"I know."

"Where are they putting you?"

"I was at Court Street. They're moving me to Chelsea, off Seventh and Twenty-Sixth."

"Good Chinese on that block. And a little Mexican place— Juanita's—around the corner." Dorie was all about lunch.

"So this is a good move."

"Lunch-wise? Absolutely." She blew her nose. "Pardon my allergies." She blew again. "Patrick, we'll talk."

"Absolutely."

"Everybody misses you. Staff and kids."

"Give them my regards."

"This is bullshit, Patrick."

"I know."

"And not about you. Remember that. Could happen to any of us."

"I know."

"And any kid."

"Luck of the Irish."

Dorie laughed despite herself and promised they'd have coffee soon. And though he knew they wouldn't have coffee or anything else soon, somehow it was Dorie's number he tapped after inserting the quarter in the payphone at 106th and Broadway. Dorie was the only person who could at once bolster his confidence and slap the self-pity out of him. She, as much as anyone, had made him a teacher. Maybe she could keep him one.

But as soon as he finished punching her number he hit the change button and heard the quarter fall through. It was almost eleven o'clock, he realized, and, indeed, a school night for her, if not for all her students.

Patrick was beyond weary, the wine out of his system, ready for sleep. He walked back home sober, if not sane. He opened their door as quietly as possible, removed his shoes and padded back to their bedroom.

Though the spring night had grown cool, Susan had kicked off her beloved comforter. With only the sheet covering her, Patrick was involuntarily warmed by a rare glimpse of her almost uncovered form, surprised by that delicious dip from rump to waist. He longed to touch her. Before he thought better of it, nearly laying a hand on that lovely hip, Chauncey jumped on the bed, circled twice, and nestled in the soft curve Susan made. She sighed and tossed an arm over her cat, pulled him to her. One eye on Patrick, Chauncey rested his muzzle on Susan's breast.

Patrick curbed his darker impulses and let the sleeping cat lie. He plucked his pillow from beside Susan's dreaming head, grabbed the red blanket from the front closet, and set up quarters on the couch. He'd finished his evening ablutions and once again bent his six-foot frame into Susan's five-foot-six-inch couch when he noticed a pink Post-it stuck to their answering machine. His girlfriend's usually impeccable private school cursive was barely legible, confirming just how crazy he'd been to think of waking her. Chauncey, he had to admit, had saved him from himself. When he finally deciphered the message, its contents were still cryptic, and distressing. *Patrick*, she'd scrawled, *who is Gunther?*

11

YOU CAN GO HOME

Yes, it was the flatness he missed. How can you miss flatness? Susan once teased. She'd spent her entire life amidst the gentle undulations of New England and the towering, manmade topography of Manhattan. Flatness equaled boring, a lack of imagination, of soul. He'd failed to explain it to her then, but he felt it now, something inside him spreading out as his plane broke the clouds and descended over the lakes, farms, villages of his native state, divided into neat, level squares. The sensation deepened as he rolled down the window of his rented Corolla and drove past the suburbs of Minneapolis, which extended alarmingly far and north into farmland. Shin-high corn stalks, endless furrows of soy and sorghum spooled out to the horizon. Fertilizer and animal smells filled the car, odors that disgusted Patrick as a boy but now smelled like home.

He was grateful for the ride and the time. His mother had offered to pick him up, just as she'd offered to pay his airfare. She was practical in all things, and generous, but even she understood that, in this instance, time and space were more important to him than money.

Mist began to fall and fog rose off the fields. Something to do with the relative heat of the air and temperature of the soil, he could hear Gunther explaining. And the nitrogen released by the crops. And he'd nod at the lecture by the boy who failed chemistry because he slept through final exams. Patrick rolled up the window, turned on the wipers, adjusted Susan's dad's tweed jacket under the shoulder strap. He cursed himself for leaving the trench coat. Susan couldn't help being solicitous, given the occasion, but he'd left her in no mood to help him pack.

The fields scrolled by as he cruised up I-94, letting a country station blare on the radio's preset. Tammy Wynette wasn't high on his playlist, but when would you hear her in the city? He was enjoying the unfamiliar familiar; he'd come home a number of times since he'd lived in New York, but never *home* home, not since his mother had moved to a condo in St. Paul, becoming office manager of the physics department at the U of M the year after he graduated from high school. God, how big Winnipee Falls had gotten! It had been the "city" to go to because it had a Walgreens; now Patrick marveled at the Burger King, Kmart, and RadioShack advertised at exit 56A.

The Falls' gain had been Peterson's Prairie's loss. The farm foreclosures in the '80s had done it, his mother said. Unlike its larger sister village, Patrick's birthplace lacked the critical mass to hold on to its downtown. His mother had wanted to drive with him because she knew how upset he'd be at the changes. As a child, he'd never liked change. And she'd been right: he swallowed hard as he drove past Morgan & Co.'s grain elevator and turned slow onto Main Street to find the Full Moon Café empty, boarded up. Anderson's Hardware, where his grandfather had worked after earlier hard times had forced him off the family homestead, was likewise vacated. Knutson's Shop-Rite, of course, was still in business. Some things were eternal. Most disconcerting, Hendrickson's Best had gone belly-up; one antique, round-headed pump still looked operational, like a one-armed sentry at a checkpoint for a war long over. The E in Best had fallen on its back, the middle prong blown off in a Minnesota snowstorm, the lone pump standing guard over HENDRICKSON'S BUST.

At the end of Main Street, still at the edge of town, Patrick pulled up to the converted farmhouse he was raised in—cornflower blue when he'd lived in it, now a faded gray, and peeling on the southern exposure. The lawn was patchy, his mother's flower beds weedy. He was glad to be alone. Shabby, she would have sniffed. Takes time to keep up an old house and a big yard, his father would've said, always withholding judgment. But, he would have added, anything worth doing is worth doing well. A bit of adolescent defensiveness snuck up on Patrick. Surely he'd taken better care of the property after his father had died, hadn't he? He'd never let the grass get that brown, the gutters droop, full of wet leaves, or let tools lie out the way he saw them, scattered and damp, back by the shed Grandfather Lynch built.

Before the current residents could come out and ask what in the Sam Hill he was staring at, Patrick pulled in and out of his old blacktop driveway—deeply fissured, he noted—and drove back toward downtown. Against his will he took a right on Evergreen and the Corolla headed in the direction of Willard County High School. How many perpetrators, he wondered, revisit the scene of their crime? Of all the aspects of Peterson's Prairie he would've changed, his alma mater would've topped the list. But it, of all places, was the same, exactly the same, as the day he'd graduated and never looked back.

It was 2:00 on a Friday. When did school get out in Peterson's Prairie? He couldn't remember; it seemed everything happened earlier in the Midwest. The Corolla crackled along the gravel bus path. He could go to the teacher's parking lot (wasn't he a teacher?) and get out, but he didn't want to risk the attention. But why not? All who remembered him would welcome a returning hero. They'd remember the second half of his high school career, not the first. How many WCHS grads went to elite eastern colleges? Became teachers in New York City? How many had the elementary school named for their father? His mother once let slip that his were the highest English SATs ever scored at Willard County High. He drummed the steering wheel. The highest because Gunther never took the SATs. Because tests were bullshit. College was bullshit.

The car inched closer to the entrance. To the left of the WCHS sign was his dad's old office. To the left of the office— boot prints? No. He squinted through the drizzle. Gunther's

oily boot prints, leading to the roof? The walls, the roof—
Gunther's spirit lurked everywhere. Patrick checked his watch:
2:15. Time to visit St. Norbert's and pay his respects to Willard
County High's least illustrious alumnus. To his earthly remains.

St. Norbert's Evangelical was the most conservative Lutheran church in Peterson's Prairie. Susan could never grasp
how religion played out in his hometown, though he tried,
repeatedly, to explain. In Darien, you were Protestant, Catholic, Jewish. If you were Protestant, you were Episcopalian or
Congregational. Maybe Presbyterian. How a town of 1,162
souls managed three Lutheran churches representing three
distinct branches of Lutheranism escaped her. But just as no
one was ever merely blond in Peterson's Prairie, unmodified by
strawberry, wheat, corn silk—some agricultural product—no
one was ever just a follower of the mad monk of Wittenberg.

Growing up, Patrick wasn't sure he really understood
Gunther's church, or wanted to. Gunther took him there one
Sunday, "for laughs," he'd said, but Patrick could find nothing
funny, not even stupid-funny, in the Hendrickson's religion.
There wasn't much to amuse in the faith of Patrick's family
either, just a bunch of rules, mostly about sex, which you could
pretty much take or leave and still call yourself Catholic. And
since sex was largely theoretical for Patrick until well into his
freshman year in college, he accompanied his parents to St. Immaculata's without qualm or interest until his father's sudden
death, after which his mother completely lost the will to make
him go.

His mother looked uncharacteristically peeved hunched
under the large black umbrella his sister held as Patrick passed
in front of St. Norbert's, spotting for a parking space near the
entrance. Identical beige raincoats aside, they looked less alike
than they used to. Erin, at thirty-three, a mother of twins, was
sturdy, no longer petite; you could envision her commanding
the ER at Hennepin County. But their mother, nearly sixty,
was still trim, elfin. Both Lynch women wore their hair bobbed
and blonde, their mother's dyed to the grain-color she'd had

all her life. The two broke into quick smiles, tempered by the occasion, as people stopped to shake hands, and, once or twice, exchange hugs. Lutherans of this order, generally German or Norwegian, weren't a huggy bunch.

Patrick found a space and hustled under their umbrella. Erin threw her free arm up around her tall younger brother's neck and gave a big squeeze. His mother's hug was firm, she kissed his cheek. "You've saved us," she chirped.

"From the rain?"

"From the gawkers," said Erin. "What's become of the Widow Lynch?"

"Today's not about us," his mother said.

"No, indeed." Patrick took the umbrella, holding it over them all.

"Poor Gunther," said Erin. "Poor Hendricksons."

"Sad," said his mother, "a waste." This was as much judgment as he'd heard from her on the subject. She'd been the one to inform him of the accident, which she did in her calm, matter-of-fact way. Just one car, she'd said on the phone. Gunther's pickup—relatively new, candy apple red—had piled into a pylon after missing the exit for Winnipee Falls, where he worked as a mechanic at the Mobil station. With unusual delicacy she posited no explanation for the accident, made no mention of alcohol or drugs. She only said she knew Gunther had been important to him though they'd "drifted apart." If he wanted to attend the funeral, she would like to send him a check for the airfare.

"I appreciate your coming, both of you," Patrick said, as he nodded back to the Lutherans filing into the church. "I know it's not easy. Being here." He turned them toward the church doors. Someone inside held a door open for them and Erin ducked in first. His mother put a hand to his forearm. They let an elderly couple pass and the door closed in front of them. She tugged him under the eaves to the right of the doors.

"Patrick," she said in her soft, clipped way, "I don't know what they'll say about him in there," she plucked a piece of lint off Susan's father's lapel, "but I liked Gunther."

"Oh, Mother." He looked off, over her shoulder. A brown Ford pickup, minus muffler, grumbled through the rain on Main. He met her gaze. "I know."

"He was a troubled boy." She was speaking to herself, barely audible above the dripping gutters. "The deck was stacked against Gunther. I felt sorry for him." The doors to St. Norbert's opened a crack. Erin. "But I wasn't going to sacrifice my son to that family. Saving him wasn't my job." She put a hand on his tie. "You were."

"And I was a big job."

She surrendered a smile.

Patrick gave his mother's hand a squeeze and they met Erin inside, where he was surprised to find St. Norbert's three-quarters full. When had Gunther accumulated so many friends? Once upon a time, Patrick had been his one and only pal. He shook the withered hand of an usher who gave him a bulletin and found them three seats on the aisle, four pews from the back. Patrick scanned the sanctuary, hoping—fearing—that he'd see familiar faces. The crowd skewed well over sixty years old; the turnout on this rainy Friday afternoon was, of course, St. Norbert's supporting the Hendricksons, longtime members. Still, Patrick picked out backs of heads and quarter-profiles and tried to imagine classmates, former teachers, with fourteen years of life in Peterson's Prairie added.

But the only person Patrick knew for sure was the guest of honor, up front by the altar in that big silver box. Beside the box, a young, rather severe, rather Aryan man in black suit and clerical collar stood importantly. Where was old Reverend Norstrand? Had he retired, died?

The young man in black waxed lugubrious about God's plan for each and every one of us, how we mere mortals were in no position to understand, let alone question it. His words penetrated Patrick's ears, but his mind was tuned to another frequency, at first indistinct but then clear as a school bell.

Alas, poor Hendrick, Gunther declaimed.

Poor Richard Burton, more like, he jabbed back.

Richard Burton, my ass. And who's the Hitler Youth in the black suit and white collar?

Who's he? Your minister, numbnuts.

Reverend Numbnuts? Never 'eard a 'im. Norstrand's my man.

And Patrick could see Gunther as he launched into his impression of Reverend Norstrand, his st-st-st-stammer, his palsied gestures at the pulpit, the excess of saliva as he reached the climax of his sermon. A parody that owed more to Jerry Lewis's *Nutty Professor* than any school of preaching and was the reason, come to think of it, that Gunther and he were invited to leave St. Norbert's the last time they were in this sanctuary together.

Erin and his mother shifted next to him in the pew. Though it was a bit cool in the church his mother fanned herself with her bulletin, a rare sign of displeasure in a woman unfailingly gracious, decipherable only by kin. It was clear the young minister had not known Gunther—how he'd lived, why he'd died—but it was clear, too, by the curl of his pink lips, the knit of those invisible brows, that he was more than satisfied with his take on Gunther's place in the hereafter. Erin pulled her dark hem primly over her knees. She turned to her brother and rolled her eyes. This was the girl he'd had chalk dust fights with Saturday mornings at Prairie Elementary, now Francis J. Lynch Elementary. He only partly restrained a grin.

Suddenly they were standing, these Evangelical Lutherans. The organist pounded the opening chords to "A Mighty Fortress Is Our God," decidedly not a hymn on St. Immaculata's playlist, but plenty familiar to Patrick. Everyone in Peterson's Prairie knew the opposing team's fight song. Erin checked the bulletin and thumbed to number thirty-seven in the hymnal. She'd sing along, as would their mother; both had sung in the high school chorus and possessed small, pretty sopranos. Patrick had inherited his father's large, croaky baritone. Effective in a classroom, but. He'd hum along.

And then the Lutherans began to sing. Nothing like this had been heard in the history of St. Immaculata's, perhaps not of the entire Holy Roman Apostolic Church. The somber, aged assembly broke into the lushest four-part harmony. On-pitch, God-fearing four-part harmony. He'd forgotten how good the music was here. Along with unyielding orthodoxy, it was their hallmark. Even Gunther could sing, sometimes breaking into quite a musical falsetto with the British schoolboys on "You Can't Always Get What You Want." Not a feel-good group, his father once said of St. Norbert's, but Lord, he conceded, those people can carry a tune. And not too surprising, Dr. Lynch instructed, from the folks who gave us Bach. A point their hymnal was proud to reinforce, stating that "A Mighty Fortress," musical cornerstone of the Reformation, was composed by the denomination's founder himself. And, Gunther would add, you had to admire a lyricist who could wedge "bulwark" into a song about divine love.

Gunther called it bullshit, this faith of his father's, but as Patrick looked around he saw tears streaming on the furrowed cheeks of these stalwart believers, trickling onto their hymnals. There was a purity, a truth in their singing. A devotion that cut to the core of whatever was good in their religion and, yes, right through the young minister's bullshit. Patrick turned and saw tears coming down the cheeks of his mother and sister and noticed, for once without shame, that his own were wet too.

The congregation finished Martin Luther's greatest hit with a swelling "amen" and wiped its tears. The young man in black stood and broke the mood of divine inspiration with some stern exegesis of the Book of Leviticus. The message, as far as Patrick could glean, was that Gunther, poor sinner that he was, may have lived and certainly died in a fashion that paid no homage to God's great gift, but he never—as far as anyone knew—knocked up any man's daughter nor had congress with any man's son, and had died, therefore, in the eyes of God, golden. You'd think Gunther would be relieved to hear the good news. But no.

How long, he moaned in Patrick's ear, *must I listen to this a-hole natter on?*

As long as he wants, Gunther. It's your funeral.

No, matey. It ain't none o' my funeral.

Oh, but it is, Gunnie. Patrick stared at the big silver box. *It is.*

The hot-dish table in the basement of St. Norbert's was the most pungent reminder. The aroma of cheese, egg noodles, tuna fish, and Campbell's cream of mushroom soup was the comfort food smell of his childhood, the staple of many a church potluck. And this odor, even more than the proceedings upstairs, took him back to his last church potluck, at St. Immaculata's, where Superintendent Lynch had been the guest of honor.

Certainly none who recognized him, and there were more than Patrick had imagined, would let him forget. His mother and sister, cornered by too many admirers, or, as Erin insinuated, the morbidly curious, had apologized and fled. They'd see him later at Erin's for dinner. Patrick was about to do likewise when Coach Carlson, his gym class nemesis and his dad's oldest friend, hunted him down as he hid behind a battered upright piano just beyond the Jell-O molds.

"Patrick," Coach called out in his throaty voice. Near retirement age, Patrick estimated, and still solid except for the basketball-sized gut covered by a plaid sport coat and wide blue tie. His face was the same only more so, textured and brown like much-used pigskin. After forty years, Coach had become the sports he taught. He looked Patrick over with a professional's eye, clearly pleased—amazed—at his lanky-but-toned six-foot physique. And perhaps there was some professional pride there, too, that all those push-ups and squat thrusts in PE had not been in vain. Maybe the way Patrick felt when he ran into a former student on the subway who'd seemed headed for trouble in ninth grade, but was now, textbooks in hand, headed for Fordham.

"You look good, Patrick," he said, seizing his right hand in a clasp that hurt and clapping his shoulder, testing his resistance. "Looks like you been hittin' the gym, son. Am I right?"

"Yeah, little bit," he shrugged.

"Pumpin' some iron, right?" Coach grinned, smacking him again.

Patrick shrugged again and looked down at his newly polished Florsheims. How could this old man, a man he hadn't seen since high school, make him feel like a skinny fourteen-year-old lost in his oversized gym shorts? And best not to tell him that his main workout was playing Ultimate Frisbee on Saturday afternoons, a recreation Coach would not recognize as a workout, never mind a sport. Tossing a plastic platter around a grassy park. What's next, he'd growl, Ultimate Slinky?

Coach continued scrutinizing him, the way adults do children: My how you've grown. Patrick tightened the knot of his necktie, pulled his shirt cuffs from the cuffs of Susan's father's tweed jacket. "And you're a teacher now," Coach stated. "In New. York. City."

Patrick moved his chin up and down noncommittally. Not a subject he wished to pursue.

"Your dad would be so proud."

Again, not an assertion he cared to entertain, but he managed to get out, thank you.

"Boy, bet you got some stories to tell." Coach rested his hands on the basketball above his belt and waited.

He would have to wait a long time. Patrick begged Coach's pardon. "Where is the men's room?"

His old gym teacher looked disappointed and said it wasn't his church, but he believed the facilities were up the stairs behind the noodle-bake casseroles. Patrick offered his hand for a final crush.

Coach's grip was gentler this time, but he sandwiched Patrick's right hand with his left. He'd done the same, Patrick remembered, at his father's funeral. Coach's eyes grew moist. He said nothing, then, "Gunther."

It was neither question nor statement, but he paused for a response. Patrick shook his head up and down.

"You were friends."

Patrick nodded.

"Good friends. Like your dad and I."

"Yes."

"We let that boy go." Coach swallowed hard. "We...we rescued you, after that stupid...stunt you boys pulled, breaking
into school. Then your father died." Coach's lips disappeared,
reappeared. "And we gave you the full court press. There was
no teacher, no janitor who'd let you do the wrong thing, give
less than your best. We didn't let you *breathe* sideways."

It was true. After his father's funeral, teachers suddenly kept
him after school for extra help, demanded revisions on papers
even after they were graded. He'd been drafted to the debate
team; the garage band he formed with Charlie Sorenson, The
Night Creatures, was chosen to play the junior prom. And he,
like all teenagers, had taken it for granted. Had viewed the extra
attention as punishment, if anything. Even as an adult—as a
teacher—he'd looked back on his upswing those final years
of high school as natural maturation. He'd grown up, become
man of the family.

"But Gunther, he was Einar Hendrickson's boy," Coach
rasped, pulling Patrick closer. "No one wanted to deal with
that S.O.B."

Patrick looked over the crowd, to the opposite corner where
the Hendricksons stood by themselves, balancing plates full of
hotdish.

"No one would deal with him, so we let his son drift away.
Smartest kid to come through here in forty years. You were
second." Coach tried to smile. "And a fine natural athlete. Nice
touch on the jump shot, good backspin."

This, too, was true. Patrick could see it, the tight backspin
on Gunther's jumper, the ball caroming off the plywood backboard behind Hendrickson's Best, slicing through the netless
hoop. Then the high-stepping backpedal and the wicked grin:
That's H-O-R-S, *amigo*.

Coach took hold of both elbows of Susan's father's tweed
jacket. "He didn't just slip through the cracks." Patrick lurched
back. Coach leaned in. "We let that boy *go*."

Patrick wanted to go, but Coach gripped tighter. And, yes, he saw Gunther clutching that rope, sprinting off the high school roof, but the scene was conflated now with James, flexing his scars and glowering at *Lord Jim* and the uncaring world, and with Josh, too, shouting that Mr. Lynch didn't dare challenge him because he was too scared of his mother, the professor.

"I don't know much about church, or religion." Coach raised his voice. "Hell, I don't go to church any more. But I do know that mumbo jumbo about God's will is a load of crap. If there's a God, he didn't plan this. *We* let that boy go. That's what I can't forgive—"

His eyes were full and he shook, shaking Patrick. Coach Carlson was about to crumble in that way of men of his generation—his father's generation—who never cried, not about their service in Korea, not about their stillborn children, but who now, in their dotage, could not make themselves stop.

"I'm sorry," Patrick mumbled, wrenching himself from Coach's grasp.

He took the stairs two at a time, flew past the men's room and out into the parking lot behind the church. Only then, panting by the garbage cans, did he reconsider the effects of water on tweed. But the rain had stopped; there were cracks in the clouds and shafts of sun fell at angles over Peterson's Prairie. The scene, he had to admit, was biblical. Well, Bible-movie. Gunther would've appreciated the visual, another excuse for his Charlton Heston routine.

A cough came from a corner of the building. A blonde woman, thirtyish, in a navy blue dress, leaned against the red brick, smoking. Familiar, but familiar like half the women in Peterson's Prairie. She looked toward him, lifted her chin in recognition. That was no woman, he realized with a twitch. That was Katie Osterlund.

Gunther whispered in his ear: *Oh, baby. What have we here?* There was something disturbing, arousing in the star of so many teenage masturbatory fantasies cozied up against the backside of St. Norbert's. As he approached, he could see that

her startling figure was gone, as was the cascade of Farrah
Fawcett hair. But, no matter, his internal response was the
same: sweaty pits, incipient hard-on. He offered a sheepish
hand that she turned into an awkward hug. Katie drew back
and, like Coach, gave him a thorough going-over, though her
evaluation paused at different spots.

"Patrick James Lynch," she blew smoke out a corner of her
mouth, "all grown up."

He cocked his head. "What's a nice girl like you doing in a
place like this?"

She snorted. He'd gotten some game since high school.
Lame game, but still.

"Buy me a beer," she said, snuffing out her cigarette against
the side of the church, "and I'll tell you."

It was fitting that he wound up with Katie Osterlund at
Dawn's Corner Taproom, always a place of fascination to
the adolescent Gunther. Whenever Patrick would walk with
Gunther past Dawn's, which even in a town as brief as theirs
occupied a notorious spot on the sketchier end of Main Street,
Gunther would stick his nose up against the smoky glass,
pondering the lurid attractions within. And if they happened
to pass by at opening or closing they'd be treated to the sight
of Dawn, a curvy brunette from exotic Moosehead Lake, who
knew as much about the effects of make-up, shortness of skirt,
and tightness of blouse on beer sales as any farmer knew about
grain feed and milk production.

It was 4:30 on a Friday and the local boys were at the bar,
blowing through their paychecks. Dawn, more solid than sexy
now, had made no concessions to time; her *décolletage* flirted
with the third button of her snug pink blouse and she fluttered
her robin's egg lids at Patrick before noting that he was sitting
on the barstool next to Katie, a valued customer if not a regular. She took in their subdued attire and asked about Gunther,
who everybody knew. Then Dawn decreed, in deference to the
solemn occasion, that the Friday Happy Hour special on low-
cal beer, the Dawn's Early Lite, was now available a half-hour

earlier. She popped open two Buds for them and sashayed over to the jukebox, inducing Willie Nelson to warble "Blue Eyes Cryin' in the Rain."

They took their beers to a quieter table under the neon Bovenmyer's display. Patrick took the sign as a *sign*: Bovey's, Gunther's favorite brew. The fuzzy-cheeked pastor had been right in one respect; forces greater than they were at work. He almost mentioned this to Katie but couldn't be certain where she stood on such matters, and they had to account for the past fourteen years before they could speak of the deceased.

"You showed up just in time," she said, sparking a lighter under a Winston. "I had to get away from that place." She offered the pack to him. He flashed a palm at her, finally able to resist peer pressure. Even from Katie Osterlund. "I keep trying to quit. Can't smoke around my son." Patrick shrugged away the confession, cool enough now not to stand in judgment. About the cigs or the son.

"It's tough to quit," he said and swigged his beer. "You're brave to try."

Katie wouldn't let that be the last word on her intentions. There was so much failure in the last fourteen years, so much to regret: dropping out of Mankato State her sophomore year; coming home, only to get impregnated by Doug Knutson, former quarterback of the Homesteaders and heir to the Shop-Rite legacy; marrying Doug, divorcing Doug; a string of inconsequential, get-by jobs. "A total flame-out," she said, "peaked on graduation day." She took a deep drag of her cigarette, let smoke trickle out her nostrils. "Turned out, being the It Girl of a graduating class of eighty-six wasn't quite the credential I thought."

"And look at you," she continued. "You went away, to an excellent college. Got your degree. Then you didn't go off to Wall Street or some fancy law firm. You teach poor Black kids, right?"

He wobbled his head to acknowledge that this was more or less the case.

"You're fucking amazing, Patrick." She sipped her beer. "Why didn't I see that in high school?"

He thought he could answer that question but was too overwhelmed by the frisson of Katie Osterlund invoking copulation and his name in the same sentence. Anyway, she saved him the trouble.

"Because I was a stupid, stuck-up, hormonal little bitch, that's why. Hung-up on biceps and broad shoulders instead of kindness and smarts."

He was content to accept the implicit compliments, though they came with unattractive implications attached. Which were all too true. Ask Coach. But he was also happy to order another round and sit and watch Katie recite the details of her fall from grace. None of which was news to him; he'd never been able to hide his crush from Erin, who'd often include some teasing "Katie updates" in their phone calls. Concluding with the latest calamity to befall his dream girl and chuckling, "It's not too late."

Now he could just look, closer than he dared to get in any class. Jesus, the pain he'd gotten gazing at her in chemistry. Blue balls didn't begin to cover it. And now as he stared into those blue eyes that complemented the navy dress, he was just being a sensitive man, a good listener. Susan had trained him well. Hello? She'd snap her fingers. Look at the woman when she speaks. You can't be grading papers and call it listening.

But, given the liberty to gaze, even Patrick could see Katie wasn't a prom queen anymore. Though she was still, as Grandfather Lynch remembered Grandma on their wedding day, "a fine figure of a woman." Only thicker in the middle now, and buxom, more aging milkmaid than cheerleader. And the cartons of cigarettes had begun to have their way with the creamy complexion.

She stubbed out a butt in the ashtray. "Here I'm rattling on with my tale of woe. Tell me about you. Tell me about your life in New York."

So he ordered another round and tossed her a few of his

old teacher war stories. Only they were new to her, magically new. Katie Osterlund was gazing at him now. He was casting the line he'd used to reel in Susan long ago. And so much simpler here: Katie didn't know Harlem from the Hamptons. Patrick felt himself caught up in the telling, in the gritty detail of it, as remote from life in Peterson's Prairie as the Serengeti Plain. Remoter. And sure there were embellishments—a few extra weapons, another gang or two—whatever he could say to make those blue eyes widen, that imposing bosom swell, he'd say. But they were unnecessary fillips; he was pleased to find how much reality sufficed. He was, in Katie's eyes, the hero of his own life.

He left out, of course, the recent unpleasantness in room 234 and its unsightly consequences. But the more he talked around it (and, to be sure, *Susan*), the more he fought the urge to match Katie confession-for-confession, to share his deepest hurts with someone with whom he shared a singular strange intimacy, someone who'd known him—well, *of* him—since kindergarten, who'd been the source of his sweetest longings, his most tortured desires. She knew him as no other woman knew him, and now he could see, by the third round of the Dawn's Early Lite, that she might want, as the young reverend would have it, to *know* him. But as Patrick's Helen leaned in to absorb his West Side *Iliad*, that snowy skin flushed pink, the glittery blue eyes a little glassy, he wrestled mightily with the better angels of his nature, fending off a new fantasy rapidly replacing the old—that fleeting image of the strip motel off I-94 he'd seen on his way up, at the Moosehead Lake exit.

He'd just launched into his set piece about the time he caught Abdul in the stairwell, jeans about his ankles, with a cutie from the Computers for Tomorrow program, when Katie began to giggle. It was funny, certainly, the way he told it, and, in the present context, with any luck, inspirational as well. But he hadn't gotten to the funny part yet.

"I'm sorry," she laughed, wiping foam from those oft-dreamt-of lips.

"What?"

"I was just remembering something Gunther said."

About time, chimed that voice in Patrick's head.

"Remember when…in biology? When he read his report on amoebas?"

Patrick smiled and nodded. He'd let her tell it.

"And Gunther said, right in front of Mrs. Geertz, with her gray bun with the pencil in it, that the amoeba was the most common…the most common single-cell orgasm?" Katie dissolved.

He laughed, took a casual sip of his Bud. It was better, much better, coming from her.

"And then the time," she continued, "the time he fell asleep in geometry? And Mr. Dietrich called on him as a punishment? And made him come to the board to solve a proof—"

"—which he did perfectly, much to Dietrich's dismay." How easy, after all these years, slipping back into the student's snarky point-of-view.

"And he finished by describing…by describing two bisecting lines," she giggled, "as bisec-tual."

One of my best, sighed the voice.

Patrick giggled with Katie. There was no doubt where the evening was headed. He'd have to devise an excuse for Erin. A good one.

"But the *best,*" she declared, pointing the mouth of her Bud at him, "was that experiment you guys did in chemistry." It took Katie a moment to collect herself. "When you guys," she swallowed, "you guys filled those beakers with the yellow and the green and the blue liquids and stirred them all together. And Mr. Jennings got all red in the face and told you to stop messing around and made you both sit down." She took a sip. "And then…later, when he was showing how the experiment was *supposed* to work, that purplish, reddish, blackish foam coming out of your beakers. It seemed like gallons of it, all over the table, all over the floor. Like some monster had puked all over the classroom." There were tears in her eyes.

He took it up. "And then when the class fell apart laughing, and Mr. Jennings was screaming, Gunther stood up and shouted everybody down, even Jennings. How can you all laugh? he said. Remember? The eruption you just witnessed, he said, was his tribute to the ancient citizens of Pompeii, to the hideous deaths they suffered—burned, suffocated—by the thousands. And he said that ooze on the floor, black and red, was a memorial..."

He looked at Katie, sober, suddenly, her eyes far away. He'd only thought of that moment once before, teaching—trying to teach—*Romeo and Juliet*. Two boys performed the Queen Mab scene, painfully, in English that Shakespeare would not have recognized. But he was riveted—*Remembrance of Things Past*—when the dread-locked Romeo mumbled, *Mercutio, thou art mad. Thou talksts...of nothing.* And Patrick was back in Jennings' chem class, April 1978, surrounded by demonic foam and his best friend's insanity.

"You guys pulled some crazy shit," Katie whispered. She popped a cigarette from the pack, sparked the lighter.

"That was Gunther's idea. They were all Gunther's ideas." Except for one. But they wouldn't speak of that.

Katie looked at her nails. They were red, a little chipped. "You know, I ran into Gunther—maybe a year ago?—right here at Dawn's." It was a different Katie talking now, older, farther away. "I hadn't talked to him in, Jesus, years. He pumped my gas sometimes. Gave me a deal when I cracked my *catalytic convertor*." She said it with Gunther's expert inflection. "He was sitting at this exact table when I walked in and, believe it or not, he was drinking coffee." She shook her head. "He asked if I'd sit with him, and I said I would, and we sat and talked. Well, he talked." She smiled to herself. "And he rambled on about politics, existentialism. Gunther stuff. Then he said he was changing his life, going to AA, reading the Bible. That's great, I said, but what are you doing at Dawn's? It was a test, he said. He'd never believed in tests as a kid, but now he did. He bought me a couple beers and just sat with me, talking, drinking his coffee." She lowered her voice as Dawn strolled by. "Horrible coffee here, he said. Another test.

"We stayed till closing and he got this look on his face. What? I asked. He said he got depressed this time of night. Would I mind following his car back to his place in Winnipee Falls? I live just past there, next exit, and he did look a little scared, so I said, fine.

"I followed him to this cute little house on Elm Street. Perfect lawn, you wouldn't think. Gonna have another cup of coffee, he said. Wanna join me? Gunther, I said, and I just stared at him. How long have I known you? I could use the company, he said. Couldn't you?

"Well, anyway, Little Doug was with Big Doug that weekend. And, I don't know, I was coming off a really bad relationship." She waved away the excuse. "And Gunther was a nut, for sure, but sweet too. And not bad looking, after he lost the goatee and that nasty black cap." A wicked smile. "And creative."

The smile vanished when she looked up and caught Patrick's expression. He could've been anywhere during this reverie, anyone. "I'm sorry," she said, and checked her red nails.

Back…way, way back, shouted the voice.

You were always so fucking competitive, Gunnie.

And competitive, fucking.

But Katie? My Katie?

Grand slam! Home team wins! Can you believe it?

"Speaking of Little Doug," Katie sighed, and it was an altogether different gear. "His sitter's on overtime."

Patrick felt some emotional breaker switch slam down. "Absolutely." He looked at his watch but didn't notice the time. "My sister's making dinner. Can't be late for that."

"Erin? Was she at the service?"

He nodded.

"Say hi for me, will you?"

"Of course."

"She was the nicest girl, and so pretty. And your dear mother too. Will you?"

Patrick paid their tab and left Dawn a tip with fourteen years' worth of interest. He walked Katie to a gold mid-80s Nissan bearing all the scars of Minnesota winter salt. She unlocked the door and turned to him. "God, Patrick, it was so good to see you." Her eyes got wet. "I can't tell you." She kissed his cheek and threw both arms around his neck, holding him uncomfortably long. His first and last real embrace with Katie Osterlund.

She started the engine and jammed it into a grinding reverse. He waved and turned but heard the window rolling down. "How does a grown man—a mechanic—have a one-car accident on a cloudless night on a highway he could drive blindfolded? Even drunk—which I know he wasn't."

She shook her head and rolled up the window. And that was his final view of Katie, turning the rusty gold Nissan onto Main Street, wiping her cheeks with her wrist.

Though so much of Peterson's Prairie had changed, the soybean field off Rural Route 17 was still there. The clouds had cleared and the furrows were revealed in all their Minnesota spring ripeness. It had grown warm and humid and Patrick rolled the cool Bovenmyer's bottle down his sweaty neck as he sat in his shirtsleeves on the hood of the Corolla. It had to be Bovey's, of course; he'd driven all the way to Bryson's Liquors in Winnipee Falls to find it. When he pointedly asked for the old liquid death, the man at Bryson's laughed and said they had some in the back. Bovenmyer's had just been bought up by Anheuser-Busch, he added, so, really, wouldn't Bud do just as well? Not for this occasion, my man, Patrick told him, reaching for his wallet.

He'd meant to drive straight to Erin's, play with the twins, help with supper. But this rental was on autopilot, determined to hit all the Stations of the Cross before he left his home state. He ceased contemplating his sister's displeasure and leaned back against the toasty windshield, enjoying the sun setting beyond the—what did Gunther call it? loamy?—the loamy field.

Patrick swiped a trickle of sweat from his cheek and his hand came away red. Katie's lipstick. He pictured that motel near Moosehead Lake and flinched in shame. The worst of both worlds: he'd betrayed Susan and struck out with Katie.

I am fortune's fool, Gunnie. He rolled the bottle across his forehead. Fortune's fool.

What was it Gunther said to him that time? Spring, senior year? He'd been running errands for his mother in his dad's old Ford station wagon, driving on fumes, forced to stop at Hendrickson's Best, something he went out of his way to avoid. He couldn't help seeing Gunther at school, playing opposite him in gym, but being alone with—served by—his former best friend was too painful.

Gunther had sauntered over, same as always, as if Patrick drove into his station every day. "What'll it be, Paddy? Regular?" He'd pulled at the goatee. A white crescent ran from the bridge of his nose to his cheekbone. "Or you gonna throw caution to the wind and go with the high test?"

He'd shrugged at Gunther and laughed, trying to be casual. "Think I'll stick with the regular," he said.

"Do what ya gotta do," Gunther said, turning toward the pump.

That was it: Do what ya gotta do. He hadn't known what to make of that. At the time he took it as judgment, a bitter summation of his role in their lapsed friendship. It was the last thing Gunther ever said to him.

But now, as he gazed out at the leafy rows of soy, Patrick took the broader view, that these last words were a final piece of Gunther's philosophy. His friend putting his lonely destiny in context. And perhaps, Patrick thought, weighing all that awaited him back in New York, his own as well.

Wasn't Gunther, in the end, responsible for that? Everyone assumed he'd become a teacher because of his parents. And true, their influence was undeniable, profound. But who, really, was the first to push him—shame him—into reading *The Count of Monte Cristo, Tom Sawyer, White Fang*? They were scattered across Gunther's stained gray carpet, under his bed with the dust bunnies and half-eaten sandwiches. Sure, sometimes it began with Patrick leafing through one of the *Classic Comics* versions, which Gunther had read in third grade. But his friend was no snob; he may have been an inbred Lutheran, but he was catholic in his tastes. The funnies, the sports section, were no less sacred texts than the editorial page. Patrick owed more of his adult life—the good part—to Gunther than he'd ever admitted before. He had, in large measure, Gunther to thank/blame for his teaching career. That was why he was here.

That, and the eulogy. All afternoon it bothered him, coming all this way and not hearing his friend properly eulogized. He, clearly, was the only one qualified to do it. But how would he begin? *Well, Gunnie, Mr. Newton was right after all—an object in motion tends to stay in motion, unless—*

Unless. He tapped the bottle in his palm.

A toast, he thought. That, he could do. And Gunther would appreciate it more; eulogies were a joke but toasts were holy. Patrick slid off the hood of the Corolla and stood. He gazed out at the loamy Minnesota soil and lifted his Bovenmyer's high. "Time flies like an arrow," he intoned, quoting Gunther quoting Groucho. "Fruit flies like a banana."

Then he took a hard gulp of Bovey's and shook his head. Don't care what you say, my friend. Still tastes like shit.

12

BACK IN THE EMERALD CITY

Kill him quick, Patrick had advised. All the greats knew it, Hemingway to Zane Grey: when you kill off the hero, do it fast. But Abdul hadn't been weaned on literature, popular or classic; his inspirations, gangsta rap videos and slasher films, celebrated the long goodbye, the slow-motion departure. Hence the last two pages of Abdul's five-page true-life crime story, a collage of high body count and mass body parts. "And, yo, Lynch," the author pushed back against his editor, "didn' you say thas how *Hamlet* ends? One big scene where everybody be stabbed to death and poisoned?" Patrick laughed. Abdul, for once, had been listening.

Whether he would be the hero of his own life was unclear, but clearly the editor of Patrick's personal narrative, unlike Abdul, was a fan of the brisk ending. Maybe Gunther, who had followed him back to Manhattan, doing occasional color commentary on his life after many years' hiatus, was editing. He'd always favored the sudden, dramatic finish. And, most comforting now, the home team always won. But the terse message C had left on Patrick's answering machine, though it promised promptness, offered no happy ending.

"Greetings, Mr. Lynch. Call me," he ordered. "It's on."

The Scribbler lifted his brows behind those round Bolshevik lenses when Patrick showed him the letter from the BOE that awaited his return from Peterson's Prairie. "Whoa, highly unusual. Expedited hearings are typically for cases of pedagogical incompetence." He gave a nod of respect. "Which yours, certainly, is not." The Scribbler was back to courting him, now that Patrick had humbled himself, seeking his counsel. Perhaps the Scribbler still held out hopes of Patrick as the star of his muckraking bestseller.

"Stankowski, your arbitrator—your hearing officer—he's a fool, and lazy. Fell asleep during a hearing last year. Snoring, they say, drooling, the works. Had a judgment vacated by the State Supreme Court the year before. Teacher got into a wrangle with his principal, who accused him of insubordination. Stankowski terminated him, boom." He slapped his legal pad. "Blanchard, the appellate judge, called his penalty," the Scribbler closed his eyes, summoning the citation, "'outrageous and disproportionate to the alleged offense' and 'wholly unsubstantiated by the evidence presented.'"

"How does he keep his job?" Naïve question, he knew. Patrick always felt like a C- student in the Scribbler's civics class.

The Scribbler shook his head. "Arbitrators are selected from a pool. They have to be approved by both the BOE and the union. Since only 17 percent of judgments call for outright termination, the public consensus is that arbitrators placate the union to keep their gig. Which is cushy, to say the least. Five sessions a month, twelve hundred bucks a session. But they have to keep the BOE happy too, so you see some draconian rulings, based more on whim than hard evidence."

"So that's why they're called arbitrators? Because they're arbitrary?"

The Scribbler stared at him. He was not one to defuse tension with humor. He cleared his throat. "And hearing officers have unfettered latitude, more than a judge. So you see awards—that's what they call penalties—inconsistent from arbitrator to arbitrator. One might give an alleged sexual predator a thousand-dollar fine and mandate some kind of counseling; another will terminate a teacher for tardiness. There aren't standard sentencing guidelines. It's all a crapshoot, who your hearing officer is.

"If they have you on the fast track, someone with juice—the Mishkins, no doubt—is forcing the BOE's hand and someone else—your principal—wants this to go away, and soon. Need-less to say, this is a PR disaster for his school. Leonard Mishkin's son injured in his building—no matter the circumstance—isn't going to get the white *bourgeoisie* flocking to his programs."

Behind the Scribbler, the Juggler was refining a new, all-pa-paya routine he'd developed in Patrick's absence. The papayas looked slippery and irregular and, despite the Juggler's impres-sive skills, seemed likely to land anywhere. Patrick knew how they felt.

"Another variable is your representation. If you can afford it—or even if you can't—you should get private counsel. I can recommend some people if you're interested. You'll have to scrape together a few grand for a retainer. The UFT, of course, will provide a lawyer to represent you. They have some good people there, but some BOE and union lawyers work with the same arbitrator as a trio for a year or more at a time, so they can get rather chummy. *They've* all got interests to protect, and none of them may be *yours*." He narrowed that left eye.

The Scribbler drummed his ink-stained fingertips on the table and let his student digest his tutorial. Patrick had stopped listening at "a few grand." Only two people in his world had that money at hand, his mother and Susan. Either woman would write him a check without a word. Both options were impossible. He'd assumed he'd throw himself at the mercy of his union, which, C aside, had been silent till now. But on the phone last night, his building rep had assured him that that phase of his ordeal was over. "Now," C honked, swirling some-thing-on-the-rocks, "we're turning you over to the big guns."

"So, has the union assigned someone to represent you?" The Scribbler thrust the nib of his fountain pen at him.

Patrick dug in the back pocket of his khaki pants to retrieve the other letter that had been waiting for him after his Midwest sojourn. *UFT* the envelope said in large block letters on the back, *Working Together!* He handed the envelope to the Scrib-bler, who opened it deliberately, as if the contents would reveal the next Miss America. The Scribbler scanned the letter and stroked his socialist chinwear.

"Sylvia Bartolino," he whispered reverently. "She's a tiger." He whistled through his teeth. The Juggler looked up; papayas bounced on the moldy carpeting. "Two words," the Scribbler said. "Be careful."

From the moment Susan picked him up at LaGuardia, Patrick knew something had changed. Flu-like symptoms had clutched him as his plane descended over New Jersey; he felt achy, sweaty, his guts tightening, regrouping, preparing for self-defense. All that Midwestern expansiveness congealed to a ball. He'd left on the worst of terms, softened only by the circumstance of leaving to bury his oldest friend. *And that, buddy,* his dead friend chimed in, *won't save you now.*

Susan greeted him in a unisex outfit—baggy jeans and Yankees sweatshirt—makeup-less, her hair seized back in a scrunchy. His girlfriend was attractive no matter what she wore, but he noted the lack of feminine effort—special lipstick, sexier jeans—that had ended their past separations, however brief. She gave him a welcoming hug, a sisterly kiss, and listened politely to the abridged version of his Minnesota odyssey as she wove through the traffic on the Triborough Bridge in the Audi borrowed from Ashley down the hall. She seemed to lean away from him even as she nodded her social worker face at The Demise of Gunther Hendrickson. Though the car smelled strongly of Mr. Paws, was Susan sniffing, too, the guilt that clung to him like Katie Osterlund's perfume, intuiting that he had cheated on her, in spirit if not in fact?

In the following days they danced, gently, around each other. Susan was, from the moment he returned, as kind, as solicitous as ever, but they lived together in her snug apartment like brother and sister, Hansel and Gretel minus the breadcrumbs and gingerbread. And Susan was gone more. She'd gotten a promotion of sorts at the shelter, more responsibility, more impact on policy. Patrick didn't understand, exactly, but he could feel her underlying excitement even as she explained it in a distant, offhand way. Now she missed dinner altogether, staying through a later shift, ordering from the Szechuan place next to the shelter.

The late May evenings turned unseasonably cool and when Susan finally did get home, she took to wearing sweats to bed. The notorious blue comforter reappeared, defending her on three sides, *Aspects of Modern Social Work, Volume 2* girded her loins, Chauncey lay circled at her feet. Patrick took his lead from Susan, a lead that led nowhere romantic—not toward so much as a quickie and certainly not toward any discussion of where "they" were headed.

Susan continued to be helpful in practical ways. One Saturday she took him down to Macy's to shop for a proper navy-blue summer-weight "hearing suit," a ritual that inevitably conjured scenes of shopping with his mother before his father's funeral, only this time it was his teaching career being put to rest. When he recapped his discussion with the Scribbler concerning the benefits of private counsel, Susan offered to speak with her dad, who, of course, was in insurance, but "knew people." Her family's financial aid was implicit. Patrick thanked her but declined the assistance, assuring her that his union was supplying him with someone who was, by all accounts, formidable.

Ms. Bartolino might be a tiger in the courtroom, Patrick thought, but she looked more like a Weeble, one of those gnome-like dolls from his childhood, so round from feet up that they rolled back up no matter how hard you pushed them. Perhaps the Scribbler was right: this is what he needed, someone you couldn't keep down.

"*Student Gives Teacher the Finger*, we meet at last," she said, rising, wiping away tuna fish sandwich with a napkin. Sylvia had to stretch upward across her desk to shake hands; she couldn't be more than five feet tall. Her pudgy hand grasped his firmly. As she sat, her rumpled black pantsuit disappeared into her large black office chair, framed by shelves of legal books. Stacks of manila folders manned the corners of her desk; the towers of file-filled banker's boxes made her cramped office smaller yet.

She ran a hand through a cap of graying shag. "So, have you always had a knack for pissing off people in high places? Or was this dumb luck?" She smiled up at him.

He shrugged, tried to smile back. People like Sylvia Bartolino—effusive, unfiltered—always made him shy. The more those of Mediterranean affects (and they comprised a large part of this city and an even larger proportion of its education apparatus) came at him, the more he shrank into himself. He had an odd sense of littleness next to this woman, a foot shorter than he. Stranger still that he couldn't recall having this feeling in Peterson's Prairie, reared among strapping Teutons and Scandinavians. Just a few days back in Minnesota had reacclimated Patrick to the ways of his native region: containment verging on the hermetic.

"Not a situation I ever imagined myself in," he managed to say.

"I'm sure not, Mr. Lynch." Her smile faded. "I'm sure not." She tapped her stubby fingers on two stacks of file folders that nearly reached her chin. "Pardon my lunch. Can I get you anything? Coffee?" He shook his head. "I'd like to walk you through the hearing process. Then answer any questions. Then I have some questions for you."

She opened a file on top of the left stack. *My case*, he realized with a jolt. Those foot-high stacks: my case. The height of them, the sheer volume, brought home how little he'd allowed himself to think about his situation as anything other than a bizarre, horrible accident. But did random accidents merit hundreds—thousands?—of pages of documentation? His mind began to swim and he forced himself to focus. *Listen, Patrick, this is your career, your life, on the line.*

Ms. Bartolino began with the charges. "Conduct unbecoming your position; conduct prejudicial to the good order, efficiency, or discipline of the service; endangering the welfare of a child; insubordination." Although his lawyer rattled off the list in the most perfunctory manner, and Patrick had, certainly, read the charges in the certified letter from the BOE, he couldn't help recoiling at each new accusation, as if they were finally real because Sylvia Bartolino had said them aloud.

She finished with the ominous conclusion of the BOE letter. "Probable cause having been confirmed based on findings of the Office of Special Investigations (OSI), penalties may be awarded by the arbitrator up to and including substantial fines and/or termination from employment by the NYC Board of Education and revocation of educator's license by the New York State Department of Education."

Patrick felt fluish again, as he had, off and on, since returning to New York. Maybe he'd get sick right on Sylvia Bartolino's legal files, including his. Especially his. She looked up from the document she was reading. Her eyes got wide. "You don't look well, Patrick. Can I get you some water?"

"No, I'm...I'll be fine." He could feel the color leave his face, pasty Irish to begin with, now surely albino next to his counselor's Italian swarthiness.

Ms. Bartolino had seen this before. "It's a lot to take in, I know. But the BOE is legally obligated to lay out the worst-case scenario." She held up her hands, like scales of justice. She threw the scales at him. "And then they hurl at you all the charges they can get probable cause on. Hoping you'll be overwhelmed, settle their way."

Good strategy, Patrick thought, it's working. As Sylvia thumbed through the Lynch files, giving an overview of the discovery process—his personnel file, interviews with his students, his colleagues, Silverstein, photos of room 234 from various angles—he was indeed overwhelmed, but less by the individual details than by the totality of it: that there was an OSI, operated by the BOE like a city-state FBI. His pits grew clammy in front of Ms. Bartolino as she flipped through file after file after file of data dug up by agents of the Department of Education whose full-time job it was to find enough dirt on Mr. Lynch to deny him the opportunity to explain to Julio what an infinitive was and why it was such a crime to split. He was back at Court Street in Brooklyn, his first year teaching, wandering the corridors of that puzzle palace, looking for someone—anyone—with the authority to issue him a paycheck. Only now he was fighting just for the right to work. "Do you have any questions so far, Mr. Lynch?" She ripped off a corner of sandwich, sipped her Diet Coke.

"Insubordination?" The moment he uttered it, he felt he was falling for that old Perry Mason trick, objecting to the red herring while confessing, implicitly, to the rest.

"I don't have all the specifications—the details that support the charges—yet. But it appears this charge is pursuant to a conference you had with your principal after a field trip to a public garden." Ms. Bartolino slipped the infamous shovel picture from a file. She looked at it, the grimace, the bulging eyes, and shook her head. "Not your best side, I'm afraid." She glanced down her notes. "After this field trip, you had a conference with Mr. Silverstein in which he warned you to treat Josh Mishkin with...kid gloves, more or less."

"I'm sorry, I still don't see..."

She shrugged. "After that, there was an after-school tutorial, with an argument overheard by students in the hallway. And apparently a chair was knocked over."

He nodded warily.

"And you expelled him from class on the day of the...the incident." She didn't say accident. Be careful, quoth the Scribbler.

"He swore and threw a wooden bathroom pass at me." Louder than he intended.

She put up her hands. "I'm on your side, Mr. Lynch. But there was an Ed Plan for the student. Detailing a three-step procedure for removal from class, which wasn't followed."

Yes, yes, but the Ed Plan didn't specify what to do after the principal visits your class, chancellor and entourage in tow, and the subject of said Ed Plan pisses off the other thirty-five kids, now prepared to mutiny en masse.

Ms. Bartolino waved one of those little paws at him. "This is what Mr. Hanrahan will argue for the BOE. Fortunately, I will be making your case. And it's a good one." She thumbed to his blue personnel file and opened it. "You are, by all accounts, an exemplary teacher. Fine academic background. Satisfactory ratings, year after year. The only letters in your file are positive, your principal noting the time and effort you put in outside of class, commending you for the leadership you've shown in developing interdisciplinary curricula." She leafed forward. "Your students seem to like you. The special investigator's interviews…even the kids that don't like you so much—or your subject—they respect you, that comes through. As far as the day of the incident with Josh Mishkin, there aren't any…" she squinted at the document before her, "…smoking guns. None of your students threw you under the bus."

Patrick couldn't picture his students throwing him under a bus. He could picture, vividly, the field trip to MOMA when Abdul had snatched Julio's beloved Mets cap and tossed it onto the subway tracks. Julio, to everyone's amusement save his teacher's, had jumped down and plucked it up, perilously close to the third rail. *That* was the moment Patrick saw his teaching career flash before his eyes, imagined himself brought up on charges, pilloried in the *Post*. But nothing—nothing!—came of that near-fatal episode.

"However, we're getting ahead of ourselves. I want to hear from you what happened second period, April 7th." Ms. Bartolino leaned back, swallowed by the black chair, a legal pad in her lap, pen in hand.

Patrick sat up. He hadn't told the full story of that day to anyone. Not to Susan, not to his sister or his mother, not to himself. Officer Rodriguez had asked questions the following day, but that was just confirming facts, facts that would determine whether or not a crime had been committed. This was altogether different; context mattered. Character and setting, boys and girls, plot should flow from them. Write what you know. Tell your story. Only you can tell your story. He could hear himself going on and on, his favorite lesson. It's your voice, your reality. Your truth.

Now came the final exam. Essay question: Have you violated Chancellor Regulations 112, 117, 121, 132A? Why or why not? Remember to supply *specific* evidence to support your answer. Be sure to begin with a topic sentence. *The question of whether or not I violated the chancellor's regulations is an interesting one, and a good example of irony, as the chancellor himself had just left my classroom...*

"It's kind of complicated, what happened," he heard himself say to Ms. Bartolino. "You see, the chancellor had just left my room—"

He heard himself rambling. Hard to do a minute-by-minute replay of a lesson in a classroom where the minute hand hadn't moved in seven years. And it wasn't a straightforward narrative, anyway, more like one of those windy Southern tales, like Twain or Faulkner or *To Kill a Mockingbird*, which he'd taught so many times. Let me tell you about when my brother broke his arm; no, first I have to tell you about my great-great-granddaddy. Oh, and there's this fella named Boo.

Where to begin his story? We were finishing our unit on *Huckleberry Finn*. Josh Mishkin was sitting by himself in the back. Back right. The teacher's right, my right. Behind the broken window. The windows, I think, were open. Josh was too cold, then too hot. Or the other way around. The principal came in. Then the chancellor and his people. Or the chancellor came first. We were almost done with our discussion. I called on Josh.

> *Multiple Choice:* Why, with thirty-five other choices, did I call on Josh Mishkin?
> a) To demonstrate that, despite his being a major pain in the ass, I bore Josh no ill will.
> b) Despite her being a major pain in the ass, I bore Josh's mother no ill will.
> c) There was a chance, however slim, that Josh would make me look really, really good in front of the chancellor and my principal.
> d) Because Superintendent Dr. Francis J. Lynch, invariably fair, forgiving, and patient, would have done so.

"Wait." Sylvia Bartolino stopped him in mid-ramble, riffled through her notes. "You haven't spoken to the special investigator yet, correct?"

"No, no. When he called, I told him I needed to speak with my lawyer first."

"Good. Don't." She set her legal pad on top of his files, put down her pen. "Mr. Lynch—Patrick—this was a traumatic event. Not just for Joshua Mishkin and his family, but for your students and you. Traumatized witnesses make lousy witnesses." Big Italian shrug. "Which can work in your favor. But even so, hearing officers, and Bill Stankowski is no exception, want to hear the accused testify, want to look in his eyes as he proclaims his innocence. A hearing is not a court of law. More…informal, as you'll see. The arbitrator is judge and jury in these cases. They use the law, but, like juries, they also use their guts. I'm sure by now you've heard Rubber Room scuttlebutt about Stankowski, how he's scattered, his attention drifts, he's biased. I know him, defended a number of clients before him. He's a fair man, generally. Went too far with his gut last year, you probably heard, threw the book at a teacher, got his hand slapped hard by the state Supreme Court." She washed down the last of her tuna fish sandwich with the last of the Diet Coke, wiped her mouth with the napkin.

"Arbitrators—and lawyers for both sides—get cynical. We see our share of troubled teachers, some overwhelmed, some, frankly, in the wrong profession. You've been in the Rubber Room, I don't need to tell you. But I'm a union girl, tried and true; Dad was a steelworker in Allentown. My job is to defend teachers, the BOE's guy, to penalize or terminate. We don't see many teachers like you, Patrick. Skilled, hard-working, but wrong place, wrong time, wrong principal. Or," she nodded at him, "wrong parents. Stankowski will want to hear you testify, but he won't. You're too traumatized to be clear, or convincing. And my sense is that, on some level, you feel responsible for what happened."

Patrick looked at his hands.

Sylvia Bartolino leaned across her desk, her round torso burying his files. "Stankowski won't hear it, but I need to: Mr. Lynch, was Josh Mishkin's injury an accident?"

No one had ever asked him like that. The answer, he was relieved to find, popped right out of him. "Yes, ma'am, it was an accident." He looked right at her. "A sad, terrifying accident."

Ms. Bartolino leaned back, patted her pudgy hands on the file stacks. "Good enough for me," she said.

Back in the Rubber Room, the jungle drums were beating. As usual, his fellow inmates kept their distance, but now they eyed him with that mixture of envy and pity saved for those taxiing on the tarmac, preparing for an actual hearing. That he was getting his so soon, and before summer break, when hearings were scarce and everything got bumped into the next school year, cemented his celebrity status.

Now that he had a UFT lawyer, Patrick eschewed the Scribbler's counsel. On his way to the men's room, the Scribbler whisked by Patrick's table, sulking like a jilted lover. But as the days passed, and May bled into June, Patrick began to wonder if he'd written off the Scribbler too soon; he'd barely heard from Sylvia Bartolino in the weeks since they'd met and his hearing was just a few days away. It wasn't clear, exactly, what evidence would be brought against him, or who would testify, for or against. He'd never been part of a legal proceeding, not so much as jury duty. Was this what you did, put your life in your lawyer's hands?

Susan kept asking, "Have you called Sylvia? When will you hear from Sylvia?" As if she and Ms. Bartolino were old girlfriends, had roomed together at Middlebury. "I can call my dad," she said. "It's not too late." Patrick had to weigh, in the balances, which fed his anxiety more, not speaking with his union-appointed attorney or speaking with Bryce, Susan's smooth, silver-templed father. Conversations with Bryce, whether in his lovely Darien home or some embarrassingly upscale Manhattan bistro, were painful. Not because Bryce himself was pain-inducing, he was as charming and smart as he was handsome. He always tried to draw Patrick out with questions about his classroom, about education reform.

But though Bryce's questions were those of a progressive, well-read man, his conclusions were chapter and verse from the editorial pages of the *Wall Street Journal*. Patrick, who was living partly off this man's largesse, sleeping with his daughter and occasionally wearing his hand-me-downs to work, never pressed his luck with Bryce beyond nodding slowly and offering a few gentle correctives to his counterfactuals. Susan, who took for granted her parents' support, and whose opinions were decidedly more *Village Voice* than *WSJ*, couldn't help rising to the bait. Bryce was happy to joust with his daughter, took pleasure from her arguments: Look at my intelligent, beautiful, grown-up girl. Susan's mother, Pepper, had the intellect to jump into the debate, but, for rather different reasons of culture and breeding, was as conflict-avoidant as Patrick, and the two would redirect the conversation toward the lively but less loaded: literature, food, what was playing off Broadway.

Patrick would not be calling his girlfriend's parents.

Susan pulled back even more from him, frustrated with what she saw as his passivity in the face of crisis. She was her daddy's girl, after all, of a people who viewed problems in practical terms, as soluble. Her father sold insurance; she offered solutions to those who had none. Once you got past a nasty wrangle over the means of production and surplus value, they were speaking from the same emotional script. Neither of them would understand the small-town, Irish Catholic ball of shame he was reduced to. Or so Patrick thought, up to the night before his hearing.

Susan got home early that evening and together they produced dinner in their galley kitchenette. It was their first cooking together in weeks, a pleasure once simple become unbearably complicated. Since he'd been home from Minnesota, they'd supplied food for themselves, or left leftovers for one another, but the proximity required for meal preparation risked too much.

That night they fell into a familiar groove: he chopped; she sautéed; Ella sang. Neither dared changing the mood with conversation. Ella took over:

For nobody else/gave me a thrill/With all your faults/I love you still

Susan made a noise, not quite a hiccup but not quite a sigh, and he realized he'd been singing along, something he only did—and for good reason—when he was alone.

She turned and there were tears in her eyes. Susan put her arms around his neck. The motion and expression were so like Katie Osterlund's that he almost confessed then and there, but that would have been confession for his own sake. And could there be confession without actual sin?

They held each other until the pork and garlic began to smoke. Susan turned off the stove and then they were on the sofa and they were tender but then on the floor and they weren't. Lovemaking—if you could call it that—like that first night she'd taken him home, turned on by his passion for educating the underprivileged, for social justice. Deploying every weapon in her sexual arsenal. It felt like battle, too, territorial, fierce: Susan pillaged him, ravaged him, sowed his fields with salt. He fell asleep—passed out, nearly—knowing he'd experienced a cleansing act of forgiveness such as never before dispensed by womankind. His callous indifference to the work she loved, his short-term alcohol abuse—his assholism—didn't matter now. As he lost consciousness, he heard the words of Oscar, his former roommate and Latin love consultant. Make-up sex, Oscar had said, it's the best, man. *Muy* intense.

He woke up on the throw rug to the sound of Chauncey masticating the garlic pork. The cat would soon be throwing up on the throw rug, but that couldn't concern him now. Patrick lay on his back, his sweetheart's slender frame draped over him, breathing deeply. The red blanket was on top of them; his boxers dangled from the radiator, Susan's bra decorated a kitchen chair.

He heard the solid thump of paws hitting floor. Susan's warm face burrowed into his neck. For the first time he felt that, whatever happened tomorrow, let the BOE do its worst, he, they, would be all right. Chauncey padded over to him, circled twice, and plopped down in the space beneath his free arm. Patrick curled his arm around, not quite touching Susan's cat. Soon all three were snoring, one happy family.

13

IN THE STAR CHAMBER

110 Livingston Street, Brooklyn. Patrick had seen it before and knew, like all New York teachers, its legend. Feared, derided—the Bastille of the New York City Board of Education. Built in the Roaring Twenties as the luxurious Brooklyn headquarters of another BOE, the Benevolent Order of Elks, it had a massive, forbidding beauty. Purchased by the city in the 1930s, it retained some of its surface charm—the Beaux Arts façade, the Renaissance Revival style—but no coffered ceilings, no egg-and-dart ornamentation could disguise its current purpose: to house—and hide—the hundreds of employees who oversaw the flow from inbox to outbox, the quotidian policies followed in triplicate. And, like the Bastille, it was a place where the miserable accused were kept and judged.

The room for his hearing, in contrast to the elegant exterior and commanding lobby, was undistinguished. A smallish rectangle, fluorescent lit, dominated by a rectangular conference table comprised of four smaller rectangular tables, creating an empty, rectangular no-man's-land in the center. Patrick, never a friend of mathematics—barely an acquaintance—felt bounded by the simple geometry of it. A puzzle room within the Puzzle Palace. He sat at the corner nearest the entrance, to the left of the black-pantsuited Sylvia Bartolino and her Lynch files. At the corner directly across from Patrick sat Hanrahan, the BOE attorney, with his own, alarmingly tall stack of Lynch files. At the head of the table, in a chair noticeably larger than the others, the arbitrator, the hearing officer, Stankowski. Just around the corner to Stankowski's left was the stenographer, a slight man with horn-rimmed glasses, expectant behind a typing machine. To Stankowski's right, down Patrick's side of the table, an empty chair. For witnesses. Hardly the *Law and Order* courtroom of Patrick's nightmares, but intimidating enough. It's a hearing, not a trial, Sylvia had reminded him. Big difference.

And Hearing Officer Stankowski wasn't the sad sack Patrick expected. A tall man, sixtyish, with an impressive head of silver hair above a gray pinstriped suit. He leaned forward in his large chair, nodded at the lawyers, then the stenographer. "Good morning," he said in a folksy way that belied the nature of the occasion, "we are on the record in the case of Patrick Lynch, SED Number 11377." He had the attorneys introduce themselves for the record, which they smiled through. Patrick had a twinge; "they get kind of chummy," the Scribbler said of the hearing crews.

The hearing officer proceeded to read the charges: "Conduct unbecoming your position; conduct prejudicial to the good order of the service; endangering the welfare of a child." After the pre-hearing conference, Stankowski, as Sylvia had predicted, dropped the insubordination charge. "The BOE," she said afterwards, "uses the same system for charges we used for testing pasta in college: throw a handful at the wall and see what sticks."

Stankowski asked Mr. Hanrahan to introduce the Board of Education's case against Patrick Lynch. Hanrahan was disconcertingly familiar—stocky, pale, a freckled forehead beneath retreating sandy hair. He could have been on the barstool next to him at Marty's. Or, better yet, a cousin, the more aggressive one, the one who blocked too hard at touch football, who drove the hardest bargains at Monopoly. The one who went to Law, not Ed, school. He wore the slightly shiny, navy blue discount suit of the public servant, an older version of what Patrick now wore. Hanrahan tugged at his lapels and raised his pugnacious Irish jaw.

Without any courtroom theatrics, the BOE attorney began reading, seated, from his script. "The Board of Education does not prefer these charges against Patrick Lynch because he is unqualified as an educator. His personnel file shows a teacher who is well-educated and skilled in his presentation of material, who even goes above and beyond to make his lessons engaging and meaningful." He continued in this vein, even quoting laudatory comments from Silverstein's observations of his classes through the years. But the more Hanrahan sang his praises, the wetter grew the short hairs on the back of Patrick's neck. He was being sandbagged, like X had done at the infamous scheduling debate. The BOE attorney came not to praise Mr. Lynch, but to bury him.

Hanrahan looked up from his script, regretfully. "But, as we all know, and as the New York Department of Education states in its frameworks, pedagogical skill is not all there is to teaching." The freckles on his Celtic brow drew together. "Not by a long shot." Patrick swallowed hard against the tightening noose. The stenographer tapped away softly. "Teachers must exercise judgment, day by day, class by class, moment by moment. Student by student." Now came the presentation of a man, Mr. Lynch, whom Patrick did not know. A man who let the challenges—yes, the irritations—of a fifteen-year-old boy get the better of him. "Who, as the specifications pursuant to the charges preferred by the Board of Education illustrate, was negligent in meeting, per federal mandate, the special needs of Joshua Mishkin, was combative with this student, in and out of class, and was unresponsive to the pleas of his parents."

Patrick felt Ms. Bartolino's round little hand on his forearm. Only then did he realize how far forward he was leaning in his chair, how hard he was breathing, and he wondered if he could be heard above the stenographer's soft tapping. Sylvia squeezed his forearm and glanced up at him. Pace yourself, Mr. Lynch, her eyes said. This is just the opening volley. Patrick looked at Stankowski, who was settled back in his chair, his lids heavy already, the grooves deep above his cheekbones. And Hanrahan, though his accusations grew sharper, harsher with each word, never varied in pitch. Patrick looked around at the three legal officials, who seemed no more exercised than the stenographer. Just another day at the office for them.

Hanrahan's tone intensified. "All of this mounting frustration with and animosity toward Joshua Mishkin culminated on April 7, in the horrific, life-altering injury of Patrick Lynch's student. A traumatic loss of a body part, his right middle finger above the second knuckle." Hanrahan was stroking his right middle finger. Stankowski scratched his. "Soon we will hear counsel for the respondent refer to this maiming as an accident. An *accident*." He hocked up the noun as if he'd like to spit and rinse.

After detailing the conflicts with Josh in class, the aborted after-school tutorial, and the showdown following the chancellor's visit, he stated that all the pent-up rage at Josh was released in that door slam. "The specifications don't point toward intent," said Hanrahan, "but they do show negligence and a tragic lack of self-control, substantiating the charges preferred by the Board of Education. This injury, this maiming, could have been avoided," he continued, "if Mr. Lynch had followed the directives in Joshua's IEP concerning de-escalation of conflict and taken into consideration Josh's impulsivity and his predictable response to the medications he was taking. Given the history of tension in Mr. Lynch's class," Hanrahan added, "putting Joshua on the spot in front of the chancellor of New York City precipitated an inevitable battle of wills. Mr. Lynch's expulsion of Joshua from his classroom, while perhaps warranted by Joshua's actions, was sudden, and the manner in which Mr. Lynch closed his door was careless—cavalier even—and, as the special investigator's report will show, done with such force that injury was not just possible, but likely."

Hanrahan's onslaught against the character of this Mr. Lynch fellow washed over Patrick until the attorney fastened his attention with his conclusion. "...and the preponderance of evidence will show that Patrick Lynch is guilty of each specification charged and that there is just cause for his termination." The heaviness with which Hanrahan landed on *termination,* the thrust of that solid jaw, gave Patrick the feeling he meant it in the CIA, not BOE, sense. That Mr. Lynch was unfit to live as well as teach.

After a brief intermission, Sylvia Bartolino gave her opening statement in Patrick's defense. She was, if not tiger-like, insistent on a different Mr. Lynch than Hanrahan had painted. She went lighter on his merits as an educator than she'd planned; the BOE attorney had deftly undermined this tack by stipulating to them. Ms. Bartolino emphasized, rather, his personal qualities: how often he met with students after school; that, on a teacher's salary, he had purchased an in-class library of used books, going out of his way to find literature of particular interest to specific students; the unofficial conferences with the school social worker about family issues raised in his students' personal narratives.

She moved on to Josh, attempting to reframe this tortured student-teacher relationship. Sylvia began by re-casting the *Huck Finn* debacle as a Great Moment in Teaching. How Mr. Lynch met with Josh and his mother to offer strategies for developing his ideas. Then meeting after school with Josh to discuss his drafts, to help refine his essay. And, finally, giving Josh a chance to present his ideas, not only to his classmates, but to shine in front of his principal and the chancellor— which he did! Plan, develop, present: not just good pedagogy, she maintained, but, given the circumstances and the needs of this particular student, the thoughtful strategy of a caring, mature professional.

"What followed the chancellor's visit," Ms. Bartolino said, throwing her brief arms wide, "could not have been predicted. As evidence will show," she continued, "it was an unusual confluence of human movement and meteorological conditions— southeasterly winds, at twenty-one miles per hour—that resulted in this horrifying, freak accident—yes, accident—for which no one was culpable." She leaned in toward Stankowski, made a professorial bridge of those little digits. "We like to place blame when things go unaccountably wrong; that's a human instinct, completely understandable." She took a deep breath. "Mr. Hanrahan has called this injury tragic." Not what he said, thought Patrick, admiring the manipulation. "We can all agree

with that. But, Hearing Officer Stankowski, let us not com-
pound the tragedy by removing from service a gifted young
educator, Patrick Lynch, who is precisely the kind of teacher
this city desperately needs."

Stankowski, looking a little woozy during Ms. Bartolino's
impassioned plea, perked up as he thanked the counselors for
their statements and ordered an hour break for lunch. After
lunch, they would hear the testimony of two witnesses for the
complainants.

Angela Wong. When Ms. Bartolino had shown him the complainants' witness list, he couldn't believe it. Leading off for
the BOE: Angela Wong. Angela Wong? Patrick thought she
was going to be *their* leadoff witness. He was probably her favorite teacher. An English teacher who didn't just see a smart,
compliant Chinese girl, not a teacher who would toss a dusty
copy of *The Good Earth* at her and be proud of his cultural
sensitivity. He saw the muscular young woman whirling her
feet through boards in after-school martial arts and later asked
if she'd read *The Woman Warrior*. Discerning the unspoken
conflict in Angela's personal narrative between herself and her
demanding immigrant mother, he'd left his own copy of *The Joy
Luck Club* on her desk and watched her gobble it up.

But he could see why Hanrahan chose her, credibility-wise,
the hard-working, studious Asian girl from Central Casting.
And, whatever Angela's misgivings, her family wouldn't have
seen it as testifying *against* Mr. Lynch. Coming from Taiwan,
they would have viewed it as honoring a request from the
government. Her parents might also have gleaned from it a
not-so-gentle suggestion by the City of New York that their
daughter's cooperation here could avoid a closer look at the
"cousins" who worked at Wong's Golden Dragon, that the
health inspector would not show up unannounced.

Angela looked pretty, as always, though girlier and more formal than usual in a knee-length black skirt, white blouse, and
black flats. Her choir concert outfit. She glanced at Mr. Lynch,

smiled nervously, then looked away. Stankowski swore her in and seated her to his right. Requiring Angela Wong to swear to tell the truth was redundant; Patrick would stake his life on Angela's honesty. He had never worried about that before. As he had in his opening statement, Hanrahan began by raising general questions that allowed for positive statements about Mr. Lynch. Angela warmed to this role, displaying her small white teeth and smoothing her shiny black hair as she confirmed all that had been said of Mr. Lynch's superior teaching skills, of his caring attitude toward his students. Hanrahan asked Angela about her grades in American Humanities. She looked down modestly and admitted that she got As but offered that it was easy to work hard in Mr. Lynch's class, since he was so inspiring and made the subject so interesting. She looked up at Hanrahan; he nodded at her and smiled. Angela's impeccability as a witness had been established.

"Angela," said Hanrahan, "let's talk about April 7th, the day Joshua Mishkin was injured." Her sunny aspect darkened, but he held her gaze. "What happened after Principal Silverstein and the chancellor left room 234? You were talking about *Huckleberry Finn?*"

"We were talking about the end of the book—the novel— and Mr. Lynch asked Jamar—"

"Jamar Robinson?" He was on their list, Patrick thought. Hanrahan's ready.

"Yes, Jamar Robinson, about what he thought of the ending."

"And where were you sitting?"

"In the front row."

"Which aisle?"

"In the center aisle." She looked off. Another Asian girl cliché.

"And where was Jamar sitting?"

She thought, pointed. "On my left side."

Hanrahan was no Atticus Finch, Patrick thought, and you didn't have to teach Harper Lee's classic seven times to see where he was headed, why he'd chosen Angela Wong to testify. She had a straight shot to the door.

"So Jamar was discussing the end of the book, the novel, and what happened then?"

"Josh started making noises."

"What kind of noises?"

"He was mumbling something. He sits in the back, at the editing table, so I couldn't tell exactly. He sounded angry."

"Why was he angry?"

"Objection," said Ms. Bartolino, without looking up from the indecipherable notes she was scribbling on her legal pad. "Witness cannot speak for Joshua Mishkin."

"Angela is describing a classroom dynamic. She was part of the class."

"Go ahead," said the arbitrator.

"Why was Josh mad, do you think?"

"Because Mr. Lynch called on him when the chancellor was there."

"Was that a punishment?"

"No."

"Sounds like an honor."

"Yes, but—"

Hanrahan smiled. "The chancellor's here, let's call on the smartest kid."

"Yes, but—"

"Yes?" He nodded. "I'm sorry, go on."

"Kind of a, you know, a dis."

"Showing disrespect, you mean? Mr. Lynch was showing Joshua disrespect?"

"No." She looked at Patrick, then back at Hanrahan. "The other kids were."

"Who?"

"Abdul and Julio."

Hanrahan consulted his list. "Abdul Phillips and Julio Aguilar?" She nodded. "What did they say when the chancellor was there?"

"Nothing. But after he left."

"Yes?"

"Just…making noises. Whistling through their teeth." She put a hand to her cheek. "I think Abdul called Josh 'professor.'"

Ms. Bartolino looked up from her pad. "Hearsay."

"Again," said Hanrahan, "she is describing how Joshua was perceived by the class. Her perception of her classmates' response to Josh, whether or not her quotes are verbatim, is relevant."

"This is not a court of law, Ms. Bartolino." Stankowski canted his head toward her. "As you well know. You can address it in your cross, counselor. Go ahead, Mr. Hanrahan."

"Angela, why did Abdul call Josh 'professor'?"

"Now she's supposed to read Abdul's mind?"

Stankowski lifted those baggy lids at the UFT lawyer. "You're trying my patience, Sylvia." He turned to the witness. "Go ahead, Angela."

"As a joke," she said.

"To make fun of him? As a 'dis'?"

"Yeah. Yes."

"So they're teasing him. He's showing off for the chancellor? Being too smart?"

"Yes." She shrugged. "And I think maybe one of his parents, his mom, might be a professor. At NYU, somebody said. And his dad's, like, a famous journalist."

"Did Mr. Lynch hear this 'professor' remark?"

"Objection."

"Did Mr. Lynch react when Abdul called Josh 'professor'?"

"He didn't say anything. I don't know if he heard. It was kind of a whisper. A loud whisper."

"But you heard it?"

"Yes."

"In the front row?"

"Yes."

"Next to Mr. Lynch?"

Angela hesitated. "Yes."

"So, Abdul's teasing Josh for being too…"

"White." Hanrahan jerked his head back. As if he hadn't left a blank next to question number four, with one right answer, and Angela, well-trained student, had given, surprisingly, the correct response.

"But Joshua *is* white." Dumbfounded.

"Yeah. But he hangs out with the Black—African-American—guys at school. And he dresses like a…" She paused, not wanting to offend. "Like a rapper. Baggy jeans, puffy jacket, Tims."

"Tims?"

"Timberland hiking boots." Hanrahan nodded. "And he has, you know, dreads." She moved her hands down her own silky tresses.

The BOE attorney looked thoughtfully at the witness. "The kids in class ever tease you, Angela? Accuse you of acting 'too white'?"

"No. Too Asian." She laughed and covered her mouth, then uncovered it as everyone, even the stenographer, smiled. She glanced at Mr. Lynch. This was the Angela he knew.

The smiles disappeared as Hanrahan homed in on the "incident." Angela described the wooden bathroom pass whizzing past Mr. Lynch's ear. "Then Josh sort of screamed out the, you know, the f-word," she said, darting a look at the stenographer, who might be printing a copy of the transcript for her mother. "I handed the wooden pass to Mr. Lynch and he took an office pass out of his pocket and gave it to Josh. Then he told Josh to go to Mr. Kupczek's office."

Hanrahan took a sudden interest in his red-and-white striped tie. "How did you know it was an office pass?"

"It's yellow and it says *Office Pass* at the top. It had writing on it."

"What writing?"

"Josh's name was printed at the top and Mr. Lynch's signature was at the bottom."

"You could see that?"

"Mr. Lynch was holding it out to Josh in his fingers." Angela mimicked Mr. Lynch, holding out an invisible office pass between her thumb and index finger. "In front of my face, kind of."

Hanrahan put a hand to his freckled Irish mug. This time, seemingly, in genuine thought. "You saw Mr. Lynch take the office pass out of his pocket." Angela nodded. "You saw the pass, with his name and Josh's on it, in Mr. Lynch's handwriting." She nodded. Patrick looked at Stankowski, suddenly wide-awake. "Did you *see* Mr. Lynch fill the pass out?"

Angela wasn't a straight-A student merely because she was a plow horse Chinese girl. She could see Hanrahan connecting the dots. And Patrick could tell, by the aggressive way she smoothed her skirt over her lap, that she resented being his pencil.

"Has this alleged office pass been entered into evidence?" Ms. Bartolino snapped. "Does it even exist?"

Hanrahan swiped a hand toward his opponent. "Witness is testifying as to what she saw."

"Continue."

"Did you see Mr. Lynch write on the office pass after he withdrew it from his pocket?"

"No."

"It was already filled in, with his name and Josh's." Angela nodded slowly. Hanrahan looked at Ms. Bartolino, then Stankowski. "So, Mr. Lynch came to class with an office pass with Joshua Mishkin's name already written on it. And with his signature." He let a moment pass, as if he needed time to make sense of these disturbing details. "Mr. Lynch came to class *planning* to throw Josh Mishkin out of room 234."

"Objection." Ms. Bartolino raised her voice for the first time. "The BOE counsel is now reading the respondent's mind. And testifying for the witness. And his language is inflammatory: no student was thrown anywhere."

"I'm not trying to read anyone's mind, Hearing Officer Stankowski," Hanrahan said, calmness itself. He'd been given a gift and was a gracious recipient. "Just trying to establish a pattern, a pattern of conflict. And a teacher's response to that conflict."

"You've made your point, Mr. Hanrahan. Move on."

He had made his point. Patrick's sides grew clammy, the way they did when a lesson headed south and a class began to turn on him. He listed toward Ms. Bartolino, who was unrumpling her black pantsuit, clicking her ballpoint pen, tapping it on her legal pad. The arbitrator's body language had changed, too—stiffer, straighter, and a harsher cast fell over those weary eyes.

Pre-filled-out office pass? He'd been doing it for years. It saved time. You knew who the usual suspects were. You never *planned* to use it, but, if you needed it, there it was: no break in the flow of the class; no time wasted rewarding a pissed-off student with negative attention. It was an expedient, not a punishment. And it wasn't about Josh; if he'd reached in the wrong pocket, he would've given him Abdul's pass. But there was no way to supply this context; only a teacher would understand. This was the missing ingredient in Hanrahan's case: Mr. Lynch's animus toward his client, malice aforethought.

The temperature in the stuffy little room had changed. If this hearing had ever been the *pro forma* exercise in due process Sylvia had previewed it as, a small slip of yellow paper had surely made it something else.

"So, Angela, after Mr. Lynch handed the office pass to Joshua, what happened?"

"Josh kind of grabbed it from him and kicked the waste basket in front of the door."

"In front of the door?"

"Mr. Lynch used it as a doorstop. Somebody stole his rubber one. The door kept slamming that day. It was windy."

"And then what did Joshua do?"

"He went out the doorway."

"Did he go to the office?"

"No. He stood out in the hall, looking at the class."

"Just looking?

"He was kind of…dancing. And waving the office pass over his head."

"Did Mr. Lynch see—" Hanrahan caught himself before Ms. Bartolino could. "Did Mr. Lynch react to what Josh was doing?"

"No. He—Mr. Lynch—was facing the class. Holding the door, with his back to the doorway. And Josh did it quiet, kind of like a, a pantomime."

"But you could see—"

"Only for a second—"

"How did you know—"

"Kids behind me were looking at the hallway, smiling." Hanrahan nodded. "Did Mr. Lynch react to them?"

"No."

"No?"

"He just closed the door."

Hanrahan waited. "Hard?"

Patrick felt Sylvia flinch with him.

Angela shook her head. "Like usual. He just kind of," she waved her hand behind her, "and moved back into the room."

"Toward you?"

"Yes."

"And then?"

Angela bit her lower lip, smoothed her skirt. "There was a big breeze, and Josh ran toward the doorway, shouting something—"

Patrick had replayed this moment a thousand times—after a third pint at Marty's, in the Rubber Room, awake on Susan's couch in the middle of the night. He hadn't watched Josh after he left the class. He hadn't. But how could he not know Josh was in the hallway? Abdul and his boys were smiling…but not at Mr. Lynch. And Josh would never leave without the last word.

And was there anger in that door-closing? How could there not be? He would never be able to weigh his responsibility for that moment, for the blood and pain Angela was now recounting, tears in her eyes. It was an instant he would take back—had taken back—in his thoughts, so many times. So full of mixed, unsure intentions, that no amount of wishing or regretting or self-justification could untangle it. Like tortured Lord Jim, he'd... *jumped...it seemed...*and could never jump back.

Poor Angela, honest and loyal, was given a brief break and some water before being cross-examined by the UFT attorney. Ms. Bartolino was gentle but thorough. No one, Patrick thought, could better clarify the angles in his classroom, what was said or done for certain versus what was an impression left by trauma. But Sylvia Bartolino, for all her legal skills, could not undo the impression left by the office pass. That fucking office pass. And after a twenty-minute break, Stankowski announced, rising, they would hear the testimony of Joshua Mishkin.

As soon as Patrick and his attorney were out in the Byzantine hallways of 110 Livingston, Sylvia pulled him into a tiny conference room, half the size of his solitary confinement at Court Street. It had the same décor, an ancient, scarred wooden table and two vinyl-covered chairs. She urged Patrick into one chair and plopped down in the other. She set her legal pad and a stack of files on the table, her hands flat atop them.

"Look, Mr. Lynch, Patrick—"

To whom was she speaking, he wondered, the innocent, terrified young man or the defamed English teacher? He noticed at once a change in Sylvia Bartolino, her tone, her posture. More, somehow, that of a broker. Or of Susan's accountant, Lonnie.

"—we have to get to the bottom line. Before Stankowski sees and hears Josh Mishkin." She exhaled heavily. "That whole office pass thing screwed us royally. I know you could see that. Sometimes things come up, small things, that you can't anticipate. But it changes the chemistry. I think I turned it around a little on cross, on the facts." She combed her shag with those little stubs. "But did you look at Stankowski? Something shifted in him that I couldn't shift back. As I said in my office, these hearings are part law, part gut. Frequently, with this arbitrator, a lot gut.

"Hanrahan is right now meeting with the Mishkins, planning his next move. Have to give him credit; he's set it up well. Got a gift and knew what to do with it." She leaned back, braided her fingers over her belly. "In a few minutes, enter the maimed, dreadlocked, Jewish boy. The lone white kid in Mr. Lynch's class, bright but learning-disabled, with high-expectation parents, who is trying to fit into the dominant African-American sensibility of the urban classroom."

A fine Hanrahan impression. And, Patrick thought, where have I heard this before? Ibid. Chapter three, *Aspects of Modern Social Work*.

"This is the kid that Mr. Lynch, a good teacher but angry beyond all management, set up for humiliation at the hands of Joshua's minority classmates, kicked out of class with a pre-signed pass, then proceeded to chop off his finger." She popped open a Diet Coke. "Next case."

Patrick felt a little sick and a little like crying. "It's that bad?"

"It's that bad right now." She took a gulp. "But this is day one. We've got a list of students to hear from. Your principal. The special investigator. This can go into next fall, next spring. Or—"

"Or?" *Be careful*, the Scribbler said.

"I spoke with Hanrahan after the pre-hearing. Quick, off the record. Standard. Just to get a sense of his view, set a baseline, if you will."

"What did he say?"

"From what he saw on paper: two thousand fine, three months suspension without pay, counseling. Then back to Garvey." She shrugged. "Or wherever."

"Counseling?"

"Anger management." She flexed the mini-bridge. "Mishkins get satisfaction, BOE saves face, Silverstein gets his school out of the *Post*. Mr. Lynch gets his classroom back."

"You already cut a deal?" He was surprised at his anger.

Fear, guilt, he had access to those. He'd never had anger to manage till now.

Ms. Bartolino thrust her palms at him. "We don't do deals, Mr. Lynch. We're the UFT. We reach settlements." She barked out a laugh. She wasn't mad; this is what she did. "And there's no settlement without your say-so. And, of course, Stankowski's."

"What if I don't want to settle?"

"Then it's game on, and we play this thing out while you cool your heels in a Rubber Room." She swiped the sweat off her Diet Coke can. "But there are no guarantees. You risk all."

Then back to Garvey? He couldn't imagine. Feeling guilty and pleading guilty were very different. One Catholic, the other criminal. Some tiny scared part of him thought, Fuck it, take it. Never set foot in a Rubber Room again. Done. Something deeper, though, told him he'd never set foot in a classroom again. *You'll always be damaged goods.* And Coach Carlson, of all people, spoke up, laid a solid hand on his shoulder: Your dad would be so proud.

He sat up straighter, squared his shoulders. "I never meant to hurt Josh Mishkin. I'm fighting this. No matter how long it takes."

"Well, all right then," Sylvia said, rising, grabbing the files and her soda. He couldn't tell if she was pleased at his decision. He didn't care.

Outside the hearing room, down the hallway, he saw Dr. Mishkin first—Mrs. Dr. Mishkin. He still wouldn't know the famous Mr. Dr. Mishkin if he sat next to him on the No. 1 local. Dr. Mishkin's back was to Patrick, the broad shoulders of her well-tailored black suit shielding him from Hanrahan. All he could see of the tall BOE attorney were his eyes fixed on that index finger pointed at his chest. Patrick couldn't see the finger, but he could feel it, how it bore in on the rib cage, filled with accusation: you, you aren't doing enough, aren't accomplishing what I want. You are incompetent. I deserve better.

But Hanrahan wasn't a public school teacher; he had a

different hand to play, and different stakes. Amid the noisy
bustle of 110 Livingston, Patrick watched their pantomime.
Hanrahan staring at the finger, arms folded. Dr. Mishkin
throwing her arms out. The attorney planting hands on hips.
Back to the finger wag. Hanrahan thrusting his palms up, tapping two fingers on his wristwatch. Dr. Mishkin's formidable
shoulders lifting, holding, collapsing. Hanrahan setting a gentle
hand on a deflated shoulder. Dr. Mishkin shaking her head,
shambling off down the hall.

So engrossed was Patrick in this bit of dumb show, he hadn't
considered the obvious source of its drama: Where was Josh?

Patrick entered the hearing room and sat next to his counsel.
Sylvia had notes on Angela's testimony in front of her and a
minute-by-minute chronology of the events in room 234, April
7, second period. A more detailed lesson plan than Mr. Lynch
had ever crafted, though, to be sure, with a less clear lesson.

The clock over Stankowski's head showed 12:58, two minutes before the hearing was to recommence. Sylvia looked at
Stankowski, who raised his eyebrows at Hanrahan. The prosecutor ducked out in the hallway, returned, shook his head at
Stankowski. The hearing officer glanced at the clock, grimaced,
motioned for Hanrahan to sit.

"We are back on the record in the case of Patrick Lynch,
SED Number 11377," Stankowski said, nodding to the stenographer. "Mr. Hanrahan, you have a witness to call?"

Hanrahan cleared his throat. "Hearing Officer Stankowski,
the Board would like to request a brief delay—"

The hearing room door opened and in stepped a young
soldier in fatigues, sporting a fresh buzz cut. The occupants of
the hearing room stared at the young man, then one another.
Even the stenographer was nonplussed. Was the fortress at 110
Livingston Street under assault? Only the Timberland boots
gave the soldier away. The boots and the short right middle
finger, wrapped in beige bandages. Josh stood more or less at
attention, waiting for a command.

Hanrahan, so recently so cocky, slumped back, thrown off

his game, off any game. So this is what Josh was doing while he tussled with Dr. Mishkin? Getting a military makeover? He shuffled some papers, reordered some files, coughed. "Hearing Officer Stankowski, the Board calls Joshua Mishkin to testify."

Josh strode to the witness chair, sat erect, hands on thighs. He looked straight ahead, solemn, as he was sworn in, grumpily, by the hearing officer. Stankowski shifted back and forth in his big chair, pulled at the lapels of his grey suit. He glared at Hanrahan. *This is your witness, counselor, the Jewish rapper that pretty little Chinese girl just described?* Patrick recalled the Scribbler's scathing description of Stankowski, how Sylvia referenced the appellate court "slapping his hand." He was not amused.

Hanrahan was nearly as altered as his witness. Gone was the restrained sureness of the interlocutor from this morning, the one who'd uncovered the damning secret. Never ask a witness a question without knowing his answer, wasn't that what they said on *Law and Order?* What would he get out of Josh Mishkin, PFC?

At Patrick's side, Sylvia Bartolino was composed, no more pen clicking, pad tapping. She merely leaned in, ready.

"Joshua, I'd like to ask you about April 7th," Hanrahan began, "the morning you were injured in Mr. Lynch's classroom."

"Objection. Joshua wasn't injured in Mr. Lynch's classroom. Previous witness established, under Mr. Hanrahan's examination, that Joshua had left room 234."

Hanrahan, chastened, rattled, restructured the syntax of his request, with diagrammatic repositioning of prepositions, as Josh ran his left hand over the bristles covering his pale scalp.

"I was sitting at the editing table when the chancellor came in," Josh began. Patrick marveled at his response. So even-toned the narrative of this young warrior, so steady the eye contact. And when Hanrahan interrupted with clarifying questions, backtracking to the failed after-school tutorial, even revisiting the neighborhood garden disaster, Josh answered patiently, completely, finishing several replies with "sir." Sir?

But though Josh's answers were respectful, and in content not very different from Angela's, Hanrahan kept tiptoeing, flop sweat emerging on the freckled forehead. This wasn't the witness he'd prepared for. Unlike Mr. Lynch, the BOE attorney was unaccustomed to teenage character reinventions. The Catholic school refugees transformed into hot mamas in the course of a weekend, plaid skirt and sweater on Friday, spaghetti straps, short-shorts, bubblegum lip gloss on Monday. Or the boy, baggy-jean badass on Tuesday, turned prep school wannabe on Wednesday: khakis, Lacoste shirt, Top-Siders, the works. Kid like that walked into class, you could barely bring yourself to call on him, bit your tongue until it bled. But Patrick wasn't laughing now.

What unnerved him wasn't so much the combat gear and barbering as the detachment with which Josh related the moments leading to the "incident." Like a film he'd seen, some scuttlebutt from a friend of a friend, and not the morning he lost a fraction of hand. Patrick was unnerved and, as Josh's English teacher, oddly offended. It's your story, Josh, he'd told him so many times. If you're not invested, who will be?

More unsettling yet was the other lanky adolescent now droning in Patrick's ear, detailing, with equal disengagement, an act of violence at another high school, as distant from Marcus Garvey as the dark side of the moon: public property damaged, blood spilt, a bright boy in a black watch cap needlessly disfigured. And a representative of another Board of Education inquiring, *Patrick, are you angry at me?* His linebacker body is still, his broad face quivering; the answer means everything. The lanky adolescent on the other side of his desk remains vague, impassive.

"Did you see Mr. Lynch's face before he…closed the door?"

"Yes, sir," said the young man in fatigues.

"What did he look like?"

"I'm sorry?"

Hanrahan reeled out some invisible line. "His expression. How would you describe it?"

Sylvia leaned forward but said nothing.

"He looked—normal."

"Normal?"

Patrick was listening now. They all were listening. The answer meant everything.

"Like a teacher."

Hanrahan nodded and scowled, a facial veto of the affirmative head motion. He tried again. "Joshua, you said earlier that when Mr. Lynch tutored you after school he raised his voice, seemed angry. How would you compare that time to when he gave you the office pass, or when he turned to shut the door to room 234?"

Josh looked at Hanrahan, then Stankowski. He even watched the stenographer type. He hadn't once looked at Mr. Lynch, though he sat straight down the table from him, much closer than they ever were in class. "It was about the same, I guess."

"The same. Can you describe that, Joshua?"

That familiar vacant look. Surely Hanrahan had memorized Josh's Ed Plan, but he wasn't used to giving wait time. Josh was searching for the right word; verbal precision was strangely important to him. His father's DNA at work, perhaps. "Consistent," he said.

"Consistent? In what way?"

"He got mad sometimes. But it was always for a reason."

"Did you feel he was personally angry at you?"

Josh swiped at his newly shaven face. "I guess, from his… point-of-view, I was making his job more difficult."

Hanrahan swelled at this, his star witness finally on script. "Can you recall anything, anything specific, Mr. Lynch did or said on April 7—or before—that showed his personal anger toward you?"

Patrick was making his own personal list. Sylvia was digging a hole in her legal pad. The second hand swept around the clock over Stankowski's shoulder.

Josh looked at Mr. Lynch. "No," he said. "Not really."

The ruddy complexion of the BOE attorney grew ruddier.

He sharpened the question in a variety of formulations, each attacking Mr. Lynch's character, his motivations, more directly. But Private Mishkin was having none of it, remaining stoical through every incursion. Hanrahan even shot a few pleading looks at Ms. Bartolino, begging her objection. Anything. But she seemed content to let him lead this witness. Let him try.

Poor Hanrahan. Stankowski stared at him, head propped up with his left hand, the grooves beneath his eyes somehow deeper than before. The prosecutor was treading water now, praying for another office pass from heaven. No one understood better than Patrick the impossibility of getting Josh to say the right thing at the right time. Mr. Lynch had only made that happen once. And look where it got him.

Finally Hanrahan went for broke, asking Josh point blank if Mr. Lynch had slammed the door of room 234 in anger.

"He was doing his job," the witness shrugged, a little irritated, a bit of the old Josh breaking through. "He did what he had to do."

Do what ya gotta do, Paddy. He could see Gunther walking away, but this time, clearly, not in anger.

Maybe that's what Josh could live with too. What they all could live with.

Hanrahan leaned back and exhaled through pursed lips, an old Schwinn with a slow leak. "Request to go off the record, Hearing Officer Stankowski."

"Granted." Stankowski nodded at the stenographer, who put his hands in his lap.

Stankowski dismissed Private Mishkin. Hanrahan and Stankowski rose and murmured in a back corner, behind the stenographer. Otherwise, the hearing room was quiet, just the soft buzz of the lights, the hum of the second hand sweeping around the clock.

"What does this mean?" Patrick whispered to his counsel.

"I think," Sylvia Bartolino lifted those dark Italian brows, "it means you're free, Mr. Lynch." She played a swift arpeggio across the Lynch files. "You're free."

14

FREEDOM'S JUST ANOTHER WORD

Frank Lynch, like all great teachers, was an actor, a trickster, a pied piper. On Christmas Eve, when his wife would haul out *A Christmas Carol* and request an excerpt, Frank would demur. Ha! That old chestnut? he'd say. Third-rate Dickens, scarcely worth the reading. And the more he protested, the more his children clamored for a performance. Soon they would be nestled at his side, giggling as their bulky daddy impersonated the spindly old Scrooge, lapping up that sugary gateway drug to classic literature.

And so those words came to Frank's son just then, incongruously, on that balmy spring afternoon in Brooklyn. *I'm as giddy as a schoolboy*, Patrick thought, bounding down the stairs of the Court Street subway station. *I'm as light as a feather.*

The No. 2 train lurched out of the station, headed for Manhattan. A frigid glance from a woman with a child on each hip brought him back to the world. Patrick begged, but did not receive, her pardon as he smiled, snapping his foot off hers. Nothing could darken his mood today. He would go back to the Rubber Room tomorrow, sure, but then only until the end of the school year—two weeks—and then, Sylvia said, Stankowski would release his report. His judgment? And then, remarkably, inconceivably, Mr. Lynch would get his life back.

Afternoon subway rides home were always a time for Patrick to reflect, and his mind—even in this mood—went to the day's events. He held fast to a support pole, shaking his head. He'd never been able to anticipate Josh's next move, but he'd never have predicted him sabotaging his own case.

And that look: he'd never forget that last look. As he left the hearing room, Dr. Mishkin standing down the hallway at the negotiated distance. Hanrahan giving her the bad news, that he wouldn't be delivering Mr. Lynch's head on a platter after all. Those shoulders drooping. She turned to her son and Patrick saw her face for the first time in a long time and it wasn't the NYU professor now, or Leonard Mishkin's wife; it was Josh's mom, anyone's mom, teary, features crumpled, making that maternal lean toward her indifferent adolescent son, begging embrace. Josh inclined just enough to permit her hands on his waist, his hands on her arms. And it was for a moment as if Norman Rockwell had captured a particularly awkward farewell: Soldier's Final Fuck You.

When her son backed away, she turned and did a quick double-take at Patrick, surprised, somehow, that he was part of the proceedings. Bitterness, yes, he'd seen that from her before. But, underneath it all—relief? He hadn't allowed himself to feel for Josh's mom, consider her legitimate pain. While his future was under siege, he couldn't spare any sympathy for the Javert who'd made his life so miserable. Had this hearing been something she felt duty-bound to pursue? Perhaps she, too, was relieved to see it ended, even poorly. Or was this mere projection on his part?

The doors beeped open at Seventy-Ninth Street. *LetemoffLetemoffLetemoffLetemoff* the conductor mumbled as passengers pushed their way past the high school students spilling in. 3:15, Tuesday, second week in June. Seniors finished with Regents exams? A guilty twinge. He should be prepping his kids for their finals.

The car exploded with teenage noise, usually an irritation on his way home from school, exhausted, no longer on the city's clock. Once, drifting off between stops, he'd forgotten where he was and snapped "pipe down" at a mustachioed youth in puffy black. The kid looked him over, shrugged to his buddies, decided the balding white guy with the stack of papers wasn't worth the trouble of taking apart.

But today was different—bring on the noise! It was all part of his celebration.

A falsetto squeal blasted from across the car. "Yo, Mr. *Leee-inch.*" Julio, waving those praying mantis arms, accompanied by Abdul and Maria. Julio's prized Mets cap was askew on his slender head, a big grin beneath it. The trio wove through the crowd, Julio pulling Maria pulling Abdul. Julio offered up a hand-slap soul-shake that Mr. Lynch failed to parse in time, fingers briefly entwining, then, mercifully, slipping away. Maria, eager but shy, shifted in her pink sneakers, tugging at a ruffly red blouse that featured alarming cleavage. Lordy. Abdul was wearing an X T-shirt—*homage* to the Malcolm unit?—with sleeves shorn to display his impressive biceps, which he was now flexing, arms crossed, behind Maria. Ah, springtime in New York. The sap was rising.

It was always awkward running into kids outside school. The protocols were broken down; how were they to interact, fellow citizens of Gotham? And his students were endlessly amused to find he had a life beyond his classroom. Last fall some of them trooped past Carmine's and saw him inside, killing a bottle of Chianti with Susan. He heard about it all week: Mr. L, oh yeah, drinkin' some wahhhhn wid his lay-deee.

But this was new social territory, engaging with a teacher who had been, in essence, incarcerated for the past two months, for an offense you had witnessed in his classroom. They glanced at each other, then at the passing tunnel walls, as if reading the graffiti. Abdul put a proprietary hand on Maria's hip; she shimmied it off, gave him a look.

"So, how you doin', Mr. Lynch?" Julio, always the tension-breaker.

"I'm doing well, pretty well, thanks. How are you all doing?"

"We're doing good—well," said Maria.

"You all ready for finals?"

They eyed each other, laughed.

He put on his teacher face. "I'm serious. You all worked hard for me this year. I expect to hear great things."

They looked down, nodded.

"And you, Julio. Are you cooperating with my sub?"

That blank face he'd seen so often in class.

"You good," Abdul muttered over Maria's shoulder.

Julio jerked his head back. "Oh yee-ah, yee-ah."

Mr. Lynch folded his arms. "Fo' reals, yo?"

The boys doubled up, shoved each other. Mr. Lynch was buggin'. Fo' reals.

Julio recovered enough to cough out, "But Abdul…Abdul got in a beef wid Sitkowitz."

Maria narrowed those almond eyes at Julio. *Not in fronna Mr. Lynch.*

Julio missed it. "Abdul say, Abdul say sumpin'…" she punched his arm, "…*nasty* in chemistry."

Abdul smirked. "*Coño,*" Maria hissed.

"And Sitkowitz get all red and say, 'You kiss yoor mutha wid that mouth?'" Julio laughed, coughed. "And Abdul say…he say, 'Yee-ah, and yoors.'"

The boys dissolved, slapped hands. Maria giggled, finally, the memory too sweet.

Patrick looked down, his hand over his mouth.

Mr. Lynch looked up. "You should show Mr. Sitkowitz more respect. He's been teaching a long time."

Abdul threw his head back. "A loooooooooong time."

"Yeah," Patrick said. "Well." It was too much effort. Today especially.

The train was slowing, coming into the Ninety-Sixth Street station, Maria's neighborhood. Even on the subway, that serious expression before she posed a question. "Are you coming back to Garvey, Mr. L?"

No time to weigh it. "I don't know. Maybe."

"Well, you should." She scrunched that adorable nose. "'Cause you're the best."

He looked at his shoes, smiled.

"You are." Abdul and Julio pushed her toward the doors.

"And yo, homeboy had it coming," Abdul said over his

shoulder. He bit his middle finger. "Kid's a punk." He pushed Maria forward.

"No," Patrick said, shaking his head. The doors beeped open. "Study!" he shouted at their backs.

"You're the best," Maria shouted back.

"Da bomb!" Julio squealed.

Abdul made that descending and exploding noise so popular when someone failed in class.

The doors closed. He watched them climb to Ninety-Sixth Street, Julio skipping up the stairs, Abdul grabbing Maria's ass, Maria swatting his hand.

The train lurched out of the station and Patrick grasped at the pole, heading home.

Fortunately, the wine shop on 106th had Susan's favorite shiraz in stock. He got a bottle of chardonnay as well, and, of course, a split of champagne. Sal on 110th was just out of roses but could make a nice arrangement of lilies. Wasn't that what he said last Valentine's? Did she complain? demanded Sal. Westside Market had salmon fillets, fresh not frozen. Some new red potatoes, asparagus, a little endive, a little arugula. No way would he mess that up.

Patrick was giddy again, picturing how he'd cook and present each dish. He even picked up candles and matches, just in case. And, still in that Christmas-in-June mood, a catnip mouse for Chauncey. God bless us, everyone. Then, on impulse, he stopped at the jewelers on 112th. They were full of rings, but no, even in this euphoric state, presumptuous. He found some earrings—purple opals—small, funky, just her style—to say thank-you. A good place to start.

He flew out of their elevator, past Ashley and Mr. Paws. Ashley laughed and Mr. Paws yapped as Patrick hallooed, tearing down the hall, nearly spilling the goodies from his bags. He set the bags down on the kitchen table, put the salmon in the fridge, dug out the catnip mouse. Chauncey would be asleep, curled at the foot of the bed on Susan's side. But he'd wake up for nip.

"Chauncey, look what Daddy brought home for yoo-hoo." He jingled the bell on the mouse's tail as he walked down the hall. Lord, he sounded like Susan. The bed was crisply made, empty, fur-free. Just like Susan's cat, to hide the one time he brought home a present. "Chauncey-boy." Jingle, jingle. Patrick looked under the bed. Not even a fur ball. He looked in the closet. No cat. And none of Susan's clothes. The mouse jingled at his feet.

He peered in the bathroom; no litter pan, no purple electric toothbrush. He walked slowly down the hall, saw the thin envelope taped to the front door. *Patrick*, it said, in Susan's lovely cursive.

He remembered, from senior year in high school, what the thin envelope meant. And he didn't have to open it to know what it said. That a girl could only take so much. That he was loved, even so. That it wasn't enough. The generous terms on which he could take leave of Susan's parents' condominium.

And he recalled again the counsel of his roommate, Oscar, the part he had edited out last night. "Only one thing better than make-up sex: break-up sex. *Lo mas fuerte.*" He'd put a brotherly hand on Patrick's shoulder. "But that's gonna cost you, *hombre.*" He pursed those plump Latin lips, shook his head. "Don't wanna talk about that."

15

BRINGING IT ALL BACK HOME

The air conditioner rattles behind Patrick, wheezing a tepid breeze over his sweaty neck. He rubs at the pollen it has deposited in his eyes. A school district like Lake Minnehaha, with all its cash, can't afford to cool the teacher's lounge. That Lutheran prairie hardiness has tracked him even to the affluent suburbs: Why waste money on creature comforts? And shouldn't we just be grateful, surviving another winter? The lime-green couch, another misbegotten economy, sags beneath him, the springs done in by colleagues seeking the same relief, complaining the same complaints.

The third-period prep crowd is scattered about the lounge, seated at tables in twos and threes. Each group has mugs of coffee and large stacks of papers—never-graded homework, untaught lesson plans—they idly sort or pitch as they discuss the real business of the day: summer. The young will be taking classes at the U, the poor will teach summer school, the well-married are packing for a season at the Lake Place.

Patrick looks down at his own damp, stackless lap. He went through his few effects last week, careful to leave Cindy Sperling's classroom as pristine as he found it. He has no school files to sort for next year, just copies of the résumé and cover letter with which he has papered the greater Twin Cities area. And a handful of rejections from communities—Edina, Golden Valley—that once sounded like Shangri-la, but now more like euphemisms for landfill. *Dear Mr. Lynch, Although we enjoyed meeting you and were impressed by your credentials* they all began. Hadn't he told his students that good news seldom begins with a subordinating conjunction?

His interviews all seemed to go well in the moment: good questions, right answers, appropriate humor, charm. But something was missing, or, rather, *extra*. The taint of his big city ordeal clung to him like that household odor you couldn't quite identify, let alone scrub away. His references, of course, made no mention of that trauma, but what *did* they say? Silverstein's backhanded, passive-aggressive compliments? Ted's gracious *apologia*? There was suspicion in the interviews; they knew, somehow, that he was burying the lede. Minnesotans had a certain awe of Big Apple toughness, you betcha, but with it came that sniffing for Tammany Hall corruption.

"We opened up the cabin last weekend," Kristie Bergquist laments, "and what do you think? Raccoons!" As Kristie details at great length and volume the hash that wildlife has made of her summer retreat, Patrick contemplates his own summer home, a boxy one-bedroom in Burnsville, in the nondescript complex where he crash-landed last August, a pad for the recently graduated and newly divorced. Clean, well-kept, cheap; big sister Erin had helped him find it. "You just might get lucky here," she'd grinned naughtily, scoping the twenty- and thirty-somethings bearing their laundry baskets in the hallway.

What he'd gotten wasn't lucky but monastic. Surrounded by his four white walls, watching the white snow fall outside his window. Celibate, except for one sleety Thursday night in February. He'd been grading papers, a working dinner at the Ground Round bar, when he noticed a woman from two floors down nursing a gin and tonic. A dental hygienist, it turned out, who wound up examining much more than his bicuspids. He woke up feeling lonelier than ever and managed to avoid her after that one night, even noting her laundry schedule. He felt, as Dorie would say, like a schmuck. A loser, unfit for a relationship. He'd followed one woman to New York City and another had driven him out.

Worse, even his mother had found romance, discreetly "keeping company" with Larry, a widowed professor of physics, whose department office she managed at the U. Patrick had dinner with them at his mother's condo in St. Paul. Not at all the awkward event he'd imagined; they were quiet and relaxed as a couple. Unnervingly so. It was the second time his mother had surprised him this year. The first had been her suggesting that he chuck the education business altogether. Why not go to law school, she said, like he'd planned as an undergraduate, before he met that Helene girl? Watching her and the professor prepare dinner—an activity she'd never shared with her husband—Patrick pondered how many other boyfriends he'd never met, that she and Erin had kept from him. And, it finally dawned on him, as she swapped spices with Larry, whispering suggestions in his ear, that he'd trapped his mother in the amber of his childhood, and that this evening was a lesson for her schoolmaster son, a tutorial in moving on.

Patrick looks up from his moist lap. Ted Sturdevant looms over him, a solid block of department chair. He waves Patrick into the Xerox room adjoining the lounge, pausing in front of the wall of faculty mail slots. All are empty, save one. This slot, beneath Mr. Linnehan and above Mrs. McPherson, is filled beyond capacity, papers drooping over the nameplate, littering the floor below. Ted points to a banker's box in the corner that Patrick assumed had something to do with recycling. "Yours, pal," says Ted, gesturing at the box, half-filled with mail. "All yours." Ted wedges his thick mitts into the edges of the crammed mail slot and extracts a four-inch mass of Scholastic catalogues, unopened envelopes, pink office directives.

He thrusts the pile at Patrick, smirking. "It's not storage space, Mr. Lynch."

Patrick squints his swollen eyelids. "Storage is the least of my problems, Mr. Sturdevant."

Ted moves to the doorway, peers into the lounge. "Actually, it's not storage I want to talk about."

"I sensed that."

Ted eyes the box. "But this does explain why you never answer my memos."

Patrick looks at the box, noticing for the first time the yellow stickie on it with *Mr. Lynch* written in the office secretary's hand and the smiley face beneath it. He shrugs. "Nothing personal." Ted leans in. "I shouldn't be telling you this, probably. It's not official yet." Patrick waits. "The school board granted Cindy a year's leave."

"She likes being a mommy."

"She was made for it." Ted looks toward the lounge. "More than teaching." Conspiratorial grin. "Anyway, we'll have to post it. And interview." Patrick nods. "But you do seem to have the inside track."

Kristie Bergquist guffaws. Oh, those raccoons.

"If you're interested." Ted clears his throat. "I know you've been looking. Thought I'd let you know before somebody else snatches you up."

"Between you and me, not a lot of snatching lately."

A guy laugh from Ted. Wife and two kids later, he misses the locker room repartee. "It's just another one-year contract," he says, lowering his voice. "Strictly on the QT, Cindy's hubby is in marketing at Dairy Queen and might be up for a promotion. In their Dallas office."

"Gotta love the winters down there. And the Dilly Bars."

"No promises, but this could turn into a permanent gig. If you're interested." Ted lands a soft right hook on Patrick's upper arm.

Patrick examines the toner-stained carpeting, then looks at Ted. "I'm interested. Thanks."

Ted flicks a look toward their colleagues. "Good. That's good," he says softly, and presses an index finger to his lips. He turns to leave.

"Ted?" The department chair turns back. His shoulders fill the doorway. "Why?" Ted lifts his brows modestly, as if he doesn't understand the question. Patrick waves his hands about the copying room. "All this?"

Ted suppresses a quip about the malfunctioning Xerox. He plants a brawny hand on either side of the doorframe. "Blame your dad."

"He's got a lot to answer for."

"Called me down to his office sophomore year." Ted folds his arms, savoring the chance to tell it. "I thought he'd found out about the beer blast at Hanson's Woods. That I was suspended, off the team." He leans against the doorframe. "Sat me down and asked me—so gently—when I was going to start acting like the bright young man I was, instead of an idiot jock." Ted laughs. "He got the second part right, anyway."

Kristie excuses her way past Ted, pretends to check her mail slot. Ted watches her return to her pile of papers.

"Part of me wanted to argue with him—What do you know, old man? Screw you." He lets out an adolescent snort. "But, you know, he had a Superintendent of the Year award over one shoulder and a trophy for All-State tackle over the other. Hard to write off that combo, even as a snotty teenager."

"Yes."

"And another part of me—a very remote part—looked at your dad behind that desk and thought *that could be me someday.*" Ted shakes his head. "Know what I mean?" Patrick does know. He is picturing the loon decoy. "Quite a guy, your dad."

Patrick lifts a hand. "*He was a man. Take him for all in all—*"

"Mark Antony."

"Hamlet. Act 1, Scene 2." Tonight, Patrick Lynch will be playing the role of Gunther Hendrickson.

"Damn. And I used to teach that. See? You were the smartest kid in school."

Patrick lets it slide. "So. You hired me because of my father. And pity."

Ted puts a hand to that square jaw. "Essentially."

Patrick tosses his unprocessed mail into the banker's box. "Works for me."

He is just going to ignore them, the two little streams, one under each arm, running down his sides. Sun is flooding through the courtyard window and even the squirrel is lethargic, resting on the largest branch of the chestnut, lazily swishing his tail, eyeing the impregnable bird feeder. It's even hotter than second period, but, with the floor fan cranked to high, not so much worse here than in the lounge. The banker's box is nearly empty now, sorted into three piles—pitch, keep, maybe—on Cindy's—his?—desk. The smallest pile, the maybe pile, is in the middle. He looks at the clock, the second hand waving at Steinbeck. Five minutes left in third period; he'll have to deal with the maybes later.

He had to get away from that end-of-year teacher's lounge chatter. Had to consider what he'd just agreed to. He breathes it in: another year—maybe more—at Lake Minnehaha. Relief, naturally, comes first—no more interviews, no specter of substitute teaching looming over the fall. But guilt is a quick second. His future is less happenstance now, more intentional. It's one thing, he thinks, to wash ashore in suburbia from the shipwreck of your life, to tell yourself that you were applying there because the city schools never hired till the last minute. True enough, but.

"That's bullshit, Patrick," Dorie said when he'd called her, unburdening in the deep mid-winter, looking out at the parking lot as snow buried his used Tercel. He'd abandoned the cause that got him into teaching, he confessed. He was just one more lackey, serving the rich. No different, he whined, than that squirrel that lived in the school courtyard, in his cozy space, fattening himself on their leavings.

"Total bullshit," she said. "Those kids need you just as much." She paused. "They need you differently." Dorie could always be counted on to bust up his pity parties, send everybody home disappointed.

"Good night," she'd signed off. "St. Patrick."

He reaches into the banker's box, grabs a last stack. He rips open an envelope, takes out a yellow flyer. *Tired? Out of fresh ideas? Let us write your lesson plan!* If only. Pitch.

Pink office slip. Mr. Lynch, call Mrs. Strohmeyer. Re: Tiffany's private school application. Dated January 17. Oops. Pitch.

Pink office slip. Mr. Lynch, call your sister. Dated June 7. Oops. Keep.

Last was a Middle School Reader's Warehouse catalogue. Too young for Lake Minnehaha eighth graders. Pitch.

Grabbing at the pitch pile, he notices a postcard stuck to the bottom of the catalogue. He snaps it off. *Cathedral of St. John the Divine*, the caption reads. *Peace Fountain*. Brother Sun, Sister Moon, and all the other creatures of the apocalypse. He leans back in his desk chair, traces the archangel with his thumb.

Slowly, he turns it over. *Miss you*, it says, in the prettiest script he's ever seen. Postmark February 21. Week after Valentine's Day, he thinks. And maybe, he calculates, the night he called Dorie. And, possibly, he shakes his head, the week of the dental hygienist.

He looks out into the courtyard, fanning himself with the postcard. The squirrel crouches on the branch, agitated, thrashing its tail. Patrick taps the postcard on his desk, sets free all the air in his lungs. He looks at the Peace Fountain, the smiling moon, and tosses it onto the pitch pile.

The bell rings. He looks at the doorway, then the courtyard. The squirrel leaps at the feeder. Patrick runs a sweaty hand over his sweaty head. He swipes the postcard off the pitch pile, slaps it on the maybes.

And Zachary Allen blasts through the doorway, tripping over his size-twelve sneakers into Brandon Rinehart, whose signature surfer highlights are now chlorine green thanks to swim team. And Kimberly Perkins shows off her sparkly, no-braces teeth to her best friend, Jessica Morrison, who darts a glance at Mr. Lynch before offering her pal a celebratory, rule-breaking chunk of Dubble Bubble as Cory Bettleman trudges behind her, hugging his writing portfolio to his chest, containing the poem he wrote last week about his parents' divorce, the one true thing he's written all year, which he will perhaps share with the class now that he can, with one foot out the door, stepping toward high school.

Mr. Lynch stands.

Fourth period tumbles in.

ACKNOWLEDGMENTS

A sixty-two-year-old debut novelist has a lifetime of people to thank: The team at Regal House Publishing, especially Jaynie Royal and my editor, Pam Van Dyk. The Ragdale Foundation, Blue Mountain Center, Bread Loaf Writers' Conference, Hen House Arts Collective and GrubStreet for providing essential space, time, and inspiration. I am indebted to my teachers at Bread Loaf, Jennifer Egan and Andrea Barrett, and to Lisa Borders at GrubStreet, for providing just the right instruction at just the right time.

My early readers, Shelly Matthews, Mel Glenn, David Fey, Tom Duprey, Janel Pudelka, Olive Woodward, Sharon Tehan, Julie McKee and the Tuesday Night Irregulars. Rob McKean, who read and sharpened every word in this book; Jane Hamilton and John White, who must be thanked together, for indispensible help improving this novel but even more for indispensible friendship year after year; Sheila McIntosh, for her patient help in manuscript preparation; Karla Baehr, whose deep knowledge of education administration was vital to this book and whose belief in this project made it possible.

Steven Brill and Mara Altman, whose journalism on New York City Rubber Rooms provided a point of departure for my fictional Rubber Room. Naomi Stonberg and Glenn Pudelka, for their legal advice and background information on education and the law.

My fellow educators at St. Benedict School in Oakland and Bret Harte Middle School in Hayward, California; Middle School 44 in New York City; and Dover-Sherborn Middle School in Dover, Massachusetts. And to my fellow educators everywhere. People think they know how hard you work. People are wrong.

My wife, Karin, and our children, Molly and Brennan, for giving purpose to this all.